The Jigsaw
and The Fan

STEWART BINT

To Jim Ody

all the best,

Stewart Bint

The Jigsaw and the Fan
Copyright ©2016 Stewart Bint

ISBN print 978-1-988256-29-0
ISBN ebook 978-1-988256-30-6

Printed and bound in the United States

www.dragonmoonpress.com

ALSO BY STEWART BINT
Published By Dragon Moon Press

In Shadows Waiting
Timeshaft

The Jigsaw and The Fan

STEWART BINT

ACKNOWLEDGEMENTS

Thank you to my editor, Sophie Thomas
and the team at Dragon Moon Press.

And thanks to my good friend, fellow novelist DM Cain,
for her unstinting enthusiasm and encouragement.

Special thanks to my wife Sue, son
Chris, and daughter Charlotte.

For my children's partners, Andrew Wormleighton and Samantha Chawner, for being so right for Charlotte and Chris.

CONTENTS

ABOUT THE AUTHOR

CHAPTER 1

In which our hero dies, and encounters a problem

ALBERT CARTER OPENED his eyes. Then he blinked. He'd seen shapes floating about his room before—but only after flopping into bed after a heavy night at The Patternmakers Arms.

This was very different though. Apart from a few hot toddies when he first went down with flu he had been too ill even to drink. And it wasn't like Albert not to want a drink. It wasn't like Albert to be ill, either. Even when the flu turned to pneumonia his doctor was not unduly worried.

"A strong lad like Albert'll soon throw this off," Doctor Fairley had told Abigail Carter. "But do keep him away from picket lines for a week or two."

It was picketing the main gates of Jebsons Glue Factory for three days in the pouring rain that had probably brought on Albert's flu in the first place. But, as Albert had said, he was the shop steward, and the management had no right to change from the soft-purple to rough hard paper in the workers' toilet without a full consultation process.

So the brothers of the Amalgamated Glue and Adhesive Workers Union downed tools and Jebsons' High Street depot ground to a halt.

Negotiations dried up and the pickets turned away everyone in sight.

Then suddenly Albert caught flu. Then pneumonia. Then suddenly he died. No vote was taken, or anything like that.

He just simply, sadly, snuffed it.

Albert didn't know what was happening. He saw the shapes on the wall and ceiling slowly solidify into human beings…or what looked like human beings. He saw the ceiling get nearer, and instinctively turned to look below. A half-strangled scream piped its way to his lips.

He was floating about the room, and there, lying on the bed below, he could see his own pale body. His throat was too dry, and the scream became entangled with his tonsils. Wildly he looked around, seeking an explanation from the figures who glided backwards and forwards over the walls.

From somewhere behind him one of the newly solidified people grasped his arm and swung him round.

"It's okay, Albert, don't worry. Everything's alright. We've come to greet you. Welcome to the Condition Of Transit."

Albert looked all around, still mystified. "W-what's happening?" he managed to stammer.

The figure spoke again. "You've left your earthly life behind, Albert. We've come to take you to see whether you go to heaven or hell."

The words went in through his ears alright, but understanding them was definitely not on the cards, and even if Albert had known what to say, his thoughts wouldn't have seen light of day without being grated to shreds on the tightening walls of his throat. It took two attempts to swallow his heart which had suddenly rushed up into his mouth.

He shook his head violently, as if to clear it. And sure enough, he thought he had the answer. "Yes, I'm dreaming. I'm delirious with the fever."

A second newly materialised figure floated forward. "Albert, it's me—your old pal Georgie." Albert looked at Georgie.

"Georgie…" was all his parched lips could muster. Georgie

had been his snooker partner at Brindon Working Men's Club
until he tried to jump off a Number 57 bus which was going
down Cemetery Hill at forty miles an hour. Georgie had been
under the influence of sixteen pints that night.

"At least he died happy," Albert had said at the funeral a
year ago.

It all flashed back before Albert's eyes, and he wondered
what people would say at his own funeral now he was dead.
Now He Was Dead! What a ridiculous thought. Of course he
wasn't dead.

He looked at all the people—if indeed, that is what they
were—who filled his bedroom, and a strange feeling deep
within him nagged unceremoniously that perhaps he *was*
dead. He didn't know what to think. He had never been dead
before, so why did he get the feeling that he might be now?
Maybe it was because Georgie looked real enough, floating
there not three feet from him, holding out his hand.

"It's true, Albert," said Georgie, gently. "The fever's taken
you. We've come to see that you're alright."

Albert made up his mind that if it were a dream he would
play along with it; throw 'em a curved ball, and all that. But
something suddenly flooded over him, like a wave of bright
light, which filled his head with the realisation that he was,
indeed, truly and undeniably dead. Strangely enough, there was
no pain. There was nothing at all. Albert just felt as if all the
cares in the world had been carefully eased off his shoulders.

Solemnly he shook hands with Georgie. But then the full
importance of the moment came over him, and his eyes filled
with tears at the thought of the good life he was leaving behind.

As Jebsons' shop steward he hadn't had too bad a time.
Albert had led many a good strike, and more than once was
carried shoulder high and victorious across the threshold

after successful industrial action. His memoirs, had he found the time to write them, would have been full of the wicked capitalist management bowing to the union's demands. The provision of a coffee machine in addition to the tea trolley, for instance; the hour-and-a-half lunch break; the fifteen minutes before the end of each shift for a wash and brush-up—it was all Albert's doing.

Sadly he reflected on those good times. "But it's no use brooding," he thought. "If I'm dead, I'm dead, and that's all there is to it."

Albert was taking the fact that he was dead with a certain amount of uncharacteristic philosophical acceptance. He felt it would not do any good complaining to the management—even if he knew where to find the management.

Then his thoughts became speech, and out loud he asked, "When's the tea break?"

"Tea break?" said one fellow, rolling his eyes. "Tea comes a very poor bottom of the list, especially in heaven. You wait until you try our vintage nectar."

By now around half a dozen people were floating about his bedroom. They seemed to be treating it like Euston Station, thought Albert, looking on in mild amusement as a man dressed in hunting pink appeared through a wall and vanished through another, hotly pursued by a bright-eyed, bushy-tailed fox.

Wonder and intrigue now filled his mind, having first chased away fear and disbelief. "What happens now?" he asked.

"You're in the Condition Of Transit. We take you to Saint Christopher, the patron saint of all travellers. He looks to see which list your name's on, to see whether your journey continues up or down. And then his Doomsday Ministry sends you on the last part of your journey."

Albert had no doubts. He had led a good trades union life.

Under his guidance the brothers rose against the tyranny of management. He fought for the poor, starving masses and was convinced his reward would lie in heaven.

For the first time since he'd died Albert suddenly felt self-conscious. What was he wearing? After all, he did not want to meet Saint Christopher in his pyjamas. Looking down, he was astonished to see he was dressed for work.

Georgie seemed to catch the puzzled look. "It's okay, Albert. When you die your soul brings with it the spirits of your life; your essence, what you were best known for. You were a great shop steward, so it's only natural that your spirit clings to the clothes in which it enjoyed so much success. You're clothed in your own righteousness, so to speak. Come on, it's time to go."

Albert's guides took him by the arms and they rose through the bedroom ceiling. The last thing he saw before finding himself in his loft, was his wedding photograph. The one Abigail kept on the dressing table. Abigail always looked stunning in photographs. But this one more than most. Radiant, was the word he used.

For a few seconds he glanced around the loft, thinking it could definitely do with a good tidying…or "fettling," as his grandmother used to say. But Albert would never tidy his loft again, for that fateful day in late April 1980 was when he shuffled off his mortal coil, at the tender age of just twenty-nine.

The haze turned to mist. The mist turned to fog. Then it was just Albert and Georgie. The others had left them. And Albert wasn't floating anymore. He was walking; walking through the dense swirling fog on soft, luscious grass. Suddenly the folds of fog were swept aside, rather like a fan closing its wing, and there in front of them stood a great crowd of people.

Georgie turned to Albert and frowned. "I don't know what this is all about. We don't often get so many newly departed spirits waiting to see Saint Christopher at any one time without a major tragedy on Earth. I wonder what's happening."

There were about five thousand people who appeared to come from all walks of life—or the life thereafter. They were thin, fat, tall, and short. Some wore cloth caps, some wore uniforms, some wore work suits, and some wore nothing at all. There was a general air of confusion as everyone stood around waiting for something to happen.

Just beyond the milling people, Albert could see a four-storey white-washed building with the legend "Doomsday Ministry" emblazoned across the frontage. At the top of the steps leading up to the large arched door sat a man with a long, flowing grey beard and matching robes. He sat at a table flanked by two more people who seemed to be doing their best to control the noisy crowd.

Georgie looked at Albert as they reached the back of the gathering.

"That's Saint Christopher," he whispered, pointing to the seated man. "He doesn't look too pleased, does he?"

The crowd was obviously disgruntled, too. Everyone was scowling and muttering under their breath. *Hmmm*, thought Albert. *Do we still breathe when we're dead?* He concentrated for a moment, and found he was still breathing. But maybe it was force of habit rather than anything else.

Then, above the noise, the voice of one of Saint Christopher's attendants was struggling to make itself heard.

"Ladies and gentlemen, please." It was a well-groomed and cultured voice but as it strained to rise above the din Albert couldn't help but feel it needed a manicure before it cracked.

"Ladies and gentlemen, you can see for yourselves that you can't cross the picket line to see Saint Christopher. We will deal with you, but all in good time. Please be patient while we draw up contingency plans."

A tall, distinguished-looking man with greying temples and an aquiline nose turned from the mass to face Georgie and Albert. He was wearing an army colonel's uniform.

"Damned disgraceful, what?" he thundered. "You fight for your country, for blighters like this, and then they thank a chap by standing there with their ruddy placards, threatening to bonk us one if we try to get past them. Don't know what things are coming to nowadays, really don't. If they'd had cold showers, bread and water, and marching drill as nippers they wouldn't be so full of all this damned nonsense now. Shoot 'em, that's what I say. Shoot the ruddy blighters."

And off he went into the bank of fog behind them.

This appeared to be way out of Albert's league. An earthly picket line he could handle, but he was sure none of his adhesive worker brothers had ever contemplated picketing a saint. It had been said, though, that they often tried the patience of one.

For a few seconds he stood there, stunned and immobile. But once over the initial shock he began to realise that being dead might not be so bad after all. Why, if there were strikes and pickets up here—wherever "up here" was—death really might be worth dying.

"What's going on, Georgie? What's it all about?"

"No idea. Let's try and get through to the front...see if we can find out." Georgie took Albert's arm again and they began to push and thread their way through the jostling mass, which was packed as tight as sardines nestling snugly in a tin.

Georgie peered at everyone's clothes and faces as they elbowed past. "I think they're all newly departed souls, just come from their earthly lives, like you, and waiting to see Saint Christopher. But there's a holdup somewhere."

Finally bursting through the front of the crowd, they found

themselves standing at the bottom step where they could clearly see the cause of the trouble. A line of people stood halfway up the steps, blockading the path to Saint Christopher, who sat looking on helplessly.

They were waving banners and chanting: "Inspectors unite. We need more staff." The banners they were holding backed up their constant drone, also demanding more staff, and proclaiming that Saint Christopher could easily afford to add to his workforce immediately.

Georgie glanced across at Albert. "Oh dear, this spells trouble. The inspectors have finally brought their dispute with Saint Christopher to a head. It's been coming for a long time, but everyone's been burying their heads in the sand, hoping it'd go away."

Georgie held up his hand as Albert tried to ask another question. "We don't go in for trouble up here. We like everything to run as smoothly as possible. There's such a big workforce, and with so many people relying on us when they're in transit, en route to their assigned place in heaven or hell, we just can't afford to waste any time."

He broke off. He knew the distant smile which crept across Albert's face would quickly disappear once Albert knew how the consequences of the strike were likely to affect him personally.

"The holdup will cause havoc, it really will," he said. "I know what's led up to it, though, and I suppose they have got a case. Saint Christopher's backroom boys have been unhappy for ages. Until a few hundred years ago his staff all came from heaven. Then the devil complained that some souls which were really meant for eternal damnation were being deliberately misrouted into heaven. For a while he locked the gates of hell and demanded a full inquiry into the way Saint Christopher ran his department. A special inquiry team was set up with representatives from both heaven and hell, chaired by an independent commissioner, and they agreed that half the staff should come from hell."

"Good to see there's fair representation," interrupted Albert. "Conditions must be good for that job...all Saint Christopher's got to do, surely, is look up a name on a list."

"Oh, Albert, you've no idea. There's much more to it than that," protested Georgie. "Everyone on Earth has to be watched throughout their lives, all their good deeds and bad deeds logged. Then, when someone nears the end of their life, an inspector has to check through their personal file. You can't leave something as important as that to a clerk. You need special qualifications to be an inspector, because it's on their recommendation, and their report, that Saint Christopher decides whether a soul goes on to heaven or hell.

"Saint Christopher himself draws up the lists from the reports, and then has to interview each soul. It's on his discretion, and his alone, whether a soul has actually done enough good deeds to warrant a place in heaven. But if those details, that essential information that he needs, hasn't been put into the report by an inspector, it'll be lost forever, and the soul finds only eternal damnation, when it really should be a case for heaven.

"If someone's not happy with a decision they can go to the Board of Appeal and their case is reviewed from the start of their life right through to their death. But, of course this takes up more time and more manpower. There are three adjudicators at the tribunal who make the final decision.

"As an appeal is usually against a verdict that someone's due for eternal damnation, the soul hires someone from heaven to speak for him, on his behalf. And there are representatives from hell, saying why they should claim the soul.

"It's a huge ministry. In fact, it's the largest we've got. But even so, the staff say they're all overworked, and they've been pressing for reinforcements for some time. It looks as if matters have come to a head at last, and the inspectors are demanding immediate action.

"See that guy over there…?" He indicated a burly giant of an angel standing with his arms folded across his chest a few paces to the side of Saint Christopher. "He's Mr. Hobday. He's responsible for all this. Unless it's resolved quickly it'll cause chaos. No-one can get into heaven or hell."

Albert's eyes widened. And as Georgie had mentally predicted, the smile at the original thought of getting stuck in a strike rubbed itself out. Albert now sat on the other side of the fence. And did he like it? He did not.

"What am I going to do?" he cried. "They can't just stop work like this and leave us all out here." He turned his attentions to the nearest picket. "Get back to work and let us through. We've got to see Saint Christopher."

The picket's face turned thunderous as he leered down at Albert from his vantage point several steps above him. "We're not going back until we get satisfaction. We're overworked, and we're not doing any more until we get some help. We've got our rights."

"What about us?" yelled Albert. "We've got rights as well, you know." He looked for support from Georgie, or from anyone. But found only blank faces. He continued, a little more lamely: "You can't just ignore us. We've not done anything to hurt you."

"Albert," hissed Georgie, urgently. "Don't say things like that to them. You'll only make it worse."

Albert threw off Georgie's restraining arm. "Worse? What could be worse than being stuck here, not knowing whether there's a place for me in heaven or not?"

"But making a fuss isn't going to help. Be reasonable, Albert. After all, they've got a perfectly valid grievance against Saint Christopher, and, as they say, they have got their rights."

"But they're putting everybody out. Why should we all suffer just because they're upset?"

For a fleeting moment Albert's thoughts turned involuntarily to the numerous strikes and pickets he had led at the glue factory. Again he saw the headlines in the *Brindon Herald*: "Sticky Time At Jebsons"; "Young Firebrand Wins Overtime Deal"; and "Pickets Get Stuck In." Again he heard the voice of Nethanial Jebson saying his firm would be forced to close down if they didn't end the strike and get back to work. And, as always, the managing director added that with the closure would come the loss of innocent people's jobs.

It was as if Nethanial Jebson were alongside Albert, the voice was so clear in his ears: "And why should the rest of my staff and workers suffer just because you're upset?"

Albert screwed up his eyes and shook his head violently. That did the trick. Old Jebson disappeared in a puff of smoke.

"That was different," Albert said aloud. "We couldn't stand for the conditions we had to work under there. We were only fighting for our rights as decent, honest working-class folk."

"What...?" exclaimed Georgie.

"Oh, sorry. Just thinking aloud."

Albert was preparing to launch another searing attack on the pickets when a group of them advanced on him and Georgie.

"Georgie," demanded one of them, somewhat menacingly. "What are you doing hobnobbing with a newcomer?"

"I'm his guide," responded Georgie quickly. "He's just arrived from Earth and is waiting to see Saint Christopher."

"So's everyone else here," said the picket. It was the one whom Albert had shouted at earlier. He had seen Georgie and gone off for a quick parley with his colleagues.

"Their guides have said they're sympathetic to our cause, and have gone on strike in support. Are you going to join us as well, or do we have to blacklist you and the spirits you bring here when the dispute's settled? No-one likes a scab, you know."

Albert stared in stunned disbelief as he heard Georgie say he would join them.

"I've no choice," insisted Georgie. "But you'll be okay. You heard them say they're drawing up contingency plans. They'll see you're alright until the dispute's over."

"Georgie, you can't just leave me here. What'll I do?"

"Sorry, Albert, but I can't afford to be blacked. Look, I must go. I'll see you when things get back to normal."

Georgie's body started shimmering and became transparent. Albert's wild cries imploring him to wait a moment fell on deaf ears as Georgie simply faded away into nothing.

Albert buried his head in his hands, wondering what would happen next. The pickets, obviously happy with their small victory, retreated to their outpost on the fourth step.

By now Saint Christopher and his two attendants were making their way down the steps through the picket line. Saint Christopher shouted above the noise: "I must ask you all to bear with us. As you can see, the situation is beyond our control, but I assure you you'll all be found alternative accommodation until the inspectors resume their normal duties.

"Places in heaven or hell have already been allocated for some of you, but not for others. However, it's impossible for us to send you on your way until the dispute is settled."

Again the crowd began shouting, but Saint Christopher was undeterred. He plucked at his flowing beard and pressed on.

"Your guides, without whom you would never find your way to your destination, have come out in sympathy, but the inspectors warn that if we try to guide you there ourselves it'll harm their relationship with us. Therefore we have no alternative but to leave you in the Condition Of Transit until the industrial action has finished. Urgent negotiations are to begin with the inspectors immediately, and we'll recall you here as soon as we can. In the meantime, I must ask you to be patient while we find a place for you on Earth as wandering spirits.

"Now, please form an orderly queue and give my assistant your names. We'll deal with each of you in turn."

An orderly queue, thought Albert miserably. *There must be five thousand people. It'll be hours before I'm out of here.*

Some segments of the crowd actually appeared happy with the idea of going back.

"I'll be able to haunt the old witch. Think of the fun I'll have sending her chairs flying across the room," beamed one old man in a peaked cap. "I'll give her some stick to make up for the years of nagging I've had to put up with."

But for others the thought wasn't greeted with relish at all, and again the protesting din rose to a crescendo. They felt that as they had made the break and crossed the great divide they just wanted to get on with it.

Albert was undecided. If they found him a decent place to haunt, he thought he could probably put up with it.

"Perhaps they'll let me be the resident spook at Jebsons," he said to himself. "I could tip the vat of glue over the foreman."

His thoughts wandered back to the day the latest dispute at Jebsons had started. It was the day he'd gone for a fifteen-minute read of his newspaper in the toilet and found a roll of rough off-white where the soft-purple had previously dangled.

"We can't have this," he thundered, slamming down a dozen sheets on to the foreman's desk. "This is dreadful stuff; a right pain in the arse if you rub too hard. As shop steward I demand we get our soft paper back."

"You ain't having it," yelled the foreman. "They've even got it in the executive john now, too. They say they can't afford to keep supplying the soft sort at the rate you lot get through it. Seventy-five rolls a week go into that workers' bog. It's a wonder it ain't blocked up with the stuff. What you lot do with it gawd only knows."

Albert refrained from saying what he would like to do with it, and opted instead for telling the foreman what he wasn't going to do with it. "Well, we're not going to use it," he said. "You can kiss my arse before I'd wipe it with that stuff. I'm going out now to tell the brothers what's happened, and if that soft-purple's not back in there within five minutes you'll have a strike on your hands."

Albert picked up his dozen sheets and stormed out to the shop floor. He fetched a handbell from his locker and shook it with all the fervour of a primary school teacher ringing out home time at the end of the summer term.

"Tools down, brothers," he called. "I'm convening a special emergency meeting of the Amalgamated Glue and Adhesive Workers Union."

It didn't take long for the workers to surround Albert's bench. He held aloft the sheets of off-white.

"Brothers, this is what the management have hung in our carsey. They've taken away the only luxury we've been allowed in the past. Our soft-purple bog roll has gone; replaced by this abomination."

There was a stunned silence. The workers could scarcely believe it.

"But I, as your shop steward, am not going to allow them to shit on us like this."

There was a cry from the shop floor: "Good old Albert. Why, if that stuff was dangling from the wall I couldn't enjoy my morning crap and decker at the boobs on page three. Ugh…the thought of having to use that stuff afterwards would really rub me up the wrong way. Put me right off, it would."

"You won't have to use it, brothers, I'll see to that. If management refuse to change it, we're going on strike."

There was a cheer from the men—but even that couldn't drown out the piercing tea siren. Albert climbed off his bench.

"Meeting adjourned for quarter of an hour, brothers. It's the tea break."

The double doors at the end of the factory floor swung open and in came Flo with her trolley. Within seconds she was besieged, and the urn became busy dispensing its thick, treacly tea into cracked and stained mugs.

Old Joe Wells took a swig with undisguised relish, letting out a loud sigh as he wiped his mouth on the back of a grubby hand. "Yer know, I've been married nigh on forty years and never had a cross word wi' the wife, bar one. And that wor when she bought two rolls of that paper. By gaw, did it make me bleed? 'Tek it back,' I told her. 'But it's cheaper,' she said. 'I dunner care,' I said. 'I ain't having it.' Anyway, she grumbled a bit and we had a right barney about it, I can tell yer.

"Well, I made her use it, didn't I?" He chuckled at the memory. "She never bought no more." Old Joe looked round with satisfaction. "So I'm buggered if I'm using it here."

After the tea break Albert strode confidently to the toilet. He was sure the management would not want another crippling strike and would have met his demands.

But if he were disappointed at seeing the cause of the trouble still dangling proudly from its askew wooden holder, now waving slightly and somewhat cheekily in the breeze which whistled in through the open window, his face did not reflect it. Game on!

He hurried back to the shop floor. "Right, brothers, it's still there. Out you go."

Albert's next move had been to storm into Nethanial Jebson's office to register his official protest. Mr. Jebson was coldly polite, but resolute.

"Mr. Carter, we are being forced to make economies and have no choice but to buy the cheaper paper. We can get it at cost price, too, and that's a big boon nowadays. I'm sorry, but there you are. You already have a lot of extra benefits not afforded to workers at other factories."

Another voice cut in on Albert's memories and he snapped back to the present. The voice was asking his name. Albert looked around and found he had finally made it to the front of the queue.

"I'm Albert Carter, from Brindon," he told Saint Christopher's attendant.

It was duly written down on the lengthy list and the attendant looked up. "As you know, Mr. Carter, we're in difficulties because of industrial action within the ministry. We'll recall you here for you to take your rightful place in heaven or hell, whichever has been assigned to you, just as soon as we can.

"In the meantime, we're returning you to Earth. We're sending you to Marlston Manor in the English countryside."

Albert looked up, aghast. He hadn't banked on anything like that.

"It's inhabited by an elderly couple, Lord and Lady Barrington-Pottsherbert," continued the attendant. "It's one of the most beautiful stately homes in Northern England. We think it'll be the ideal place for you to wait until we're ready to recall you." He carefully wrote *Marlston Manor* alongside Albert's name.

Albert began to get worried. Marlston Manor sounded diddly squat like the bundle of fun he'd hoped for. "Couldn't I go to my old factory, Jebsons? I know my way around there. I don't think this Marlston place—"

The attendant raised his hand. "Mr. Carter, you're holding up the queue. I'm sure you'll find Marlston Manor most acceptable. Now, if you'll please close your eyes we'll send you on your way."

Albert started to protest—but suddenly his whole world went crazy. Closing his eyes was the last thing he wanted to do, but felt he must, to shut out the blindingly white light hurtling past as he flashed through space, seemingly at a million miles an hour.

For several seconds they remained tightly shut. Then it was all over, as swiftly as it had begun.

There was no *bang* or jarring of bones, not even a gentle thud. But his feet were once again on terra firma. Of that, there was absolutely no doubt.

CHAPTER 2

In which we learn of forbidden love

GINGERLY ALBERT OPENED one eye and peered from left to right. Then he opened the other one.

There in front of him stood Marlston Manor, with the quiet English countryside rolling away in green folds to its distant rendezvous with the morning sky. The sky itself looked as if God had tipped his marmalade jar upon it and spread the rich golden contents thickly over the wispy clouds.

Albert was on a hillside looking down to the magnificent house. From his elevated perch the house appeared to stand guard over a shimmering lake whose waters distorted an upside-down world of trees and sky.

To the back of Marlston lay a tightly packed wood, the trees as close together as a clock's hands at midnight.

From his distance of around quarter of a mile the large stone blocks from which Marlston was constructed looked to be in need of sandblasting, but there was no denying the building's opulent splendour. Ten double-hung sash windows adorned each of the three floors on the southern-facing frontage which was topped by an imposing crenellated roof with turrets at either end. Ten stone steps rose from the sweeping gravel drive to a central door beneath a triangular-capped portico supported by six gothic pillars.

Gradually Albert began to make his way down the hillside towards the manor. The grass was wet with the early dew and had already begun to grow again after its long winter's rest. The seasons were coming early this year—the sign of a good summer, despite there being only one swallow overhead.

The morning stillness echoed eerily in Albert's ears. He was used to the hustle and bustle of Jebsons, or at least to the noisy chanting of a picket line before television cameras and radio microphones. The quietness of the countryside, broken only by the dawn chorus which had lingered a little that day, rang unnaturally to his soul.

His pace quickened until he stood at the top of the ten stone steps before the imposing oak front door. His outstretched hand stopped just short of the large metallic bell push.

If there was one thing Albert hated it was doorbells. He had had quite a row about them with his wife, Abigail, not long after their wedding. She had wanted one on the front door of their first two-bedroomed terrace house in Brindon, and Albert had said no.

As the thought flashed across his mind, it was accompanied by a powerful image of Abigail's smiling face, Abigail's beautiful, high cheek-boned face framed by shoulder-length dark hair. The face he would never see again in the living world.

His deep dislike of doorbells could be traced back to his early childhood, when his favourite pastime had been ringing old Mrs. Jackson's bell and running off before the ninety-year-old cripple could get to the door. For a week or two everything had gone according to plan. But one day he was on his usual escape route through the alley at the side of her house when she surprised him by coming out of the back door instead, and catching him by the hair.

Albert had always thought of her as an old witch and when he saw the broomstick propped up by the drainpipe it confirmed his worst fears. His eyes widened as she reached for it, her other hand still firmly entwined in his dark brown locks.

A few moments later he had ruefully been rubbing the seat of his pants after the somewhat overenthusiastic way the broomstick had dusted them, in the hands of the witch herself.

Whenever Albert had tried to sit down during the next few days he was none-too-gently reminded of old Mrs. Jackson's bell, and he grew to hate it. His hate intensified and was not confined just to Mrs. Jackson's. Day by day Albert's hatred of the doorbell spread to other people's, until he hated every innocent doorbell throughout the length and breadth of the land.

Then he had his sixth birthday and forgot all about it.

It was only when Abigail came home with one in the third week of their marriage that the memory of his sore posterior was promoted from his subconscious.

The argument had ended with Albert putting his foot down firmly—not just figuratively, but with all the physical vigour he could muster, right in the middle of the bell's delicate works.

And here he was, years later, dead, and about to ring one. And at the home of a wealthy lord and lady, as well. *What could be worse,* he thought, *than having to spend the next goodness knows how long with privileged capitalists who had been born with silver spoons planted securely between their teeth?*

Albert felt he hated the Barrington-Pottsherberts even before he had met them. They stood for everything that he, as a good working-class trades unionist, despised: money, a title, and a mansion that could house with ease dozens of his hard-working brothers.

"Better get the introductions over," he said to himself, reaching out once more; this time for the brass knocker. Again he stopped just short of touching it. Not through a deep-rooted hatred of brass door knockers (although there was that time in Oldham with that pair of big knockers…but no, that's another story); this was something much more fundamental. What was he going to say to whoever came to the door?

For the first time he began to weigh up exactly what he was doing there. He was a ghost destined to haunt the mansion until he could take up his rightful place in the life thereafter. Perhaps Lord and Lady Barrington-Pottsherbert would not take too kindly to the idea of Albert stalking their ancestral corridors. They might be just as much against Albert being there as he himself was. As far as he knew, though, ghosts did not have to ask the hauntees if they minded the haunters doing the haunting.

But then again, he did have only strictly limited knowledge of the subject.

Albert's hand reached out again for the knocker, all thoughts of hesitation now banished to the dark recesses in the back of his mind. After all, he had never been one to wait if he could leap in feet first. He never liked the proverbial iron to be anything but boiling, and striking had always been his catchword. Albert's questions regularly came after his actions—never before.

He firmly intended to grip the knocker and send the sound of his presence echoing madly along the oak-panelled walls of Marlston Manor. And no doubt that's exactly what would have happened, if it were not for just one slight hitch. His hand went straight through the knocker. And straight through the solid wooden door.

Albert snatched it back with a yell. After a quick examination which yielded neither cuts nor bruises, he tried again. His pointed finger hovered on the brink, then slowly entered the knocker to the first knuckle. Somewhere along the line it had slipped his mind that his body was still at home in Brindon—unless it had been carted off by the undertaker already—and this was just his ethereal spirit.

This time he did not withdraw his hand, but followed it

through with his arm, his leg, his whole body. He walked through the closed door as if it were not there, and stood looking around the great hall.

For a few moments the splendour was overshadowed by the thought of what he had just done. Then, to make sure he really had done it, he did it again. This time straight through the outside wall. There was no doubt about it. One second he was savouring the licking tongues of sunshine as they inched their way over the treetops; the next he was halfway through the wall; then he was back inside Marlston.

A wide staircase swept up to a gallery where a number of Lord Barrington-Pottsherbert's illustrious ancestors had been commemorated on canvas.

Albert was right when he decided that the man walking down the stairs was not the lord himself, but a butler.

Albert started towards him. "Excuse me, I wonder if…"

It was an eerie feeling when the butler did to Albert what Albert had just done to the door and wall. Albert had never let anyone walk over him, so it was inconceivable that he should let anyone walk through him. But that was what had just happened. The butler definitely occupied the same space as Albert at the same time, while being totally unaware of it.

Albert swallowed and stared hard at the retreating back. Then, from somewhere overhead, someone spoke to him.

"It's okay, mate, he'll never see you."

Whirling round and peering up at the gallery he saw a youngish man leaning over the balustrade. He felt sure the butler must have heard the man call out to him. But a quick glance assured him that was not the case. The butler was just closing a door behind him at the end of the corridor.

Then the man was running down the stairs, two at a time, and he was speaking again. "Why, hi there. It's good to see a new face round here. Popped in for a chat, have you?"

"Well, actually, I…er…I…I've dropped in to stay for a while, if the truth be told. Do you live here, then?"

"Lived here for the last sixty years," said the youngish man, who looked as if he had not yet seen his twenty-fourth birthday. "Came here when I was eight. My mam was the cook here, God rest her soul." He swiftly made the sign of the cross over his heart. "Which is more than he's doing for mine."

Instantly Albert grasped the meaning. He was quick on the uptake, like that. "You're dead, then, like me?" he stammered.

"For forty-five years," replied the youngish man. "And you?"

Albert related the tale of the inspectors' strike, and how he was to live at Marlston until the dispute was settled.

Marlston's resident ghost pursed his lips and expelled a breath, half in a whistle and half in a whoosh. "That's going to cause some problems," he mused. "Crikey, the backlog's going to be enormous. Boy, it'll take some sorting out, will that, I can tell you. Anyway, your misfortune is our good fortune. It'll be just fine and dandy to have you around, even if it is only for a short while."

Albert was intrigued to know why the man was still at the mansion having been dead for so long.

"Forbidden love, mate, forbidden love," said the youngish man in reply to Albert's question. "Look, sit down. You're a fellow ghost, come to live here for a while. I suppose it can't do any harm me telling you all about it."

So Albert sat on the stairs alongside his newfound friend and listened as the sad tale unfolded.

It seemed the young man's name was Bobby Lewis, and he had arrived at Marlston with his widowed mother. By day he attended the nearby village school and in the evenings earned his keep at the mansion by helping out whenever he could.

He left school at the first opportunity and worked full-time at Marlston as a gardener and handyman.

All had been well for several years, but a week after his twenty-first birthday he met the local magistrate's daughter.

"And a prettier creature you never did see," he said. "I was walking through the woods one day and she came riding down the path on her chestnut horse, her long blonde hair flowing out behind her. What a stunning vision she was. Straight from heaven and paradise itself, I'll swear it.

"Anyway, we stayed chatting for a while and arranged to meet the following day."

As Bobby's story unfolded it became clear he had quickly fallen in love with the beautiful Daphne Pride—and Miss Pride had reciprocated his love.

For months they kept their relationship secret, but Bobby decided they could not go on hiding their love from the world forever, and asked her to marry him. At first she refused, saying they ought to wait a little longer. But eventually she succumbed to Bobby's persuasions, and he went to her house one morning to ask her father's permission.

"For a magistrate he certainly had a fine command of rich Anglo-Saxon swear words," grinned Bobby. "If he'd known his daughter was listening behind the door he'd have shrivelled up with embarrassment."

Mr. Pride JP told Bobby he had never been so insulted in all his born days to think a common working lad should have serious designs on the apple of his eye.

It was at that point that Daphne had burst into the room, crying. She threw herself into her lover's arms and sobbed that he was the only man she would ever look at. Her father remained unmoved, and ordered Bobby out of his house.

For the next few weeks they continued to meet in secret,

excitedly making plans to elope. All might have gone well, had it not been for one unnoticed mistake. Unnoticed, that is, until Bobby climbed the ladder to Daphne's bedroom window ready to help her down, and whisk her off into the night.

Bobby had set the ladder about six inches too far to the side, and when Daphne threw the window open its frame caught the ladder a glancing blow. With a shriek Bobby and the ladder parted company from the window ledge, and after the law of gravity had its say, they made a sudden and rather sharp contact with the neatly trimmed lawn.

Lights appeared in upstairs rooms and before Daphne could get down the stairs to Bobby, her father's thunderous face was silhouetted at his bedroom window.

"I thought I warned you to keep away," he bellowed before disappearing from view. When he reappeared seconds later it was through the French doors, just after his daughter had run out across the grass to Bobby.

Levelling his shotgun, he peered menacingly along the sights. "I'm too soft with you, you young whippersnapper. I ought to pepper your backside with this grapeshot. If I ever see you round here again trying to entice my daughter away I'll blast you to kingdom come. D'you hear me? This is your last warning. Now, off with you, before I change my mind and rid the world of you."

Roland Pride JP turned to his daughter. "And as for you, my lass, I'm going to teach you a lesson you'll never forget."

Bobby looked across at Albert, his eyes now ablaze as he recalled those dreadful moments from years ago.

"That night she hanged herself from the oak rafters of her bedroom. The news spread through the village like wildfire, and it wasn't long before I heard it.

"Village folk said her father blamed me and that he'd sworn

vengeance on me. Some said he was after me with his shotgun. Well, I hid broken-hearted in the woodshed for hours. I had plenty of time to think about it all, and I decided that without my beloved Daphne life wasn't worth living. I wasn't what you'd call a religious man, but I somehow knew that night that there was only one way for me to ever be with her again."

Bobby told how he had made a hangman's noose from strong garden twine and hanged himself in the shed.

"It turns out that here in the afterlife they regard suicide as one of the ultimate sins, but because we'd led otherwise good lives we weren't condemned to hell. They reckoned it'd take one hundred years to cleanse our souls and purge the sin, so here we are haunting Marlston Manor for one hundred years. But at least we're together, and we know there are places in heaven for us at the end of it all."

"Which is more than I bloody well know thanks to the strikers," said Albert, somewhat bitterly. "It's all this waiting about that'll kill me." He smiled at the irony of what he had said, and looked hard at Bobby. "But can't you do anything about it? I mean, one hundred years seems a hell of a long time just because you committed suicide. Haven't you taken this up with anyone—protested—made your voice heard?"

"Well, no," said Bobby. "Daphne and I had a lengthy interview with Saint Christopher who showed us the error of our ways. He said we should really consider ourselves lucky that we weren't being packed off to hell. But for our otherwise blameless lives we should have been."

"Typical management attitudes," sneered Albert. "They make it sound as if they're doing you a favour. You don't want to stand for that. If I were you I'd make the most of this strike and while Saint Christopher's not too busy get up there and tell him straight that you're not having it. I'll support you."

Bobby looked horrified. "We couldn't do that. It'd be a sure way of booking a passage to hell. You don't go round messing with Saint Christopher."

But Albert was not deterred. "If we'd all had that fatalistic outlook we'd still be in the dark days when the bosses ruled everything. Since you've been here, my lad, times have changed in the world. The bosses still seem to be the bosses, but it's only on paper. The trades unions have gradually amassed so much power that we could now bring the entire country to a standstill if we wished. Our industrial muscle lies in the fact that we no longer accept the outdated claim that he who pays the piper should call the tune.

"Gone are the days when the bosses could treat you like dirt." Albert's eyes were overshadowed by a dim faraway look. "If only the bosses could realise that, and treat their workers properly all the time; there'd be no industrial trouble at all.

"Our solidarity can see us through any crisis. Don't forget lad, that if all the Indians ganged up on their chief their arrows would soon polish him off.

"And it's just the same for you. You don't have to accept what Saint Christopher says just because he's the boss. After all, your places in heaven were won by your good life on Earth. What happens now you're dead surely can't alter that. You stand up for yourself, lad. If you feel you want to leave here and go to heaven now, you tell Saint Christopher."

During Albert's lifetime it had often been said by his critics and the unkinder members of society that he had less grey matter above the neck than did a chicken in an egg. But his heart had always been in the right place, they said, more or less to the left; which was a constant source of amusement to those in the Brindon Labour Party who thought they were possessed of a quick sense of humour.

Had they been dead, like poor Albert, and witnessed his attempted indoctrination of a forty-five-year-old ghost, even they might have done a double take. The big advantage of a trades unionist is their strike potential, and all Albert's friends and contacts had been such fodder. If the ugly face of capitalism had failed to meet their demands they had withdrawn their labour at the drop of a hat.

But Albert—of whom it had once been said, again by those prepared to cut deep, that the gleam of light shining in his ear was a glimpse of daylight filtering through from the other ear—had not realised that Bobby's strike potential was somewhat limited, if not nonexistent.

Bobby stood up and took half a dozen paces across the great hall before turning sharply to look at Albert, still seated on the bottom step.

"You just don't understand, do you?" he asked, shaking his head slowly. "It'd be terrific if I could do that, but it…it's just impossible."

Albert could not see it. But as he did not subscribe to the view that those who will not see are perhaps amongst those who are none so blind, he thought Bobby was being a mite pedantic.

The grandfather clock under the stairs made its proclamation. At Marlston on a weekday morning, eight chimes indicated that bacon and eggs, sausages, mushrooms, and devilled kidneys were assembled for muster in the dining room.

Bobby asked if Albert had seen Lord Barrington-Pottsherbert yet, and on learning that he still had that pleasure ahead, declared himself to be in charge. He led the way through a closed door to the dining room and they waited for His Lordship to put in an appearance.

April was the time of year Lord Maxwell Filchester Barrington-Pottsherbert and Lady Sylvia Amelia Barrington-

Pottsherbert hated the most. There were other months they hated as well, but April took the prize because it was then that, by popular demand, they were forced to reopen Marlston to the gaping public.

While the front door was reserved for family and friends, garish arrows painted on white signs outside led the two-pounds-fifty-pence-a-timers from the spacious car park at the side of the house to a door by the ice cream kitchen.

It was the third day of the 1980 season and the lord and lady had so far kept themselves very much in the background. They lived in half a dozen rooms in the West Wing, but the other sixty or so rooms were regarded by the tourists as being theirs when they paraded through with fervour, day after day.

Each day they trooped noisily among the maze of rooms, leaving their chewing gum on light switches, door handles, and velvet chair backs, until Riley, the butler, was on the verge of tearing out what little remained of his hair.

There was an army of cleaners, of course, but Riley liked to be on hand personally to supervise the operation.

In two and a half hours the first cars and coach parties of the day would be crunching their way over the gravel parking area and the treadmill would again begin its daily grind until seven o'clock.

Hundreds, if not thousands, of enthusing mums, moaning dads, crying or snotty-nosed kids with fingers and mouths smothered in mint choc ice or orange ice-lolly, doddery grandpas, wobbling grandmas, pointing aunts, loudly dressed uncles, senile great-aunts, and ancient great-uncles would all descend on the endless corridors from their suburban semis, the council estates, and the bijou villages.

A resounding slap on the back of hands or legs was the usual sequel to a young sticky paw being aimed at the priceless

Ming vase on the shelf in the cordoned-off-with-twisted-red-rope-and-keep-out-strictly-private area that the rascally siblings had crept into. And the sequel to the sequel was a few moments of bawling while Mum professed to never having been so embarrassed in all her born days, Dad pretending not to notice and saying how beautifully turned were the legs on the Queen Anne chair, and the elderly couple behind muttering to themselves that in their day children had known the meaning of the word *discipline*.

Such was a normal day in the life of Marlston Manor, and Lord and Lady Barrington-Pottsherbert felt their enormous leisurely breakfast was the only way to start it.

In the dining room Albert eyed the dishes of hot food enviously. His usual breakfast had been a bowl of shredded wheat and two rounds of toast and beef dripping, which shrank into insignificance alongside the appetizing bacon, eggs, mushrooms, sausages, and kidneys.

Bobby and Albert perched on the window seat and watched Lord and Lady Barrington-Pottsherbert begin their meal with more than a little vigour.

Bobby suddenly leaped up with a worried frown. "Daphne'll be wondering where I've got to," he exclaimed. "I told her I was just coming down for my morning stroll. Come on, Albert."

He stood quite still and closed his eyes. Instantly his body began to fade from sight, and Albert could see the laden table right through Bobby's shirt.

"Here, hang on," cried Albert, alarmed. "What are you doing?"

Bobby opened his eyes again and was instantly solid to Albert's eyes once more. "We live in an attic room," he said. "I'm going up there now. You'll share with us while you're here, won't you?"

"But wha...what did you just do then, when you started to

disappear?" Being a novice in the art of successful haunting, Albert had only just mastered the thought of walking through solid walls and doors and having butlers walk through him. The idea that he could make himself disappear merely by closing his eyes was one that had not yet become the inkling of an electrical impulse in the deepest wiring system of his mind.

Bobby had had forty-five years of practice, and quite rightly regarded himself as something of an expert.

"It's merely concentration," he said. "You close your eyes and think hard about where you want to go." His eyelids drooped, and he was gone. "And instantly you're there." This time his voice came from behind Albert. Albert whirled round, and there in the corner stood Bobby, who had gone from one side of the room to the other without moving—just by closing his eyes.

And all the time Lord and Lady Barrington-Pottsherbert were making great inroads into their breakfast, blissfully unaware of the incredible goings-on around their table.

"Come on, have a go," urged Bobby excitedly. It was the first time he had had to teach a fellow ghost how to move himself with a thought, and he was positively enjoying it.

"I call it gleeking. Come on, you'll soon get the hang of it."

Although Albert was on the right lines, his first few attempts could hardly be called an unqualified success. First of all he thought he wanted to go to the other side of the table. He did go to the other side, but a touch too far, and his legs disappeared inside the sideboard, leaving his head, chest, and arms poking out of the top, like a pig's head on a plate with the front legs left on.

"A bit more concentration; that's all that's needed," laughed Bobby. Concentration to Albert was working out a spot-the-ball quiz or doing the picture crossword in his nephew's puzzle book for the under-tens. Or, if he were really pushed, it could be stretched to aiming for treble-twenty during a darts match at Brindon Working Men's Club.

Eventually, though, he was able to control his thoughts with a modicum of ease. Enough to attempt to think himself up to the attic with Bobby, anyway.

He opened his eyes and felt it was more through luck than skill that he found himself standing in the attic alongside Bobby and the most beautiful girl he had ever seen. Well, someone who would run a close second to Abigail, he thought, swallowing a lump in his throat. Abigail. His Abigail, who had lost her love with Albert's death.

Albert was introduced to the stunning Miss Pride and expressed a sentiment of being extremely honoured and pleased to meet her. Bobby explained Albert's temporary plight to her, and how he was going to stay with them for a while.

Daphne enthused as much as Bobby about having a new face around the place and someone new to talk to.

"The life of a ghost is very boring," she said sadly. "There's nothing to do, no fun to be had anywhere."

Albert studied Daphne when he thought she wasn't looking. She was certainly the most attractive girl he had seen, with her deep blue eyes and flowing hair the colour of ripe corn. He could see why Bobby had been prepared to commit suicide all those years ago to be with her again.

Looking around his new home, Albert could not say with all honesty that he was impressed. A foot-and-a-half of light shone lethargically in through the tiny window in the ceiling. But it was enough to show up the dust and cobwebs which had made themselves at home. The room itself was quite large for an attic and Albert thought it probably capped much of the West Wing. Where the corners were not full of bundles of newspaper tied up with string, they were full of wooden chests, chairs, and a large bed.

Until he knew better, Albert thought the bed was where Bobby and Daphne slept, and he wondered where he could rest his head. In his naivety and lack of experience of being dead, he had yet to learn that ghosts did not sleep. Neither did they eat or drink. It is only the body and physical brain which are recharged through sleep and food. The spirit needs no sustenance.

If Albert's friends, workmates, and fellow trades unionists could see him now they would consider he had found Utopia. He had no work to do, and to them that was everything. But it was not long before Albert fell prey to the ghosts' nightmare as described by Daphne—boredom.

"There must be something to do," he moaned.

"Very little," Daphne told him grimly. "For us, the first ten years were the worst, but it shouldn't be too bad for you. You know you'll only be here for a short while. We've still got more than fifty years to go."

Bobby felt he ought to change the subject before Albert started on his indoctrination again. "Why don't you have a look around the house first of all, and get to know it? Practice your gleeking a little."

Albert felt his gleeking could certainly do with a little practice, and thought the suggestion the best he was likely to get.

He gleeked from room to room, but failed to appreciate the fine antiques and art, along with gold and silver, which abounded everywhere. He thought the gold taps in the Barrington-Pottsherberts' luxury en-suite bathroom to be both vulgar and ostentatious. Likewise, the sunken bath.

The three racehorses in the stable were more to his fancy, though. Albert had often partaken of a flutter. Indeed, his local bookie regarded him as a valued client, as it was his dead certs more frequently being dead than cert that paid for the bookie's powder-blue Mercedes.

Albert spent much of the day exploring his new home and its grounds. He sat in a chandelier in the King Charles I Room, looking down as the trippers filed past the four-poster bed with its silk curtains and sign proclaiming "Charles I slept here in 1644."

He spent some time sitting on the counter in the ice cream kitchen, pulling faces at the customers who stared right through him, unaware of his ghostly presence.

He stood by the lake as cheeky schoolchildren skimmed stones at the swans. He gleeked into a glass cage and put his arms around a stuffed fox, stuck his tongue out and blew raspberries.

Then he was bored again. *It does seem to be a waste of time doing all this when they can't even see me,* he thought.

Time passed. He stood up from the circular seat around the summer house. Instead of gleeking, he decided to kill a few more minutes by walking back to the mansion.

As he crossed the car park the last few straggling vehicles were snaking their way along the drive back to the road. Marlston was winding down for the day.

The door to the ice cream kitchen opened and a harassed-looking man emerged lugging a huge bag over his shoulder.

Intrigued by the appearance of the man with the bag, Albert followed him round the side of the house, through a door marked "Private," and along a brightly-lit corridor to another door also announcing that privacy was required. The man knocked and went straight in without waiting for a response. He closed the door quickly behind him, but, of course, closed doors now presented no deterrent to Albert. As

Albert strode through he heard the man with the bag telling a man with big ears sitting behind a desk how pleased he was that the day was over.

"We've taken a fair bit, I can tell you. We'd sold out of banana and raspberry flavoured lollies before four o'clock. Rushed off our feet, we were."

The man with the ears took the bag and rattled the money inside it. "Good," he said. "I should think His Lordship can afford that portable telly for the bathroom with this."

Portable tellies in the bathroom and gold taps were too much for Albert. He thought that if he threw his three-bedroomed council house and its gardens open to the public he would not even raise the price of a pint. And he would be right.

"Why should this Lord Whatever-His-Name-Is get away with all this?" he cried, too incensed to realise that neither the man with the bag nor the man with the ears could hear him.

"It's the privileged few having it easy again and getting money for nothing. And you two are helping him."

They carried on their conversation oblivious to his ghostly rantings and ravings. "My God," shouted Albert. "I wish you could hear me. I'd tell you a thing or two."

The man with the ears stopped talking and looked up. "Who said that?" he asked, a puzzled frown creasing his brow.

"I don't know. It seemed to come from over there," said Bagman, pointing in Albert's direction. They peered round the office tentatively, rather like a big game-hunter seeing a fast-advancing tiger and realising he has left his rifle at base camp.

"You ought to be bloody well ashamed," continued Albert. Then he suddenly realised he was not talking into empty air after all. "You can hear me?"

They seemed to have heard him as soon as he wished they could.

"Of course we can hear you—where are you?" they wanted to know.

Albert gleeked to the opposite corner. "I'm here." By the time they whirled round he had gleeked again, and this time stood between them. "I'm here now." Their eyes wide, they turned to face each other. There was no-one else there.

"It must be a trick of some sort," said Ear-man.

Albert would have liked to stay and play a little longer, but felt he could put his newly discovered powers to a much better use, and needed to talk with Bobby and Daphne first.

***

"For the last time, no," Bobby told Albert firmly, after hearing Albert's request. "We have to purge our sins. If we get involved in this sort of thing we'll be here forever. It'll go against you, as well, if you carry out this harebrained scheme."

"But how much money has he taken from the tourists today?" Albert proclaimed to the horrified sweethearts as he declared his intentions. On his gleeking around the house he had noticed with distaste a white Rolls-Royce snuggling up to a racing green Daimler in the garage. To say nothing of the Range Rover and Mini Clubman sitting forlornly at the back.

"It's scandalous. They must have taken thousands, one way or another. It's no wonder they can afford all these luxuries and be able to live it up like this. And the money's coming out of the pocket of the working man. They're parasites, these people, nothing but parasites—and I'm going to put a stop to it."

But it looked as if Albert would have to embark on a one-man crusade, because both Bobby and Daphne said they were having nothing to do with it.

"Okay," Albert said. "If that's the way you feel. But something's got to be done, and I intend to do it. With or without your help I'm going to be a proper ghost and do a ghost's duties. I'll scare every last tripper away from Marlston Manor—you see if I don't. From now on a hostile spirit will haunt these ancient corridors. And that hostile spirit is me."

CHAPTER 3

In which we meet two angels at a limpid pool

ALBERT SPENT HIS first night as a sleepless ghost pondering over the coming days. How should the phantom of Marlston make his entrance? What powers could he summon to aid him? There was a galaxy of things he must find out. He knew he could make people hear him just by wishing it...and it was only a simple thought that lay behind the art of gleeking. So perhaps a thought could help in other areas, too.

He mentally told a chair to rise from the ground. It didn't. He told a bundle of newspapers to scatter themselves over the floor. They wouldn't.

Harder concentration brought the same dismal result, and Albert imagined his old class teacher from Brindon Secondary Modern School standing over him.

"Come on, Carter, stop daydreaming, lad, and listen to me. You're useless—what are you? Useless. It's like trying to milk a bull to get you to understand anything."

Albert could picture the end-of-term reports: "Chair Lifting, could do better, more concentration needed; Newspaper Scattering, poor, not got a clue." And the final remark: "I hope your boy enjoys his holiday as much as I'm going to enjoy mine."

At school, though, he could always copy someone else's work or talk his way out of a seemingly impossible position. He used to spend all the time he should have been doing homework thinking of a new excuse as to why he hadn't done it. Once he had even told his maths teacher that he was doing exactly that.

"I was too busy thinking of something new to tell you, sir," he had pleaded, "that I didn't have time to work out those percentages." And the maths teacher was so impressed with the excuse, because he had not heard it before, that he let Albert off.

Albert wasn't to know at that early stage in his disruptive life that percentages would later figure heavily in it. If he'd worked harder on his percentages perhaps a few strikes over pay could have been avoided at Jebson's. Albert could work out percentages as long as they were nice round figures such as twenty-five or fifty percent. But management always offered something silly like four-and-a-half percent, or point-eight of one percent. And because he could not work out how much more money that would mean in his pocket each week he turned the offer down.

But here was something he had to do without peering over anyone's shoulder. Somehow he must find out for himself how to be a proper ghost. Ghosts he had heard about always rattled chains or carried their heads under their arms. He could do neither. He pulled at his head, but it remained as firmly attached to his neck as it had always been. He shook his belt, but a belt rattling sounded nothing like a chain.

Inspiration, like opportunity, knocks but once, and then usually at the back door. And Albert had known once before what it was like to be inspired. It had happened on that memorable night when he needed a treble-nineteen and double-seven to win an important darts match. He had thrown them perfectly. Perhaps that had been Albert's once-in-a-lifetime inspiration.

But no, it happened again, here at Marlston Manor. It washed upon Albert, leaving him feeling rather weak at the knees. He regarded it as a flash of genius. He knew there were still many mysteries yet to be presented to him in the afterlife, let alone be unravelled, but he was sure he had solved one, at least.

"Of course," he exclaimed. "When I wanted them to hear me, they could. So if I want them to see me, they'll be able to see me."

***

Somewhere in the great beyond, at a place far removed from the humble earth where the mists of time are perpetually kept at bay, two angels stared into a limpid pool.

The waters had shimmered and sparkled, and by the magic of some unimaginable spell, all that had transpired at Marlston in the last few hours had been seen in their depths. The first angel caught his wandering halo with the tip of a shining wing and proclaimed the folly of giving men like Albert an inkling of logic. He was Nethanial Jebson's guardian angel, Wallace.

Albert's guardian angel, Mozelbeek, turned to him and said that had God been less sparing when dishing out brains for certain angels, heaven would perhaps not be such hell to live in. Mozelbeek was sure Wallace was to blame somehow for Albert catching his death in the torrential rain that had suddenly been unleashed upon Brindon and the picket line. After all, Wallace had been seen talking to the clouds.

Mozelbeek's problem was that he couldn't prove it, which was just as well for Wallace. To deliberately change the course of destiny and lead to a soul departing from Earth before its pre-ordained time was unprofessional conduct at its worst. It was seen as wilfully depriving another guardian angel of his duties, which the rule book said was intolerable and called for expulsion from the Alliance of Guardian Angels, more commonly referred to as the AGA.

It was said that without an Alliance card it was impossible

for even a fully-trained and highly-experienced guardian angel to find work in his own field, but no-one had dared put it to the test in crossing the powerful Alliance. Mozelbeek couldn't prove anything because he had been at an AGA Executive Committee meeting at the time and was not around to see exactly what happened.

Mozelbeek and Wallace had sparred throughout history using mortals as their pieces in a gigantic chess game. They had each had failures and successes with the mortals they guided. Hitler, for example, would never have committed suicide if Wallace had been allowed to jam the gun as he had wanted. But in those final days of the Second World War, Wallace had been under close scrutiny to ensure he did not overstep the boundaries of his duty.

It was Mozelbeek who had sent the spider to Robert the Bruce, and launched Sir Winston Churchill on a spectacular, overachieving career through Parliament.

Now Wallace and Mozelbeek were again pitting their wits. Mozelbeek had scored a handful of minor victories when Wallace's charge, Nethanial Jebson, had bowed to the demands made by Albert, Mozelbeek's charge. So when no-one was looking Wallace played the ace from up his sleeve.

But in reality the ace turned out to be quite the joker, leaving Wallace with a more difficult task. The rulebook requires an angel to keep his charge until that soul had entered heaven or hell, meaning Mozelbeek would stay responsible for Albert during his time on Earth as a ghost. A common fallacy down the ages was that everyone has a separate guardian angel; but as there just aren't enough guardian angels to go round, many have to look after more than one soul at any one time. Whether it was the long arm of coincidence or a mischievous trick of Destiny's, Wallace did not know. What he did know, though, was that he didn't like it. He was also the guardian angel for both Lord and Lady Barrington-Pottsherbert, and therefore still had Albert and Mozelbeek to contend with.

So when he heard Albert work out the secret of making himself visible to mortals he knew the Barrington-Pottsherberts were in for a hard time—and announced it unfortunate that Albert had been blessed with a little logic.

***

Albert was not to know that his next discovery was made courtesy of a little prompting from Mozelbeek. He saw Daphne Pride pick up a chair and move it to a spot where the moonlight shone in through the attic window. Remembering how his own hand had gone straight through the door knocker when he tried to grip it, he wondered how Daphne could pick up a chair.

"It's just the same as all our other powers," she explained. "You think you want to pick something up, and you can. It's easy."

Albert tried it, and she was right—it was easy. He practiced for a while until he was sure he would be able to do anything to scare away the visitors to the manor. He could speak in a disembodied voice; while still invisible he could pick things up and make it look as if they were floating about the room by themselves; he could make himself partly visible, a see-through spectre; he could make himself fully visible. In fact, he felt he could do absolutely anything he liked. He smiled. He was going to have a fine old time as the Ghost of Marlston Manor.

***

At sunrise Albert stood outside on the hill, marvelling at the wondrous powers he had discovered since he was there just twenty-four hours earlier.

He was beside himself with excitement and could hardly

wait for the flock of visitors to arrive. He had not thought any plan through to a conclusion but had decided how to begin as soon as the chance came his way, and from then on the sweet music of success would be played by ear.

Albert was not a man given over to emotion unless he was putting the downtrodden workers' case in a pay claim to the unrelenting management. But it was with new feeling that he saw the beauty of the sun peeping over the green horizon.

It was as if the sun had been frustrated with coming up over the power station every morning with Albert still in bed missing it all. The sun told Albert how glad she was to see him. "Sometimes it's ever so lonely," she complained. "While the morning birdsong is lovely for a while, it does get a bit monotonous after a few million years. I was even grateful for the pea-brained dinosaurs' attention when they ruled the earth, but mankind seems to take me for granted. I often say that one day I won't rise at all. And I would, as well, but mankind would only say I'd gone on strike and light a candle until the dispute was settled."

If Albert had known the tune of "For The Beauty of the Earth" he would have hummed it. But even "All Things Bright and Beautiful" eluded him, so he was left to sing "The Red Flag." It served its purpose; the sun enjoyed the music, although she said she had never risen for "The Red Flag" before.

Albert was waiting in the office when Ear-man came in. As the man sat down at his desk, Albert reached over and picked up a pen. He waggled it in the air before lodging it rakishly on one of those huge ears, then watched with glee as Ear-man leaped from his chair, the pen clattering to the floor and rolling out of sight under the desk.

"My God," yelled the man, whom Albert was later to discover was the Marlston estate manager. His eyes wide with fear, he leaned heavily on the filing cabinets. After all, not everyday did pens wave themselves about and find his ears attractive. His wife's fingers found his ears attractive, and by an amazing coincidence the first time she had playfully tweaked his lobes had been at the very same second that Albert's adventure with the big knockers had occurred in Oldham.

Before the manager could do anything else, Albert scattered a few papers about for good measure, then gleeked into the dining room where the Barrington-Pottsherberts were in the middle of breakfast. He snatched Lady Barrington-Pottsherbert's forkful of grilled mushrooms which was en route to her mouth and hurled it at the fireplace.

When His Lordship related the tale down the years he always exaggerated what happened next. "Well, I thought the old girl had gone mad," he would say. "I was just about to ring for Riley when this hideous creature climbed in through the window. I pounced on him straight away, of course, and we rolled around the floor locked in each other's arms for all of five minutes before the blighter hit me on the head with the coffee percolator. That smashed into a thousand pieces and I went out like a light. No recollection of him getting away, or anything. But I can tell you that Sylvia and I only just escaped with our lives. Strange business all round, what?"

Although many stranger things were to happen at Marlston over the next few days Lord Barrington-Pottsherbert never connected them to Albert's first visitation, and to this very day believes his breakfast was interrupted either by a burglar or by a fiendish yeti which happened to be passing and disliked grilled mushrooms so much that it threw his wife's at the fireplace.

What, in fact, happened, was this: Albert cried, "Geronimo!" and started pulling the curtains about. Lady Barrington-Pottsherbert fainted on the spot, and her brave hubby was making a quick escape bid to the door when he tripped over the rug and fell full-length onto the breakfast trolley, which, not having the benefit of brakes, crashed into the wall, smashing the percolator and bringing the crown of His Lordship's head smartly into contact with said wall, knocking him out.

As Riley helped the elderly couple into chairs, the door burst open and the estate manager, Mr. Cochran, hurtled into the room yelling that a pen and papers had taken leave of their senses in his office.

Riley mumbled something about it always pouring, never simply raining, and politely suggested that Mr. Cochran should go away and tell the pen to behave itself, because he had more important work to do in sorting out everything and everyone in the dining room.

***

Wallace fumed as he watched Albert create havoc. "He could have induced a heart attack and killed them both in one fell swoop," he raged at Mozelbeek. "I've never seen anything so disgraceful. That spirit is disturbed. Only spirits authorised to walk the earth should become disruptive like that. He'll alter the whole fabric of the universe if he keeps this up for much longer."

Wallace was right, of course, but there was little he could do to stop Albert. And short of appearing at Marlston and telling Albert he was a naughty boy or dragging him away to a remote desert island, there was little Mozelbeek could do, either, even if he wanted to, which he very probably didn't.

Wallace's fears for the safety of the fabric of the universe referred to the balance of life. Albert was now swinging that balance dramatically. Had Albert stayed in the background and not made his presence felt all would have been well. But the problem, for the angels and the fabric of the universe, was that he insisted on becoming known to those who were still alive. And as well as having more than a little unnerving effect on mere mortals who were not used to seeing or dealing with ghosts, Destiny had set out the fate of the universe on the assumption that most spirits enter the kingdom of heaven or the kingdom of hell almost as soon as they move out of the earthly realm.

It was usually known before someone died if their soul would have to walk the earth, and enough moves were made to correct the balance if they needed to show themselves as ghosts. But perhaps Destiny had not foreseen Albert Carter. Maybe she had thought he would live quietly at Marlston Manor until Saint Christopher recalled him. Had Destiny done her homework properly? Could it be said that the danger to the equilibrium of the universe had been caused by Destiny herself? She had given Albert the freedom of Marlston, and did she now have a problem on her hands?

"Hmmm. Gotta do something about this," Wallace said to himself, as he slipped a serious and responsible thought past Mozelbeek and into Albert's mind: a thought that perhaps his actions could have drastic repercussions on completely innocent people.

"It's a very fine balance," the smuggled thought told Albert. "And you're going to upset it."

The Condition Of Transit was only a marginally lower plane of consciousness than were heaven or hell themselves, but it was enough to make the universe top-heavy if too many spirits in it announced their existence to the world.

It turns out, Wallace had chosen an unfortunate time to kill Albert off, as there were already plenty of spirits who denounced the closed shop of heaven or hell and chose to stay on Earth as ghosts.

Unlike Wallace, Mozelbeek was sure Albert's little excursions into the realms of the ghost world would not do any lasting damage. He would not be long at Marlston and the balance could be corrected when he was recalled to Saint Christopher.

And the angel was pleased to be able to play another hand against Wallace. The game was not yet over—Mozelbeek was determined to win the last few battles before he lost Albert forever. But, of course, he had no idea who was looking over his shoulder at the cards in his hand.

***

Albert felt the principle for which he was fighting, against the Barrington-Pottsherberts' greedy capitalism, was far more important than upsetting a worldwide balance, and he banished the intruding, smuggled, thought.

He watched intently as a shaking Mr. Cochran opened the combination safe in his office to get enough money for the cash floats at the entrance, the ice cream kitchen, the snack bar, the tour-of-the-gardens gate, and the souvenir shop. Albert had not worked at his uncle's grocery store on Saturday mornings and during the school holidays without knowing that a float was necessary when the day's trading began.

He had seen the safe in Mr. Cochran's office last night; he had seen a bulging money bag taken to the office and quickly connected the two. All that remained for him to do was to find the combination and he could put his plan into working effect.

Mr. Cochran transferred a fair amount of money into a leather hold-all, put the rest back into the safe and clanged it shut. He spun the combination as if it were the wheel of fortune and hurried off on his round of tills with the hold-all. Albert rubbed his hands with glee. This was better than he had hoped for. The combination was still fresh in his mind as he reached for the wheel. In a couple of minutes he had the money bags out on the floor beside him. Should he leave the safe open or should he add further to the mystery Mr. Cochran would face later by closing it?

He plumped for the latter, and the door clanged shut with a satisfying and resounding ring. Had Albert known Mr. Cochran planned to take the previous day's takings to the bank after making sure each till had a good float, he may well have waited in the office to watch his face when he found it gone. As it was, he decided to wait in the Charles I Room and put the money bags under the four-poster.

Meanwhile, Mr. Cochran was distributing money at the tills as Marlston gradually yawned into another working day.

The steady stream of two-pound-fifties began to cross from pockets to tills as the daily routine began again. The noisy hubbub of visitors even penetrated into the Barrington-Pottsherberts' private living quarters as Riley tried to persuade the couple that they must have been the victims of an hallucination. After all, he felt his feet were planted firmly on the ground, so why shouldn't everyone else's be? Burglars and yetis, indeed.

He only had His Lordship's word that someone else had been in the dining room and he did not see how they could have got in or out. The window was firmly locked and no-one had come past him in the corridor. "No, indeed," he said to himself. "They've imagined it."

Just a few moments later Mr. Cochran's face was an absolute picture. Certain parts of his body definitely slumped towards the office carpet: one physically—his jaw dropped—and the other was in accordance with popular legend—his heart sank. It was if a giant crab held his stomach firmly in its powerful grip when he opened the safe and found the money gone.

Frantically he searched the office but all the time he knew it would be to no avail. He could clearly remember putting the money back inside. No way had he not put it in. And yet there was no doubt about it, the cupboard was bare.

For a moment he began to question his sanity. What with pens and papers developing a life of their own, and now the money disappearing, perhaps he was starting to go bananas. No, there must be a rational explanation, he thought. But what would the others think? They might investigate further the question "is old Cochran going bananas?" And they might come to an altogether more disturbing conclusion than the one he reached.

Then he remembered the disturbance in the dining room, and also how someone had spoken to him and the ice cream manager the night before.

"It's an elaborate robbery," he cried, and ran out to find the Barrington-Pottsherberts.

With it being the schools' Easter holiday there were plenty of families who decided to incorporate a visit to Marlston in their day trip to the countryside, and before long the crowds were flocking through the mansion and going on the garden tour. It was a bit early for the hot dog and hamburger man, but the ice cream kitchen was already doing a roaring trade.

Albert lay on the bed where King Charles was said to have slept and savoured the fun he was soon to have. "Not long now," he told himself. "Just a few more moments, then off we go."

He watched the people as they passed through the bedroom on their way to the stuffed wildlife display. They paused for about five minutes to look at the priceless antiques and famous bed. Once, an inquisitive nine-year-old wandered too close for Albert's liking, and a nifty tweak of the nose by a ghostly hand was enough to send him sobbing back to Mummy.

Albert stretched, then stood up. The time had come,

he decided, for the Ghost of Marlston Manor to make his presence known to an altogether unsuspecting world. He smiled as he reached under the bed for the money bags.

The smile froze on his ghostly lips. He was sure he had put the bags in that corner. So where were they? He lifted the cover and peered into the gloom. Not only was there no chamber pot to be seen, there were no money bags either!

A terrified grandmother saw the corner of the bedsheet mysteriously raise itself. She was not to know it was really Albert lifting it. Even if she had known she would probably not have believed it. And Albert knew how she would feel. He stared in the same disbelief at the empty spot on which he was absolutely certain he had placed those money bags not an hour earlier.

***

At the exact moment Albert learned that the bags had gone from under the bed Mr. Cochran was pouring out the story to Lord and Lady Barrington-Pottsherbert about how they had disappeared from the safe, and how he and the ice cream manager had heard the mysterious voice the night before as they discussed the day's takings.

Mr. Jackson, the ice cream manager, was called to corroborate Mr. Cochran's story. "That's right, Your Lordship," he said. "The voice told us we ought to be bloody well ashamed of ourselves. And it kept coming from different parts of the room. Just like a ventriloquist throwing his voice, it was, sir. He was good at it, too."

"He's good with safes as well," added Mr. Cochran. "I wasn't gone more than twenty minutes and he'd cracked the combination lock and fled with the money."

Lord Barrington-Pottsherbert jumped up. "Let's go and investigate at the scene of the crime. Look for clues, and all that."

They made their way to the office in the forlorn hope of finding discarded cigarette ends, footprints, fingerprints, and other clues detectives in cheap paperback novels take one look at before confidently naming the guilty party.

"Let's see if there's anything in the safe that the burglar left behind," said Mr. Cochran. "When I saw that the money had gone I didn't bother to look inside carefully, I just ran straight out without even...closing...the...safe...door." His voice trailed off as he looked down and saw the safe door firmly shut and locked.

"I...I know I didn't c-close that door," he stammered. "It was wide open when I left it. Now look at it."

Feverishly he dived towards it, his fingers frantically twisting the combination first this way, then that way, then this way and that again, until the tumblers all fell into position and the door swung open. He peered inside and a strangled cry escaped his suddenly parched mouth.

If ever the moment had to come when the earth would crack open and gulp him deep inside he wished that moment could be now. For there on the shelf in the safe, grinning cheekily back at him as if they had never been away, sat the money bags.

Lord Barrington-Pottsherbert pushed him aside and hauled the bags out on to the desk. He pulled the cords loose at the top and out tumbled a variety of coins and notes.

"What the devil are you playing at, Cochran?" he shouted angrily. "Wasting my time like this. If someone's stolen my money, what's it doing here, eh?"

"I just don't understand it," moaned Mr. Cochran. "It wasn't there a few moments ago, sir, I swear it wasn't."

"I'll see you later," growled His Lordship, and he strode out of the office, closely followed by Her Ladyship.

Mr. Jackson gently eased Mr. Cochran into a chair. "Are you absolutely sure the money wasn't there earlier, George?" He laid a soothing hand on George Cochran's shoulder.

The angels could have taken bets on which way Mr. Cochran would react. Would he be indignant and angry at the veiled suggestion that he had lost his marbles, or would he simply break down in tears?

As it was, he chose the latter. "Well, I didn't think it was," he sobbed. "I opened the safe door to get it out ready to go to the bank, and it wasn't there. I'm sure it wasn't." He stared unhappily at the bags and the mound of money on his desk, then put his head in his hands.

While this was all going on in Mr. Cochran's office, Albert was still upstairs in the Charles I Room, too angry and puzzled to sob, but he knew without doubt that he was in no danger of losing his marbles. He had definitely put that money under the bed, of that he was completely sure. What had happened to it in the meantime he had no idea, but he did know there would be a perfectly rational explanation for it. All he had to do was find out what it was, and the money would be close on its heels.

He pondered awhile. The money was needed for part of his plan, but he certainly had no intention of remaining idle until it turned up. Oh dear, no—there were many other ways and means for the Ghost of Marlston Manor to make his presence felt.

Albert smiled to himself and gleeked.

CHAPTER 4

In which a suit of armour goes wild, and a queen is sacrificed

BOBBY AND DAPHNE were worried about their own position at Marlston. Although it was Albert causing the trouble they had agreed it would look bad for them to be there while it was all going on. When the time came for them to be recalled for Saint Christopher to see if they had purged their sins of long ago, they feared they might find further charges against them. Charges of having been involved in the Marlston hauntings.

They had spent all night wondering what they could do, and decided their best course of action would be to try and sabotage Albert's schemes. What they could actually do, they were not sure, but they felt they must give it a go, so at least on their Judgement Day they could tell Saint Christopher they had tried to stop him.

They kept a close eye on him, and when they saw him take the money from the safe they felt he must want it for part of his plan. Just how he could use it they had no idea, but they agreed they must get it back from him if they could.

So they were highly delighted when he slipped it beneath the four-poster and then lay down on the bed. It was a simple matter for Bobby to gleek under the bed, and then gleek with the money back to the office. He, too, knew the combination, and in a matter of seconds the bags were back in their place in the safe.

The couple might have been a little upset if they had seen the disturbing effect the money's reappearance had on Lord

Barrington-Pottsherbert and Mr. Cochran, but they had gleeked back to watch Albert.

Albert had gleeked from the Charles I Room down to the side entrance hall where the visitors were queuing with their two-pound-fifties. Bobby and Daphne were careful not to let him spot them as they appeared in the hall. They knew of the power they didn't have. The power of ghosts to make themselves visible to humans was all very well…but what they didn't consider to be very well right now was the fact that ghosts can't make themselves invisible from each other. So they had to crouch down behind the cashier's desk as Albert made his way towards a suit of armour which stood at the bottom of the sweeping staircase like a guard at Buckingham Palace.

He had spotted the armour immediately and thought that perhaps it would make his debut even more spectacular than his original plan would have done. But he made up his mind that the money would still play its part eventually. *First things first, though,* he thought, and thrust his hand through the breastplate inside the suit. It was completely empty. A quick examination revealed that the legs had been locked solid to keep it upright, but that did not deter him. Thanks to his recently acquired ghostly powers he reckoned it would be a simple task to bring the armour to life. His limbs filled the metallic arms and legs as he stepped inside. With the locked legs, it was no use trying to get the armour to walk, but, to his delight, a swift thought enabled him to move off in it, floating an inch or two above the ground.

Gingerly Albert moved his left arm. And the left arm of the suit creaked into life. But as it did so, the evil-looking axe which was held in the right hand, leaning on the left arm, clattered to the floor.

There was a stunned silence as heads turned towards the armour.

"Oh," gasped one woman. "Frightened the living daylights out of me, that did." If that was enough to scare her, there's no telling what Albert's next action did to her. Slowly he raised both arms and issued a low-pitched moan that lingered in the air for several seconds: "*Oooooaaaaaooooooh.*"

He floated towards the horrified visitors, this time turning his moans into what was at first a barely legible message. He felt good; he had the attention of everyone in the hall and thought it best not to waste any time.

"Beware," he cried. "There is evil in this *hoouuuse.* I'm here to protect *yooouuuu.* Leave here immediately or you will come to *haaaarm.*"

The crowd didn't move. They couldn't. They were rooted to the spot in fascinated horror. Then one of the more sceptical teenagers piped up: "There's a bloke in there." He ran forward and pulled up the visor, fully expecting to see an embarrassed face squirming inside. It was empty. There was no head to be seen, but there was no mistaking where the voice came from. It came from where the head should have been.

"You have been warned," boomed Albert in as low a pitch as he could muster. "There is danger here. It has been lying dormant and still across the years, but has now awoken, and is moving through the house. You're all in danger. Leave now or regret it for all eternity."

The brave youngster was suddenly faced with the very real prospect of having made a ghostly mistake, and let out a yell.

"Ohmigawd, there's no-one in there." He dropped the visor shut with an echoing clang and ran for the door. The otherwise stillness in the room lived on for a few more seconds, but died a horrible death as everyone glimpsed the truth the teenager had seen. No volcano had seen an eruption like it. People were crying, screaming, and howling as they fled from the room, down every corridor they could find and out of every door the hall could provide. Some hurled themselves up the stairs, some clambered out of the windows, but one thing remained firmly implanted in each and every mind—and that was the maniacal laugh resonating from the empty suit of armour as it floated down a passage towards the ice cream kitchen.

The cashier leaped from her seat, babbling hysterically, staring down the passage after Albert. In the three years she had been taking the entrance money, the suit of armour had never so much as even whispered. She looked hard, almost disbelievingly, at the empty spot on which it had, until now, eternally stood.

Bobby and Daphne leaped up, too. "We've got to stop him," cried Bobby. "He'll frighten everyone away at once unless we do something."

Albert was really enjoying himself and felt it would not take long to achieve his objective. When he clanged through the door everyone froze as solid as the ice cream they were queuing to buy. Eyes and mouths wide, they looked on as Albert floated over to the counter and sat down on it…the locked legs sticking straight out in front of him.

"I'm here to warn you," he boomed, lifting the visor himself this time to reveal an empty interior. "You must leave this house of evil at once."

Like a row of standing dominoes toppled by a light finger pushing the foremost one, a fire of hysteria blazed through the queue. And just to fan the flames a little more, Albert let out a blood-curdling cry and started pirouetting around the room, the armour creaking and groaning as it went.

The hordes of people who had fled from the entrance now stood trembling in the car park. No-one tried to deny what they had seen, even if they didn't want to believe it. There was no doubt that the suit of armour had been empty—and they were sure it hadn't been suspended on wires from the ceiling.

There was a feeling of intense, but frightened, excitement. No-one had seen a ghost before, but now they were outside in the bright sunshine, things seemed a little different. From all round the crowd, people could be heard telling each other how it wasn't as frightening as it had seemed when they were actually face to face with the armour.

"Well, I wasn't really scared of it, of course; I just felt it was a father's duty to get the wife and kids out. They were terrified. That's why I ran out first, trying to clear a path for them."

They were just beginning to pluck up enough courage to go back in, at least to demand their money back, when a new round of screams emerged from within the ancient walls. Albert had found another crowd to pass the time of day with, this time those looking at the glass cases full of stuffed animals and birds in the wildlife exhibition. It was wildlife of the human variety which flocked down the stairs and out of the door a few seconds later.

Bobby and Daphne had caught up with Albert as he arrived at the exhibition. Everyone was already as still as the animals on display as they stared at the armour partaking of its ghostly dealings. The young lovers gripped Albert's arms and Bobby began to issue a stern warning. "Albert, get out of this suit of armour immediately. You don't know what harm you're causing by doing this."

The punters couldn't see or hear Bobby, of course—but they were readily witnessing Albert's side of the ghostly conversation, and that was more than enough.

As Albert shook his arms free, every joint of the armour rattled anxiously. "Get off me," he cried. "Don't stand in my way now." He gleeked, armour and all, to the other side of the room, determined that Bobby and Daphne would not stop him.

His gleeking had an even greater effect on the speechless witnesses, who now knew how the rabbit felt as it stood in the middle of the road paralysed by the glare of the oncoming headlights. To see a suit of armour floating about the room by itself was bad enough, but when it suddenly disappeared, to instantly reappear in another part of the room…well, the whole world could have exploded and no-one would have taken their horrified eyes off Albert at that moment.

Bobby and Daphne closed in on Albert again. "If you don't stop this, you'll regret it," shouted Bobby. But Albert ignored him. He gleeked to just inside the door, not so much as to stop the first hysterical screamer from making a premature getaway, as to escape himself from their clutches. "Leave me alone. This has nothing to do with you, so don't get involved."

"It's got everything to do with us," countered Daphne. "We've been here all these years without a hint of trouble. What right do you think you have to come here disturbing us and these people?"

"These people are being exploited," Albert shouted, oblivious to the fact that everyone could still hear him. "They're decent working folk who've been duped into putting money in the already overflowing and bloated pockets of the wealthy parasites who live here."

"But they don't have to come here," said Bobby. "They choose to pay, because they want to come. No-one's forcing them. Why should you try to stop their enjoyment—and who are you anyway to say they shouldn't come?"

"They've been indoctrinated by the capitalist society we're fighting against. It's not right that people like Barrington-Pottsherbert should have all this wealth, and then grab even more from people coming to see it. It's wholly indecent."

Albert floated up to the ceiling and shook the armour violently, shouting over the top of the rattling and banging: "I'm warning you all to leave this house *nooow*. Do as I say before it's too late."

His movement from the door, coupled with his ghostly warning, had the effect he desired. As if of one voice, the crowd became a screaming mass, almost falling over each other as they scrambled for the exit.

Albert was left alone in the room with Bobby and Daphne. He smiled at Daphne from underneath the raised visor. "Well thank you," he beamed. "I'll wager you making me shout like that has frightened them more than if I'd just been warning them."

Bobby and Daphne realised he was probably right. "Look, Albert," said Bobby. "Let's keep calm and talk this over. You don't know what you're doing. You've not been dead two days yet, and already you're causing more disruption and upset than we've had in all the time we've been here."

"Yes, you've told me that," protested Albert. "But as I've told you, I'm not going to stand back and watch all this happen without doing something to put a stop to it."

"But can't we get it through to you that these tourists obviously want to come here…and you shouldn't be plaguing them like this?"

"We'll see how much longer they'll want to come here," grinned Albert menacingly. "I think I've done very well so far in frightening them away. I'll just go and see what they're up to now…make sure they're as terrified as they should be."

He gleeked down to the deserted hall and stood the suit of armour back in its original position. Then he changed his thought that was keeping him inside it, and stepped out. Picking up the axe, which still lay where it had fallen, he also put that back where it came from, resting on the left arm, then pulled the visor down.

"Thanks for the help, pal." He patted the armour on its head. "I'll see you later." He wandered out to where everyone had gathered in the car park. By this time they had been joined by Mr. Cochran who had heard the noise and come out to see what was going on.

Mr. Jackson, the ice cream manager, was out there, too, and was wildly relating to Mr. Cochran how the suit of armour had sat on his counter and then started flying about the room making terrifying noises. There had been enough strange goings-on at the manor over the last couple of days to convince Mr. Cochran that everyone was right. He believed they must have seen a ghost, and decided to take charge of matters. He called for silence.

"Ladies and gentlemen, I apologise for any disturbance and for any fright you may have had, but it's all due to circumstances beyond our control. Could I ask you to be patient for just a few more moments, please? Lord Barrington-Pottsherbert himself will be informed of the situation immediately." He nudged the ice cream manager and whispered: "Come on, Cyril, we've got to get to the bottom of this, and pronto, or we'll have no tourists left."

Albert floated after them towards Lord Barrington-Pottsherbert's study.

"A ghost," roared the angry nobleman. "Don't be ridiculous. Never heard such a load of bally nonsense in all my life."

"It's true m'lord," protested Mr. Jackson. "Not only did the visitors all see it, but I saw it, too. Gladys said it was the suit of armour that stands by the side entrance. She saw it all happen."

A distant look came over Lord Barrington-Pottsherbert's face. "One of my ancestors, Sir Bartlewood Barrington, died in that suit in one of the early crusades in the Holy Land," he murmured. "So is it just conceivable, do you think, that he's come back to haunt me?"

"The spirit did say this was a house of evil and warned everyone to get out," said Mr. Jackson. "Do you think your ancestor's come back to tell us of some terrible danger we're facing?"

"Blowed if I know, but I suppose we'd better try to calm the visitors down first of all. We need to think of something to tell 'em. Can't have 'em thinking they've seen a ghost, it'll scare 'em all away and do untold damage to our trade." Lord Barrington-Pottsherbert strode out of his study, heading for the car park.

"Now listen to me," he ordered when he was sure of everyone's attention. "I'm told you've been having a spot of bother with one of my old suits of armour. Let me assure you there's nothing to be alarmed about. I've got one of my young nephews staying with me and it was just one of his practical jokes. He's done things like this before with electromagnets.

"If you all go to the sandwich bar at lunchtime I'll see to it that you get a free meal to compensate for your shock."

Albert smiled and left them to it. Some were still understandably shaken and didn't believe Lord Barrington-Pottsherbert's unlikely explanation. They were demanding their money back as Albert gleeked to the sandwich bar to check out the lie of the land for his next plan. Oh yes, when they came to collect their free lunches, what a chef's surprise he would be able to serve them. And what better way to dish it up than in a suit of armour? His smile broadened as he thanked the twist of fate that had taken the money bags from him and given him the armour instead.

Bobby and Daphne felt crushed and defeated. They had made matters worse. Instead of stopping Albert from frightening the visitors their efforts had only heightened the horrors the mere mortals were having to face.

"At least we tried, darling," said Daphne, taking Bobby's

arm. She shuddered as someone walked over her grave, and said: "Famous last words, I suppose."

"At least we tried, darling" had been the famous last words as many a brave soul parted company with its body throughout history, culminating with the extremely recent demise of an American stuntman and his good lady. The demented and now late lamented wife had uttered them to her husband as they plummeted to their deaths after attempting to make love on a tightrope suspended high above Niagara Falls.

Daphne hoped their fate would not be the same when their time came to be summoned to Saint Christopher. After all, darling, they had tried.

***

Lord Barrington-Pottsherbert put up notices diverting customers from the usual side entrance to the main entrance instead. Gladys was in no fit state to collect their money, however, and was being comforted by Lady Barrington-Pottsherbert and a glass of brandy in the library. So one of the young girls with a stouter constitution was brought in from the ice cream kitchen to deputise.

Mr. Cochran joined His Lordship in peering round the jamb of the oak door. First of all His Lordship's head appeared at forty-five degrees to the upright, with just his right eye, right ear, and half a nose and mouth coming into view to anyone who might have been in the hall. And peering over his shoulder was Mr. Cochran. They saw that the hall was deserted. But there, in its usual spot, stood the offending suit of armour, now doing nothing in the least offensive. Lord Barrington-Pottsherbert prodded his estate manager on the arm.

"Go and see if it's alive, Cochran."

"Me, Your Lordship?" stammered Mr. Cochran. "Why, I'm even afraid of the spooky movies on TV. And, after all, sir, he is your ancestor. Far more likely to be friendly towards you than to me."

"Oh, very well, come on then. Can't be doing with all this namby-pamby dithering and dallying. I'll come with you." Lord Barrington-Pottsherbert pushed the protesting Mr. Cochran in front of him towards the now docile armour. "Sir Bartlewood," he called gingerly. "Sir Bartlewood, are you in there?" Mr. Cochran wondered if he saw a slight movement of the metal head, but dismissed it as being his imagination, which, in fact, it was.

Slowly they inched their way forwards until they stood just two feet from it. With one swift movement Lord Barrington-Pottsherbert flicked up the visor. "There you are, look. Empty," he cried triumphantly. "I don't think it's ever moved from here. They must all have imagined it."

"But so many people claimed to have seen it," said Mr. Cochran. "Including Gladys and Mr. Jackson. Surely all the visitors wouldn't have suddenly imagined it at the same time…would they?" he finished rather feebly, wilting under the aristocratic glare.

"There's something funny going on here, Cochran, that's for sure, but whether it's a bally ghost or just some scurvy bounders trying to pull a scam, I don't know. We've got to find out what it is, though, and quickly, because whatever it is, it isn't doing Marlston a scrap of good."

Albert had gleeked from the sandwich bar to watch Lord Barrington-Pottsherbert. Should he bring Sir Bartlewood's armour to life for a special performance now, or should he wait and see his plan through unaltered? He decided to carry on as planned and leave the armour until the sandwich bar would be packed with his former victims claiming their free lunches. But he felt he ought to give Lord Barrington-Pottsherbert and Mr. Cochran a little aperitif.

He let out a whooshing whistle, rather like the wind scurrying through trees and old barns. That lasted for several seconds and pinned the mortal men to the ground. Then he changed it to a wild, lingering laugh, hurling himself invisibly at a chair. He clattered into the furniture, sending it skidding madly across the floor, coming to rest by the grandfather clock. His laughter paused just long enough for him to cuckoo a couple of times while opening and shutting the clock door. Then his laughter rose to a crescendo as he sent a marble bust of Lord Barrington-Pottsherbert's great-uncle-on-his-father's-side flying up the stairs, to come bumping its way back down again, settling, eyes up, at the feet of the trembling pair.

This had a most spectacular effect. His Lordship and Mr. Cochran stared into each other's terrified eyes for a fleeting moment. Then with one sound and one movement in perfect unison, rather like a second-rate song and dance act, they ran yelling from the hall as if their tails were ablaze.

Albert's laugh turned to a natural one, its echo following them like a shadow down the corridor. They did not stop running until they found sanctuary in the library, where the brandy had turned Gladys's hysteria into a giggling fit.

"Why, Maxwell, whatever's the matter?" Lady Barrington-Pottsherbert jumped up as her husband and Mr. Cochran dived frantically for the decanter.

"The ghost," panted Lord Barrington-Pottsherbert, draining a glass. "There's a ghost here. There is. We've just heard it."

The next thing they heard was a thud as Gladys stopped giggling and slid off the settee in a dead faint. Her recovery from seeing the armour and hearing its booming warnings suffered a severe relapse on learning His Lordship's news.

Lady Barrington-Pottsherbert clutched at her not undergenerous bosom. "Oh my goodness, how dreadful.

Whatever are we going to do?"

Their thoughts were interrupted some ten minutes later by Riley. The butler's gentle and unmistakable four taps came at the door. There was a scuffle and shouting outside, before the door burst open amid a flurry of arms and legs. In rushed Giovanni, the Italian chef from the sandwich bar, accompanied by a now agitated Riley.

"Your Lordship," began Riley. "I'm so sorry, sir, I just couldn't hold him. He's gone stark raving mad, sir."

"Youra Lordaship," cried Giovanni, his tall floppy hat perched to one side of his flushed face. "Come-a quicka. There's a suita of armour in my sandwich bar. The people, they are a-screaming and a-shouting. They say it's a ghosta."

Gladys had started to come round, but fell back with a moan. Again, that was definitely not the sort of news to kick-start her stalled recovery...a sort of triple-dip setback.

His Lordship put a comforting arm around Giovanni's shoulder and wondered who was trembling the most. "Now tell me all about it, Giovanni."

"Noa, noa," cried the excitable Italian. "You acome-a. The people, they go a-mad."

Lord Barrington-Pottsherbert turned to Mr. Cochran. "Cochran, go and sort it out, and for God's sake, calm 'em all down. Tell 'em my nephew's been at it again."

"But Your Lordship..."

"Good God, man, what are you dithering for? The ghost won't hurt you. Friendly sort of cove, he seems. You heard him laughing earlier. It's not as if he was moaning. Blighter must be friendly to have been laughing so much. Get off with you; you can see I can't come. I've got to look after Giovanni and Gladys.

"Now go and sort it out, and for the love of might, don't put your foot in it."

While Albert had been assuming the role of cuckoo in the grandfather clock he noted it was lunchtime, and had stepped back into Sir Bartlewood's metallic suit as soon as Lord Barrington-Pottsherbert and his henchman fled down the corridor. He decided to make more use of gleeking this time. There was no way Lord Barrington-Pottsherbert could fob the tourists off with the line about his nephew and electromagnets if he gleeked a time or two.

A family of four had been just about to tuck into their steak sandwiches when the armour suddenly appeared out of nowhere alongside their table. The teenage daughter stopped with her hand halfway to her mouth. Albert relieved her of her sandwich and flung it up in the air.

"This is your last warning," he cried to the dumbstruck assembly who looked on in total disbelief. "I've told you before to leave this house. There is pending danger here. For your own sakes, leave *noooowwww*."

Giovanni stared with terror in his eyes. The room had been instantly turned upside down. Food, tables, chairs, drinks, and cutlery were all upended as a stampede for the door began. Screaming children were pushed aside as everyone made a mad dash, crying that the ghost had returned. Suddenly Albert was between them and the door, holding his arms aloft, beginning his wild laughter again. The pushing mass screeched to a stop. Then heads whirled as the wicked sound came from the window instead. That was when Giovanni had made a dive for the door and set out to hunt for His Lordship.

And now, while Giovanni was having a comforting glass of brandy, Mr. Cochran stood trembling outside the sandwich bar. He could hear the hysterical cries coming from within. But it was the other sound which chilled him to the core, the sound he'd heard in the side hall not half an hour earlier; the sound of Albert's laughter. Mr. Cochran's adrenalin washed his courage from off its rocky hidey-hole and swept it along to his heart where it exploded into his brain.

Right, he thought with renewed vigour. *It's now or never.* Grasping the handles, he swung the double doors open with a flourish. And what a sight there was to greet him. It was as if the proverbial bomb had been helped by a hurricane after a bull had been given free rein in a china shop. People were scrambling over one another in total blind panic. Children were crying, hamburgers were being trampled underfoot, and no-one quite knew what was going on. Many were cowering back towards the window staring aghast at the suit of armour standing between them and the safety of the door. Some were holding tables and chairs in front of them as if the armour were the lion and they its tamer.

It was the first time Mr. Cochran had seen the armour touched with the spirit of life. Albert whirled round, smiling to himself as he witnessed Mr. Cochran's wide-eyed, jaw-dropped expression of frozen terror, which washed upon the poor manager like a wave breaking over him in the sea.

Albert decided to experiment, and tried gleeking while in the middle of issuing a spectral missive. The first half of his grim prophecy—"This is my last warning to *yoouuuu*"—was delivered from near the door, while its finale—"There is only death in this house for those who linger"—was almost drowned out by the extra screams caused through him gleeking right into the heart of the seething mass of bodies.

Mr. Cochran leaped aside like a shop manager who has just unlocked the doors at bargain time, as everyone stampeded for the exit. By the time the bottleneck cleared itself through the door, Mr. Cochran's adrenalin-fuelled courage was at its zenith. With a thumping heart he peered into the sandwich bar again, where the armour was standing by the still-sizzling frying pan which now contained nothing but the charred embers of a couple of steaks. Inching forward, he called in a half whisper: "Er…Sir Bartlewood?"

If Albert had the foggiest idea what Mr. Cochran meant by that name he may have responded differently and played along. As it was, however, he felt his wicked laughter was becoming quite a trademark, and brought it back into the game.

Mr. Cochran swallowed his pride at the same second his courage evaporated, and he tore down the corridor back to the library and a glass of brandy.

***

Mozelbeek peered glumly at the black pawn in Wallace's open right palm. "Hell's bells," he said to himself. "I knew I should have gone for his left hand. And he knows I prefer white; he's got an advantage right from the off in this game."

Wallace placed the white pawn from his left hand and the black from his right back onto the chessboard, wondering which of his eight pawns and two knights he should move first.

"Well, you're going to have a difficult time explaining this one away," he said. "Albert seems intent on breaking every rule in the book." He made his first move:

P–K4 ——

"Not at all," countered Mozelbeek. "He's merely following the convictions of his heart. And whether those convictions are right or wrong, he's got to be admired for sticking to his guns. Which is more than I can say for that old scallywag in your charge, Lord Barrington-Pottsherbert." Mozelbeek calmly played his response:

—— N–KB3

Wallace swallowed the bait and angrily tried to pull himself off the hook. "What do you mean by that? What's wrong with

76

him?" He slammed another piece down without really thinking.
N–QB3 ——

Mozelbeek: "Where do you want me to start?"

—— P–Q4

Wallace: "He's only defending his home and there's nothing wrong with that. An Englishman's home is his castle, you know."

PxP ——

Mozelbeek: "But what about all the lies and deceit he's bringing into play to keep the truth from the people who've paid to visit his home? Doesn't paying two pounds fifty give those tourists a right to the truth, instead of being told a pack of lies? This little escapade's taught me a thing or two about the aristocracy, I can tell you."

—— NxP

Wallace: "Paying two pounds fifty entitles them to a tour of the manor, no more, no less. It certainly doesn't give them a right to know everything that's going on. Lord Barrington-Pottsherbert has every right to make decisions which leave the punters in the dark."

KN–K2 ——

Mozelbeek: "Even if that decision is based on dishonesty?

—— N–QB3

Wallace: "There are certain things it's better for the people in charge to keep from the run of the mill. Lord Barrington-Pottsherbert knew how scared these people would be to think there was an unfriendly ghost in their midst. He was trying to keep them calm. It would have been better for them to have gone home thinking there was nothing amiss, instead of being terrified out of their wits as they were."

P–KN3 ——

Mozelbeek: "He was more concerned abut losing his trade. If word gets around that people have been scared half to death no-one'll visit his precious home. Then he'll have to do some work for his living instead of just sitting back and watching the money roll in through his inherited silver spoon."

—— B–N5

Wallace: "The fact that those people voluntarily pay their money and take pleasure from looking at the treasures of Marlston Manor means nothing to you?"

B–N2 ——

Mozelbeek: "You have to accept that sacrifices are part of the pursuit of excellence. Collateral damage. Albert's fighting hard for a principle. That's all that matters. And his campaign is clearly worth supporting when you take one or two things into account."

—— N–Q5

Wallace: "Oh, yes?" His voice oozed, dribbled, and dripped sarcasm. "Such as?"

BxN ——

Mozelbeek: "Well, how suspicious everyone is of the others. Riley didn't believe Lord Barrington-Pottsherbert when Albert disturbed them at breakfast. His Lordship didn't believe Mr. Cochran about the money disappearing from the safe, just because it was back when he looked. Also, the fact that they all think it's Sir Bartlewood's ghost, simply because it's his suit of armour…it all adds up to show that you shouldn't believe everything just because of its outward appearance."

—— QxB

Wallace: "It also shows up the human race for the pathetic, frightened weeds they are. Look how they're all so afraid of something they don't understand. The Condition Of Transit is a plane of existence higher than earthly life, but every time mortals see a wandering spirit from it, they go mad. They're a bunch of sheep, nothing more, and it's our misfortune to have to watch over the ignorant heathens. Sometime I wish I'd taken up horticulture instead. I see there's a good job mowing the lawns in the western quarter of heaven, where the grass really is greener."

NxQ ——

Mozelbeek had to agree. "Yes, I sometimes think I'd go loopy if we hadn't had fun locking horns together, while guiding our mortals down the ages. You might be a bit of an old bugger, but I'm glad to have you around." Nostalgia started to glaze his eyes, but only for a second, before normal service was resumed and his fighting spirit emerged again. "But don't let that fool you. I'm going to fight as fiercely as I can for the short time I've still got Albert. It's the first time I've had a hostile spirit, and I certainly don't intend to let his powers go to waste." Mozelbeek turned his attentions away from the cosmic game of chess between them that had already lasted for thousands of years, to focus instead on the small-scale tussle on the marble board in front of them. He saw that Wallace's last move had been a fatal mistake…the trap was about to be sprung. He checked the white king.

—— N–B6 check.

Wallace had no choice in his reply.

K–B1 ——

And Mozelbeek gleefully hammered home his win.

—— B–R6 checkmate.

He sacrificed his most powerful piece to win the game with underlings working well together. He was pleased.

But it had shown Wallace that the power to snatch victory in their latest earthbound battle could still be his. Albert may have more abilities than Lord and Lady Barrington-Pottsherbert, but if Wallace employed those limited abilities better than Mozelbeek guided Albert to use his greater power, he could still emerge victorious.

For Mozelbeek it held a different message, though. His sacrifice had worked because his opponent had made a mistake. All he had to do, he told himself, was to keep a clear head and not make an error. Then he would be the one emerging victorious.

CHAPTER 5

In which dark plans are laid

WHAT MADE ALBERT go back to Mr. Cochran's office after returning the suit of armour to its home at the bottom of the stairs once more, he didn't know. But as he didn't know of Mozelbeek's existence he was hardly likely to realise the suggestion was implanted in his mind by his guardian angel. He just knew that he had an irresistible urge to go.

There on the desk sat the money bags, left by Mr. Cochran when he'd run to the car park to see what all the noise had been about. Albert couldn't believe his eyes. He didn't know how the money had got back to the office from under the four-poster, but when he came to caring about that, now he'd found it again, he gave diddly-squat.

Gleefully he scooped up the bags and gleeked back to the Charles I Room with them. It was deserted. Word had spread like wildfire about the mysterious haunting, and all the visitors quickly departed, even those who hadn't seen Albert in action and didn't believe in ghosts anyway. They didn't want to see something that might change their minds. But Albert had no doubt that the afternoon tranche of tourists would soon be arriving, and his postponed plan could be put into action then.

Oh, happy days.

By now Gladys was sitting up once more, having fainted yet again when Mr. Cochran burst back into the library crying out for brandy and wildly relating how Sir Bartlewood had cleared the sandwich bar as effectively as if he had yelled "Fire!"

Lord B-P looked thoughtful as he rubbed his hands backwards and forwards across his chin. "Well, I just don't understand it, Cochran. What's he trying to do, d'you think?"

"He must be trying to warn us of some terrible misfortune that's coming our way, sir. Or, I suppose he could just be trying to scare everyone away—but I can't imagine why."

"I must look up my family history and find out exactly what this Bartlewood chap was like," said Lord B-P. "There could be a clue to his behaviour somewhere in those ancient papers. Now then…we took them out of the library a couple of years ago, didn't we? They're in your office, aren't they, Cochran?"

"Yes, that's right, sir. I'll go and fetch them."

Mr. Cochran couldn't resist going the long way from the library to his office, to peer cautiously around the door into the hall. And sure enough, the suit of armour was back in its rightful place. He repressed a shudder while hurrying past it without another glance. He felt decidedly better, even managing a smile, as he threw open the door to his office and strode inside. Abruptly he stopped as his eyes fell on the empty table. He knew without a shadow of doubt that the last time he saw the table it had been covered with the money bags.

And now, for the second time in a matter of hours, the money had mysteriously vanished. He closed his eyes, exhaling a long, restful sigh. It was the only outlet valve he could think of, and without it he may have leaped up and down and torn out his hair.

He flopped down heavily in his swivel chair and stared at the table, willing the money to come back. But it didn't. It was under the four-poster, with Albert lying on the floor alongside, to make sure it didn't don its wandering boots again. After all, it had a purpose in his plan, making it well worth guarding.

***

Many inspectors in Saint Christopher's ministry rebelled against the influence of their colleagues who had joined them from hell. Ever since the Special Council had agreed that half their numbers should be representatives from there, they felt the whole setup had gone downhill.

"Deteriorated rapidly, old boy," was the usual thing to be heard coming from the occupants of the large padded armchairs in the exclusive Heaven Club. "Never been the same since we joined up with those blighters. Why we couldn't have carried on as we were, I don't know. Should have left them to it, and kept ourselves separate."

The Angel Marshall had just happened to be passing by on his way to refill his glass with the Premium Nectar that was provided at ridiculously subsidised rates at the Heaven Club bar. "Couldn't agree with you more," he butted into the conversation. "I've seen exactly the same thing happen on Earth. We were rolling along very nicely, got people to Oxford every year. Then they joined us up with the secondary modern down the road. Ruined us, it did."

The Angel Marshall had been a grammar school headteacher.

Like the Alliance of Guardian Angels, the Association of Inspectors' Unity was affiliated to the Afterlife Professional and Workers Council, and there was a clause in contracts for posts in both those areas that operatives be members of their relevant united bodies. The inspectors' industrial power had grown ever since Mr. Hobday joined their ranks. Mr. Hobday had originally been a boiler inspector in hell, who felt that charting the courses of several human lives on Earth would make a restful change from watching over ancient and cantankerous boilers to ensure they kept the place at the optimum temperature. After an intensive training course he managed to bluff his way to a guardian angel's job, rising quickly to gain a seat on the AoIU's General Purposes Committee.

Mr. Hobday had led his team to the confrontation with Saint Christopher in his usual articulate manner, demanding that something be done to relieve the "intolerable workload caused by the management neglecting to provide an adequate workforce."

Although several of the older inspectors disagreed with the way Mr. Hobday was running the dispute, he had been democratically voted their leader, so they had no option but to withdraw their labour along with the rest. But they still had access to the limpid pools whose mystical waters showed life on Earth. Inspector Baines glanced up from the pool, looking across at Inspector Staniforth.

"Albert Carter's upsetting the whole balance," he muttered. "He's wreaking havoc at old Barrington-Pottsherbert's place, and both their guardian angels are just letting it happen."

Staniforth cast his mind back across the ages. "Wallace and Mozelbeek should never be allowed to guard mortals who might come into contact with each other on Earth," he agreed. "It's a well-known fact that they spar with each other, using their human charges as pawns. Separately they're brilliant, but put them together and they're incorrigible." His expression changed as an idea turned itself over in his mind.

"Hmmm, I wonder…There's not much we can do from up here, but I think I know of someone who could put a stop to Albert's antics."

A few moments later Inspector Staniforth was furtively whispering his idea to Wallace. Wallace's wings bristled throughout their every fibre.

"Excellent," he whispered back. "Why didn't I think of that? If that doesn't stop our notorious Albert Carter, nothing will."

Inspector Staniforth beamed as he went on his way to set the wheels of his plan speeding along their track, all the time thinking of the promotion that may well come his way when this whole unpleasant episode was over.

***

Albert's antics had come to a full stop of their own accord. But only temporarily. As soon as the afternoon visitors arrived, the Ghost of Marlston Manor would be back in action.

Mr. Cochran had to call once more on his limited courage as he stood outside the library door. Clearing his throat and straightening his tie, he marched in.

"Ah, Cochran, any luck? Did you find…?" Lord B-P broke off as he saw Mr. Cochran was empty-handed—no file of family papers.

"My lord, you're never going to believe this, but the money's disappeared again, sir."

Lord B-P's face turned a bright pink, having first filtered through greeny-grey and puce. But he'd heard and seen enough today to believe absolutely anything. "What?" he thundered. "Good God, this is beyond a joke. I'll dismantle that ruddy armour, you see if I don't. Why the devil can't it tell me straight what it's up to, instead of all this damned messing about? If it's got something against us, why won't it come out in the open with it? I can't be doing with all this skulking about. D'you realise it's never dared show its face to me? When it was up to its tricks with the clock in the hall it did it without moving that blasted armour. It can't face me, that's its problem. It knows I won't be afraid of it, what?" He looked round proudly and triumphantly, then strode towards the door. "Sylvia, look after that girl and get her fit for work this afternoon." He indicated Gladys, who by now was feeling the effects of at least half a bottle of brandy rather more than she was feeling the effects of her fright.

"And Cochran, you're coming with me. We're getting Bartlewood out of the way before the afternoon visitors arrive.

85

Don't want to let him scare anyone else away, do we? Word'll soon get round, y'know, and we'll have no visitors left."

The determined, square-jawed look came over Lord B-P's face, indicating to Mr. Cochran that protesting was futile. Once His Lordship had made up his mind, neither fire nor earthquake could change it. Sir Bartlewood had to go. That was all there was to it.

Lord B-P marched purposefully up to the armour and prodded it firmly. "Bartlewood, are you in there?" he demanded, lifting the visor and peering inside. When it became apparent no-one was at home he turned confidently to Mr. Cochran.

"There, he's gone again. Got a yellow streak in him, that's for sure. Puts his point when I'm not about, but stays quiet when I am."

He slammed the visor shut like a bank cashier pulling down their blind for lunchtime when you finally reach the head of a half-hour queue. "Right, come on, to the attic with him." He gripped the head, pulling it towards him. "Get the legs, Cochran, and we'll be off. Hurry, man, it's nearly two o'clock; the tourists'll be here soon." They manhandled the innocent suit of armour up the stairs.

Bobby and Daphne looked on helplessly. There was nothing they could do, short of appearing to Lord B-P themselves and trying to explain what was going on. But they wondered if that would only add to the confusion. And they'd be right.

Bobby turned to his beautiful lover of long ago. "We've got to keep a careful watch on this and if there's anything we can do to help Lord Barrington-Pottsherbert we must do it instantly without hesitation."

Daphne nodded and smiled. It might not be doing much towards purging their sins, she thought—in fact it was probably landing them in even hotter and deeper water—but at least it broke the monotony of their endlessly same days and nights.

Lord B-P sent Mr. Cochran down for a torch. He had never bothered to have electricity connected in the attic. In fact, he had never been in the attic at all for as long as he could remember. He looked at the suit of armour, totally devoid of all life, spirit, and soul.

"What is it you want?" he muttered, more to himself than to the deaf earplates on the headpiece. "Why are you doing this to me? Good God, I wish I knew." Sadly he stared hard at the lifeless metal, shaking his head. "Here I am, rolling along through life, not wishing to hurt a fly—oh, well, perhaps that's not strictly true; I did step on a spider the other day—and here you are trying to stop me earning my livelihood. Why, Bartlewood, why?"

Faced with a total lack of response, he turned away and peered up through the open trapdoor into the blackness of the attic. A flicker of a smile nervously creased his cheeks for a fleeting second. "But you'll be out of the way up there, right enough. That should put a stop to your little games."

Mr. Cochran came panting up the back stairs, torch in hand.

"Right," said Lord B-P. "Let's get this hunk of whatever it is into the attic, then we'll get down there and stay with them all afternoon, just in case…" He broke off, looking uncertainly at the armour.

Slowly they heaved and grunted the armour up the steep ladder to the attic. With a crash it toppled over, through the square trap.

"Oh, at last," puffed Lord B-P, shining the torch like a lighthouse all around the attic. That same foot and a half of lethargic light which Albert had noted miserably when he first arrived at his new home, shone listlessly in through the tiny window. "Must get this place tidied out sometime," mused Lord B-P. "Might be able to use it for something, you never know." He clambered down the ladder after closing the trapdoor, and stowed it away in its cupboard.

"I feel better, now, Cochran, with that blighter safely out of harm's way. I suppose we'd better start looking for that money, too. We can't afford to lose a whole day's takings. I wonder what could have become of it? Still, it turned up last time, let's hope it does again."

***

"Forever the optimist," said Mozelbeek. "But it does go to show that those who think they're in charge of a situation often can't face up to the truth."

"That's only because the truth is hidden from him," said Wallace. "He still thinks the ghost is his ancestor."

"But even so, carting the armour away is hardly likely to stop a ghost, whoever he is. It proves another point, too: that those in charge can't always cope."

"It's hardly an eventuality that crops up regularly in the day-to-day running of Marlston."

"He should be prepared for any eventuality," countered Mozelbeek, quickly.

"He's handling it in the way he sees best," said Wallace, philosophically.

"Yes, going round in circles and getting back to square one. Marlston Manor is on a slippery downward slide and it won't be long before Albert is in complete control there."

Wallace turned away with a smile.

***

Lord B-P and Mr. Cochran stepped out of the door marked Private, and into the afternoon sunshine.

The sun was still humming "The Red Flag" to herself, looking out for Albert to join in the chorus. Lord B-P and Mr. Cochran hurried across the car park to where all thirty-eight members of a women's institute from Barnsley were getting off a coach.

"Good afternoon, ladies," beamed His Lordship. "I'm Lord Barrington-Pottsherbert. I'll be taking you on a guided tour of the house myself, today."

Ooohs and *ahs* and "*Sshhh*, it's His Lordship himself," rang down the coach as the ladies queued to alight.

Albert peered out from under the bed as the visitors began to traipse through. He wondered whether to use the armour again, but decided against it this time. Lord B-P and his staff would be more confused if he did something else.

With the afternoon wearing on the visitors became more thickly spread, and at last Albert felt it was time for action. Remaining invisible, he clutched the moneybags and crawled out onto the Persian carpet.

The reaction was mixed, but the effect was stunning. "Coo, Mum," wailed a kid. "Look at them bags." There were about twenty people in the room, and instantly all eyes were on the bags which pulled themselves along the floor before suddenly flying onto the window-ledge. Altogether there were four bags. Albert put two down and started juggling with the others. The children started crying, proclaiming that they wanted to go home. By now Albert was used to the hysteria and terror his ghostly actions caused, but even he could not have foreseen the mad scramble to get out when he hurled a bag across the room. He had hoped some people at least would have waited a while longer. After all, he had something to tell them, and he considered it rather rude that they wanted to leave before he was ready.

"Stop," he boomed, gleeking to the door with one of the bags raised in his hand. The time had come for the first public showing of the Ghost of Marlston Manor's true form, and the rush for the exit stopped as they found their way barred by a shadowy, transparent figure. "Go from this place of evil and take with you this message—spread it far and wide. Tell the world that disaster lies ahead in this house and for all those in it." He threw back his head in a wild laugh, then abruptly loosened the cord at the neck of the bag, throwing it into the air, scattering notes and coins as it went.

The people, no longer paralysed with fear, tore their eyes from the spot where Albert's wispy form had simply vanished, and dived about the floor scooping up the money into their handbags and pockets. For a few seconds their terror seemed to evaporate. Albert's idea of redistributing a little wealth was working, although he had hoped that people would not have been quite as afraid of him as they were. He wanted to play cat and mouse awhile longer, to gradually work up an uncontrollable panic in them. Instead, they had been terrified right from the start and Albert had no chance to talk to them further or perform any more ghastly tricks. Yes, he mused to himself, he had much to learn about being a ghost. He really was quite a novice.

Their pockets bulging, they ran out, bumping into those on the way in, who had gone to the stuffed wildlife exhibition first.

"It's haunted," they cried, pushing their way through. "There's a ghost in there. For God's sake, don't go in."

But human nature being what it is, they failed to heed the warnings and rushed in to see for themselves. Taking one look at the dancing moneybags, though, they quickly turned tail. Suddenly the bags were in front of them again, ushering them back into the Charles I Room.

Albert's constant gleeking around the room had the effect of making the moneybags shoot and dance faster than the eye could see, from one wall to another, from one window to another. He was determined these people were not getting out without sampling his wares. As they stood trembling, huddled together in the middle of the floor, an unseen hand slammed the door shut and turned the key. And almost instantly the door at the far end of the room also swung shut and locked itself. Both keys dangled and waved in the air, then flew low over the terrified, ducking heads of Albert's eight prisoners, clattering against the window panes, before simply disappearing into the proverbial thin air as Albert dropped them into his trousers pocket.

Gradually he willed himself to become a grey shadowy figure again, to the gaze of the unwitting ghost hunters. A shaking finger pointed towards him from the cowering group as they edged their way back from him. "What the devil's that?"

Albert paused to attain his favourite booming pitch and tone, and then he was off in full swing again: "The stars foretell danger here. The Angel of Death is even now on his way to kiss all those he finds beneath the roof of this evil house. I have awoken from my slumbers to come and warn you. Heed my words carefully, O mortal men, and leave this place with all speed."

As Albert stopped, a pin dropping would have sounded like the loudest thunderclap that ever there was. All eyes were on his shimmering presence, all ears horrified by what they heard, all mouths dry and gaping, and all hearts and lungs had almost gone into hibernation.

"Oh, you are naughty," said the sun, peering in through the window. "Come out and play later, won't you?" And off she went behind a fleeting cloud, happily humming "The Red Flag" to herself again.

Albert ignored the interruption and turned to his guests—

who were blissfully unaware that the sun knew that tune, let alone wanted Albert for a playmate. Had there been any babies with the group, they might well have heard the sun's friendly invitation, because rumour has it amongst mankind that children under eighteen months old can talk with the birds, the sun, and the clouds. The problem is, goes the legend, that when they reach that magical age their power fades, then disappears altogether. And they're too young to remember anything about it.

Albert was now feeling pleased with himself, and rather proud of the success he was having with his haunting.

"The Angel of Death is hovering near, and I'm told the devil himself rides piggyback."

What happened next startled even Albert for a second or two. As he finished speaking there came an urgent hammering on the door, and a melee of shouting.

"It's the Angel of Death," cried the panic-stricken crowd, and fled across to the other door, trying to bang and kick their way out.

Albert started his trademark wild laughing as he recognised the voices on the other side. With the bedroom resembling a mass of screaming hysteria, he reached into his pocket for the key. As he threw open the door, in rushed two rather hot and bothered figures. Some of the crowd hardly dare turn round to face what they were sure would be the cowled black angel. But those who did almost sobbed with relief, as they saw nothing more spectral than Lord B-P and Mr. Cochran.

Albert thought it was about time he introduced himself to his host. "My lord," he mocked. "Your visitors are just leaving, I believe." He spread his arms and hurled an open money bag into the midst of the group. Lord B-P stared at the shadowy figure. Albert materialised fully, all the way to human form for a few seconds, to let his unwilling host get a good look at his face. "Look carefully, Lord Barrington-Pottsherbert; you'll be seeing plenty more of me." Albert glanced across at the visitors who had been emptying the bag. Now their fear was back, as they gazed upon Albert's flickering shape. With another laugh, he disappeared completely. There was only the lingering echo to tell that he had ever been there at all.

With a gasp of horror the freed captives rushed past the protesting Lord B-P and Mr. Cochran, not stopping until they reached the relative sanctuary of the car park.

Albert still had two money bags of yesterday's takings. Untying both cords he hovered above His Lordship and the manager, showering the contents all over them.

His outline again stood out against the wall as the petrified pair brushed aside the falling coins and notes. "Listen to me, Barrington-Pottsherbert, and listen well. This is only the beginning. Your fear shall know no boundary by the time I, the Ghost of Marlston Manor, have finished my task."

Before Albert could even so much as draw breath to launch his laugh, their nerve reached the end of its elasticity, letting go with a *thwang*. Trampling the remaining money into the carpet, they ran from the room, their last recollection being of an unknown ghost whose purpose at their home, they couldn't begin to tell.

CHAPTER 6

In which our protagonists meet face-to-face, and hostile ghosts gather

IN THE STUDY Lord B-P called a council of war with his wife and Mr. Cochran.

"Either that ghost isn't Sir Bartlewood after all, or the portrait in the gallery isn't a very good likeness of him."

Mr. Cochran was a little more decided. "I'm convinced it isn't Sir Bartlewood. The ghost was wearing modern-day clothes and didn't look at all like the dashing cavalier Sir Bartlewood was supposed to be."

Lord B-P sighed. "Yes, I suppose you're right," he said. "I think I was just trying to put off the evil question a while longer. If he's not my ancestor, then who on Earth is he?"

"I didn't really get a good look at him, sir, but he certainly doesn't look like anyone I've ever seen before."

Lady B-P felt she wouldn't mind having a ghost in her home if it were one of her husband's illustrious ancestors, but she wasn't too happy with the idea of stranger. "What do you think he can want?"

"Don't know, m'dear, but he certainly wasn't very friendly towards us. He seems hell-bent on scaring everyone away."

"Oh dear," sighed Her Ladyship. "Do you think the tourists'll mind?"

"Mind...?" mocked Lord B-P. "They've been terrified out of their bally wits. If we don't stop him soon we'll never get another tourist at Marlston again."

Mr. Cochran said he knew it was a different kettle of fish when they were actually face-to-face with the ghost, but he thought the thing to do was to stand up to him and let him see they weren't afraid.

"As you say, Cochran," responded Lord B-P. "That's all very well while we're sitting here, but will we still feel the same when the air's full of that hideous laughter, and there's a shadowy, misty figure not two yards from us?"

"I think we ought to try to talk to him, my lord, to find out just what he wants here, and why he's suddenly turned up out of the blue like this. I think if we stick together, the three of us, that'll be better than just one of us facing him. Safety in numbers, and all that."

"Oh, I don't know that I want to meet this character…" protested Lady B-P.

But she was instantly stumped by her husband's winning googly: "Now he's got a foothold here there's every likelihood that the blighter could creep up on you when you're alone and least expecting it. No, the thing to do is as Cochran suggests; the three of us go and find him. That way he'll know we're not scared of him, and he might go away. And it'll be a help if we can discover what he wants. If we can give him what he wants it might just get rid of him. We've got to do something though, and quickly, before he wrecks the whole business."

Mr. Cochran looked thoughtful. "I wonder where the suit of armour comes into it? I don't think the ghost will take too kindly to us having hidden it."

"Good God," gasped His Lordship, clutching at his throat. "I'd forgotten about that. D'you think we ought to get it down again?"

"Well, I don't know about that," said Mr. Cochran. "At least while it's up there it's out of the way and the ghost can't use it.

And another thing, we could perhaps use it to bargain with. If he wants it back he'll have to talk to us – that sort of thing." Mr. Cochran felt himself beginning to take control. Maybe a promotion would be on the cards if he handled it properly. "It always pays, my lord, to have something to bargain with in these matters. Much better than going in with nothing. It means he'll have to listen to us, if nothing else."

"Yes," mused Lord B-P. "That's a thought, isn't it? Okay, Cochran, we'll do it that way. Now, let's go and find the blighter." He paused. "Um, exactly how do we find him?"

"We don't, sir. We go to where the tourists are and wait for him to find us, which I'm sure he will, sooner or later."

The visitors who had already seen the ghostly antics were well on their way home by the time Lord and Lady B-P and Mr. Cochran were waiting downstairs in the main entrance hall, for another wave of guests to arrive. The diversion was still in operation as Lord B-P felt it was too much trouble to change it back today.

Normally there was a continuous flow of tourists through the mansion, but today things were quieter. There was actually an unaccustomed breathing space for Lord B-P's usually overworked staff. Even Giovanni found time to sit and relax for a few moments—but he needed it more than most. He felt he would never fully recover from the shock of seeing his sandwich bar turned upside down by a malicious ghost.

Gossip and rumour flew thick and fast among the staff about Marlston's new and unwelcome visitor. When Riley went down to the kitchen he found the young kitchen maid. Tracey; the parlour maid, Miss Simms; and Mrs. Brass, the cook, discussing it over a glass of cooking sherry. (At least he hoped it was the cooking sherry, and not His Lordship's best aperitif.)

"Oh, Mr. Riley," called Mrs. Brass, as he came down the stairs.

"Do come and join us. We'd welcome your valued opinions. We were just having a little conflab about this 'ere ghost His Lordship's found. What do you think we should do about it? Should we complain, or ask for more money, or what?"

"I'll tell you what I think," said Riley, confidentially. They all leaned forward, elbows resting on the table, chins resting in their palms, expectantly. "I think…it's none of our business, that's what I think." He folded his arms, adopting his snooty look-what-the-cat-dragged-in stance. "If His Lordship's got a ghost, then it's up to His Lordship to do with it as His Lordship pleases. I hardly think you'll be called upon to cook for the ghost, Mrs. Brass, or you, Miss Simms, to have to dust the parlour before His Lordship entertains it with a glass of his finest sherry"—Riley noticed that Mrs Brass paled noticeably at that, and downed her drink swiftly—"or you, Tracey, to have to scrub the floors after it's been in wearing muddy boots.

"And I certainly can't see myself ever serving it cognac from a silver tray…I'm sure it has nothing to do with spirits—ha, ha, ha." He laughed long and hard at his little joke, wishing for all his might that he could think of one of his big ones.

With a genteel cough, he continued: "So I think we could very well ignore these rumours, even if they were true."

"What d'you mean; if they're true?"

"My dear Mrs Brass, neither you nor Tracey, nor Miss Simms, nor I have seen this so-called ghost. All we're going on are the rantings of a few drunken tourists and that old fool Cochran. I should prefer to witness this phenomenon myself before passing judgement. But I'll tell you this: if there is a spook here at the manor it has absolutely nothing whatsoever to do with us. It is Lord Barrington-Pottsherbert's affair, not ours. And I'll thank you to remember that. Now come on, drink up ladies and let's have you back at work."

But Tracey was not to be put off. She'd been through the ghost-train once at Brighton funfair and didn't want to feel the clammy hand of fear rubbing her spine again. "Why, Mr. Riley, we'd never be able to sleep safely in our beds at night with a ghost wandering about loose. No, we've got to do something now and find out just what's going on."

"And they're not just rumours, Mr. Riley." It was Miss Simms's turn this time. "Gladys on the door saw that suit of armour come to life. Dreadful, she said it was, chasing people with a sword trying to cut their heads off, it was."

"Yeah," said young Tracey. "I don't want it coming into my room with its chopper out."

"Now ladies, you know Gladys's penchant for stretching everything to its limits," said Riley. "You'll all be safe, I assure you. If this ghost really does exist outside the oversensitive minds of certain of our staff and visitors, it can't possibly have a quarrel with us. Its argument must be with Lord Barrington-Pottsherbert, if it's with anybody."

"But we work for His Lordship," protested Mrs Brass. "Perhaps it's a bit ignorant if it comes from a long way back in time, and doesn't understand. It may think that because we're here in this house we're a part of Marlston, and why ever it's cross with Lord Barrington-Pottsherbert, it's got to be cross with us, too."

"Don't be silly, Mrs Brass. Just because we're in His Lordship's employ doesn't mean we've got to suffer when he's got a difference of opinion with anyone, least of all with a ghost."

"You know that, Mr. Riley; I know that; and I daresay His Lordship knows that. But does that mean the ghost'll know it too? Just you answer me that, Mr. Riley, just you answer me that."

***

Wallace looked up and waved his hand over the limpid pool. As the scene in the waters faded, he glanced around for

Mozelbeek, who was attending to his vase of Christmas Roses. "This is ridiculous," he moaned. "You ought to do something, Mozelbeek. It's just not on that he should disrupt everyone's lives at Marlston like this. Even the staff are getting worried. They think that because Albert's fighting a battle against Lord B-P they'll be dragged into it, too. And they could be right, the way Albert's mind's working at the moment."

Mozelbeek put down his watering can. "My dear fellow, but isn't that the way of life on Earth today? Times have changed since we were mere mortals, you know. No longer is man obliged to perform his so-called gentlemanly conduct.

"After all, when Albert was alive his arguments with Nethanial Jebson frequently led to other staff and workers at the glue factory being laid off; staff and workers who were in no way connected with his disputes. Why should he change his tactics now?"

With an exasperated oath Wallace turned back to the pool, bringing the drama being played out at Marlston into its waters once more. He had a feeling things were going to start heating up for Albert pretty soon, and he wanted to be around when they did.

***

It was as big a surprise for Albert when he gleeked back to the attic for a rest and found the armour up there, as it was for Bobby and Daphne.

"What have you brought this here for?" he demanded. "If you're trying to hide it from me you could find somewhere safer for it, I'm sure. Or didn't you think I'd come up here again?"

"There's no need to be nasty," said Bobby. "It's got nothing to do with us, we didn't put it here."

Obviously Albert did not believe them. "Oh no?" he mocked. "Did you not? You've already tried to stop me once. I wouldn't put this one past you, at all."

99

"You know we wouldn't do anything to change the earthly pattern of things," said Daphne. "And moving this armour up here will certainly change things in the house. After all, suits of armour don't just disappear. Someone will want to know why it's gone and where it is."

"Well, how else did it get here?" was what Albert wanted to know.

"We know as much about it as you."

"That's a likely story. No-one else would put it here, would they?"

"That's as may be, but someone did, because we didn't. Look…we'll take it down for you if you like and put it back in its place."

"No, leave it, now it's here," mused Albert. "I'm sure it'll come in handy again soon."

Bobby glanced across at Daphne. She seemed to understand the look; they must do something to persuade Albert to stop.

"Albert," she began. "I know we've tried before and you didn't want to listen to us, but for your own good, as well as for everyone at Marlston, please, please stop this ridiculous game."

"Game!" exploded Albert. "Game!" His eyes sparked fire. "This isn't a game, it's deadly serious. How many times must I tell you? I'm not doing this for fun. I'm doing it to save the working classes from being exploited by shameless parasites like the Barrington-Pottsherberts."

And so the battle flared once more until Albert gleeked in exasperation back to the hall, muttering to himself, "You'd think those two would have more sense than to meekly accept their punishment of being stuck here for one hundred years. I wonder what I can do to make them see sense"

Daphne said to Bobby, "I wonder what we can do to make him see sense."

***

Wallace shrugged and wondered what he could do to make the three of them see sense. "If only they would spare a moment to break off their single-track journey and look at the opposite point of view," he said to Mozelbeek, who had now forsaken his Christmas Roses and was taking a tiny pair of pinking shears to a somewhat overgrown bonsai tree.

"Each of them is quite right in thinking the other isn't seeing sense because they have differing views of sense," continued Wallace. "Sense to Albert in this case is seeing his point and agreeing with it, just as sense to Bobby and Daphne is stopping the world for a minute and getting off, instead of just ploughing on regardless.

"Sense dominates their own individual worlds, which at the moment are rather like roundabouts. If they each jumped off awhile and looked at the other roundabout they may see the opposite viewpoint a little clearer than they can while they're still dizzy from going round on their own.

"And the worst that can happen is that they'll jump back on later, but at least they'll have tried. If you're too close to the heart of matters you may get a distorted view. Far better sometimes to stand back as an outsider, looking in."

Mozelbeek nodded without answering. He knew Wallace was right, but didn't want Wallace to see that. He focused his attention again on the bonsai, snipping here and there, until it gradually retained its oval shape.

***

As Albert arrived in the hall he saw Lord and Lady B-P and Mr. Cochran standing by the cashier's desk. Gladys was back in her place, keeping remarkably quiet about what she had seen. Although she was trying to forget about it at that precise moment, it would be a great story to tell her grandchildren.

She felt if she did not thrust it to the back of her mind and concentrate on her job she was likely to start screaming again.

The girl who had been standing in for her was dispatched upstairs to collect the money from the Charles I Room. Lord B-P wondered for a fleeting second if the taxman would believe that a ghost had scattered at least half a day's takings to a group of visitors who had stopped to scoop them up before fleeing from the house in terror. Then he wondered if the taxman might believe that the ghost had scattered a whole week's takings…

But other problems were a trifle more pressing. The ghost itself, for starters. The taxman and his pressures paled into the background compared to the pressure the ghost was piling on. And Lord B-P mused on the fact that the taxman could very well forget all about him soon if the ghost weren't stopped, because he'd have no visitors left to pay their two pound fifties.

Albert had told Bobby and Daphne he was not haunting for fun, but a smile flickered across his ghostly lips as he saw Gladys sitting there, with Mr. Cochran and Lord and Lady B-P standing stiffly alongside her desk. No-one spoke. They were all trying to steel their nerves for the next encounter with the supernatural.

Slowly Albert started to pull the desk sideways.

"Oooh, look," cried Gladys. "Me table's going."

Mr. Cochran frantically held on to the table's legs, trying to drag it back. Albert eased off slightly, allowing Mr. Cochran to pull it back almost to its rightful place, before yanking it again, more swiftly this time. Mr. Cochran was jerked forward with a yell, and sprawled across the table, sending the cash register and rolls of tickets flying off with an almighty clatter.

This startled Lord and Lady B-P into action. For Lady B-P it took the form of widening her eyes as if to match her hanging jaw, before screaming her way up the stairs. But His

Lordship was determined not to give in this time, and hauled the table back again with Mr. Cochran still squirming on his stomach trying to get off.

"Leave my bally table alone, whoever you are. My God, if ever I get hold of you I'll tear you limb from limb. I'll send you scuttling back to hell or wherever it is you've crawled out of; just you see if I don't." He then proceeded to unleash a string of choice phrases aimed at the ghost's personal habits and parentage.

"My word," chuckled Albert, after first stopping to ensure his voice could be heard. "Talk about the aristocracy having blue blood—you're certainly turning the air blue."

His jibe was ignored by the angry lord, who had now reached the end of his tether, snapped it, and was running free in a violent temper.

"Come on, show yourself, you cowardly cove. Now we've taken your suit of armour you're not so keen to show your face, are you?"

"But of course I am," smiled Albert, instantly appearing in front of Lord B-P. It was a good job he had taken the precaution of only looking solid and not actually materialising fully, because Lord B-P forgot his delicate upper-class background for one instant and swung a vicious right hook at him, of which any professional pugilist would have been justifiably proud. The fist disappeared inside the smiling face, only to come straight out of the other cheek, flailing harmlessly in the air. Albert instantly solidified his hands to haul Lord B-P on to the table, alongside Mr. Cochran.

"Now listen to me," he boomed. "You are powerless against me, you can do nothing. I have a mission here and you won't stop me. Do you understand? You may as well pack your bags and leave here now before the going gets rough."

Albert was enjoying himself. "When I unleash my full fury upon your miserable hides you will be only too glad to leave this place and never return."

Like every true Englishman Lord B-P felt his home was his castle, and rose to defend his lair like an angry fox. He leaped off the table, lunging for Albert once more. And, of course, he shot straight through him, crashing heavily into a chair. Gripping the chair leg he swung it around his head, then hurled it with all his might towards the grinning figure. But it was Mr. Cochran who had to duck as the chair passed straight through Albert like a knife through butter.

To give him his due, Lord B-P was not for putting off this time. "Why don't you fight like a man, you young puppy?" He grabbed Albert's hands, and to his delight found something solid to grip at last. He pulled sharply, and Albert felt himself spinning off balance before he could react.

But then, react he did. Albert swung his legs up into the air and dangled upside down with another grin. Again Lord B-P grabbed for his foe's hands, but gripped them for only a second as they lost their solidity, reverting to their normal ghostly air-like texture. Albert flipped the right way up as Lord B-P pulled at nothing.

"Calm yourself," he roared. Lord B-P, his spirit broken, his fighting force now evaporated, sank onto the table beside his manager, who hadn't dare move a muscle, not knowing who offered the more terrifying sight—the grinning ghost or the angry lord.

"What do you want from us?" he managed to ask, rather feebly.

Albert decided the time had come to let the cat out of the bag. "I represent the underprivileged working classes. You, Lord Barrington-Pottsherbert, are the very summit of the over-privileged upper classes we so often have to fight to get a fair and decent living wage. You have all this wealth, this enormous house, and yet you are greedy. You want more. You take money from the pockets of the underprivileged who want to look at your inherited house, to gaze upon its unearned treasures."

Lord B-P sat bolt upright, unable to believe what he was hearing, as Albert continued: "You don't know what it is to bring home just a few pounds at the end of each week, knowing it isn't enough to feed and clothe your family and keep them warm. We often have to make a choice—food or heat. To you, the hardships of the working man are but a nightmare you might occasionally have after overindulgence of the port and Stilton at supper time.

"You've no idea what the real world's like. You have a wonderfully sheltered life here at Marlston Manor with none of the financial worries that frequently drive working people to suicide."

Lord B-P could take no more without a little retaliation. "You don't know what you're talking about," he snapped, his spirit restored. "Marlston Manor is mortgaged to the hilt to find money to keep it going. Parts of it are falling to pieces because I just can't afford the repairs. Times are hard for me, too, you know. The money I get from my visitors hardly covers the day-to-day running of the manor. Its overheads are enormous—what with paying my staff, heating bills, lighting bills, and everything else. "

"Hark," interrupted Albert, cupping his hand around his ear. "Are they violins I hear? My heart bleeds for you, it really does."

But Lord B-P ploughed on, undeterred. "I'd love to be able to sell up and move to a cottage in Harrogate, but Marlston is part of England's heritage. It'd break my heart to see it turned into offices or flats. I'm patriotic, you know, and this house is a part of England that must stay unblemished for the benefit of every true Englishman. It gives the so-called underprivileged workers, to use your own words, a great deal of pleasure coming here to look over a piece of real England.

"This house represents what England once stood for, and will stand for again if people like you don't get in the way—beauty with a firm and solid foundation, all that's glorious and wonderful. I'm preserving this ancient monument to the good old days when England really was great, for the benefit of the people you're now frightening away."

Albert had heard enough. "A very pretty excuse, Lord Barrington-Pottsherbert, for your parasitic greed. Let me tell you…"

But what it was that Albert wanted to tell him was lost to both the spirit world and to the world of mortal men forever, as he heard a voice behind him calling his name.

"Albert Carter, stop this at once!"

Albert broke off and whirled around. What a sight there was to meet his eyes. Standing by the open doorway were a dozen people, if indeed they could be called people.

Lord B-P and Mr. Cochran stared in the direction in which Albert had turned to look. The sun streamed in through the door. Their blank expressions told Albert they could see nothing else, and he realised he was looking at a gathering of ghosts.

There were ghosts and ghouls of all shapes and sizes. Some young, some old, some with chains around their wrists and ankles which they clanged alarmingly at him. There was even one rather bedraggled looking spirit with its head tucked under its arm.

Albert quickly surveyed the bunch. There were two spirits dressed in seventeenth-century period costume—one man, one woman, both aged about forty—who seemed to be at the front. But suddenly the bedraggled spook in rags with its head under its arm stepped forward.

"Stop this at once, I say," it cried. Albert shuddered at the horrific bunch facing him.

"Who…who are you?" he stammered.

"Just a minute," said the head. "Let me get on the same level as you." Gently gripping his head behind the ears, the ghost carefully lifted it up and placed it slowly on his neck.

"That's better. Right, down to business. You must be Albert Carter?" Without waiting for a reply the head ploughed on: "It's come to our attention that you're haunting this place without the proper authority. We've been informed that you're here awaiting your place in the afterlife. In other words, you haven't applied to come here as a ghost through the proper channels, namely the Ministry of Hauntings. So therefore you have no right to be here, doing this.

"We've been told that because of your irresponsible actions about one hundred bona fide ghosts have had to be recalled because of the danger to the natural continuum of the universe."

"What on Earth are you talking about?" interjected Albert.

"You are meddling with something you know nothing about—and it could have seriously dangerous repercussions on innocent people and spirits. You're already preventing one hundred of my colleagues from performing their normal haunting duties."

"I don't give diddly-squat about that," shouted Albert angrily. "I've got a job to do here, and I'm going to do it. You're not going to stop me."

The ghost started forward. "You bloody fool," he shouted, but the rest of what he had to say was lost in a yell, then a thud, as his head fell off and rolled towards Albert.

Albert shot back in a panic.

"Damn!" cried the head, as the rest of his body darted forward to pick it up. "I hate it when that happens." He shook the dust from his hair, perching the head again on top of his neck.

"We're here to put our case to you and to ask you to stop this unlawful haunting immediately. We all come from various hauntings and haunted spots throughout the country. Although we've personally not yet been affected by your actions, our colleagues have. They've been recalled from Earth to wait in Limbo until you've finished here, so they can't come to see you themselves, and we're asking you ever so nicely on their behalf to bloody well pack it in.

"We're proper ghosts; you're not. We've got ministry authority to do our haunting; you haven't. And the longer you keep up this silly game, the more ghosts are going to get recalled—including us, and we won't like that, will we?"

As he started to turn to the others behind him, his head fell off again. "Bugger." Quickly he scooped it up, sat down on a chair and plonked the head on his knee, looking up at his fellow ghosts.

"We won't take too kindly to that, will we? I can tell you for certain that I won't."

A mournful, lingering response of "*Noooo, we won't*" came from the gang of ghosts as they started waving their fists at Albert.

"You understand, of course," continued the head, glaring up at Albert, "that we're here to persuade you peacefully. We don't want any violence, or anything like that, do we chaps?"

The gang advanced menacingly as Albert started to back away. "Now wait a minute." He gave a nervous laugh, which sounded remarkably like the dying squeak of a mouse. "Listen, fellers, let's not be too hasty about all this. This is my business after all, and nothing to do with you. It's between me and the people at this house. There's no need for you to get involved at all, you know."

The head and his body leaped up. "Here, hold this a sec." He gave his grisly top to the seventeenth-century man, then swiftly turned to pick up a chair, which he hurled at Albert.

Lord B-P and Mr. Cochran had had enough. Throughout the amazing conversation they had only seen and heard Albert. But that one side alone had been enough to convince them to get back to the relative safety of the study. Now, with the flying chair they needed no second opinion and fled down the passage.

Poor Gladys, forgotten by everyone in the panic, had slid to the floor in yet another faint when Mr. Cochran fell across the table. Now she started to groan and sit up. But in her half-conscious state she was able to see Albert and the other ghosts as blurry shapes. It was a toss-up between snapping wide awake or sinking once more into oblivion, which, of course, oblivion won.

Albert dodged the chair, stepping backwards over her prostrate form as the evil-looking horde came menacingly towards him. One ghost took about eighteen inches of chain fastened to his wrist and pulled it tight, advancing on Albert all the time. Slowly, slowly…

The spirit took his head back from the seventeenth-century man and tucked it under his arm once more, raising his other hand. "Okay, okay, that'll do. I think he gets the message." With a leer, the pig-like eyes stared up at Albert from his elbow. "I've told you, Albert Carter, we don't want any violence. Not if we can help it, anyway. Now be sensible and stay quietly in the background for the rest of your time here, eh?"

"You can't intimidate me," cried Albert, recovering a little of his composure. "This argument is between Lord Barrington-Pottsherbert and me. It's got nothing to do with you at all. Now get back to your own place of haunting and leave me alone." Before they had a chance to do anything, he disappeared. But even as he gleeked up to his attic he was sure he hadn't seen the last of his unwelcome visitors.

***

It was Mozelbeek's turn to fume this time. "However did they get to find out what was going on?" He was sure it had something to do with Wallace.

"Search me," said Wallace, innocently. "I've been here all the time, as well you know. Don't blame me."

Some time earlier Inspector Staniforth had scuttled away from Wallace to talk to a friend at the Ministry of Hauntings. The ministry took a dim view of an unregistered spirit appearing to mortals as a ghost, and usually instigated immediate steps to bring the offender to justice. But Inspector Staniforth knew that in Albert's case there was very little that could be done officially because Albert was still in the hands of Saint Christopher's ministry, which was why he approached his friend instead of official sources.

"Yes, I see the problem," his friend had said. "And I think I know of one or two ghosts who might fancy an away-day to Marlston from their resident haunting spots. They'll soon sort Albert out."

Inspector Staniforth's friend never liked visiting Earth. He found it to be a rather sordid and squalid place of late, full of people who weren't very nice to know.

However, there was one rather pleasant little inn in East Anglia that he didn't mind popping down to every now and again. It was right in the heart of a quaint little village. The small, compact lounge had low black beams in the ceiling, a log fire always crackled away in the grate, and the public bar was very similar. There was just one problem with the inn. It was haunted. They do say that on wild, windy nights when clouds scurry in front of the moon and trees bend under the unrelenting wind, a lonely, bedraggled figure can be seen walking up the stairs with his head tucked under his arm. On reaching the top of the stairs he walks slowly along the gallery before disappearing into the end bedroom. Who he is and why he's there, no-one knows. The landlord and his wife have seen him several times after locking up for the night, but he never troubles them, so they leave him alone.

Inspector Staniforth's friend arrived at the inn and floated down to a bricked-up room concealed beyond the cellar wall, where the headless ghost spent much of his time waiting for wild, windy nights. On hearing the trouble Albert was causing everyone, the headless ghost said he would get some friends together and they'd go and sort him out. Such was the tale of how Albert came to face a horde of angry spirits at Marlston on an otherwise pleasant and rather sunny afternoon.

***

Lord B-P shakily emptied yet another glass of brandy. "This can't go on," he muttered. "Word'll soon get round that the place is haunted by an evil spirit, and that'll be the end of us all."

Lady B-P shook her head sadly. "If only we could stop people coming here while we find a way to get rid of this dreadful creature."

Mr. Cochran frowned thoughtfully. "There's one thing that might just work." He scratched his forehead and tugged at one of his large ears.

A smile crept over Lord B-P's lips as he listened carefully to his estate manager's plan. Gleefully he rubbed his hands. "It's a great idea, Cochran. You go and find the paint and placards while I ring the evening newspaper. And remind me to give you a rise on payday."

CHAPTER 7

In which our hero finds an incredible hiding place, and meets himself

IMAGINE FOR ONE moment there are fairies at the bottom of the garden…and someone tells you there aren't.

Then imagine you'd never even dreamed fairies existed, and someone tells you they're there, parachuting on the thistledown.

Either way, you're likely to be rocked to the very core, and in defence of your own belief you'll swear they're lying to you. It'll shatter your cosy little world if you do believe in fairies, or soften the harsh realities if you don't.

A pound to a penny, or even to an old shirt button, you don't believe in them, and wouldn't even if your next-door neighbour's wife stood on her head in the nude and told you she'd seen them sitting on your bird-table feeding crumbs to the sparrows not ten minutes since.

But some people are more easily led. All through their lives they clamour to be different from everyone else, to stand out from the crowd. Then when they get the chance they've been waiting for, alarm bells start ringing inside them. Sometimes those bells are hidden so deep it's impossible to hear them, but their inescapable message is hammered home anyway, into the very fibre of their own sub-conscious. And the warning they ring out is reminiscent of those lazy sweltering days in the holiday sunshine when the coastguards warned not to swim against the current.

In other words, it's no use going against the tide, and if you don't want to get carried along the way the water's going, you shouldn't get in, in the first place. Or another way again: if no-one else believes in fairies, you'll look pretty silly if you do. Unless, that is, you're prepared to make a stand and argue with such unswerving fidelity against the rest of the world, and you really must go in for a swim, there seems very little point in trying to go upstream.

Albert had never even thought about attempting to go the other way. As far as he was concerned there was only one way, and he was dutifully traversing it. He had always fit in with his fellow crowd of workers and seemed to get on fine. If it came to a show of hands at a union meeting early on in his life he always voted with the rest, without even thinking about it. He joined the Amalgamated Glue and Adhesive Workers Union the day he left school and started at Jebsons. At the first couple of meetings he hadn't a clue what was going on or what they were talking about, but when it came to the vote he put his hand up with the others.

The more he thought about it, the more he realised he didn't have to think about it. And everyone else felt exactly the same way. So they elected someone to do their thinking for them—their shop steward. He was able to put their collective voice to the management and he told the management he was just the workers' mouthpiece. They did all the thinking, he said, and he was just the voice who conveyed it.

It was more than merely a circle with no beginning and no end, never knowing the start from the finish; it was more like an onion. In an onion each ring has a smaller ring inside it, or a larger ring outside it, depending on whether you're inside looking out, or outside looking in.

When Albert became the shop steward he stepped up a ring from one of those where the ring above does the thinking, to a level where the thoughts come from the ring below. And he soon began to realise what power he had at his fingertips. He started to have ideas of his own that the men should get an extra thirty pounds a week, that they should start work later in the morning, have a longer lunch break, and leave earlier at night.

The men went along with his every idea, not so much because they actually agreed with him (though ninety-nine percent of the time, they did, of course) but because they had voted him into the position of coming up with these ideas and felt it would be wrong if they went against him.

And the more Albert saw of the management—their luxurious board room with green baize on the table and the deep-pile carpet, the executive suite with its own dining room, the bottles of claret, and rare steaks—the more he thought the workers deserved a better deal.

Here in the afterlife he brooded on the injustice of it all. He had spent his working life fighting for his fellow men, and as soon as he passed into the next life and tried to keep it up he was picketed by a group whom he felt should know better than to do that to him.

He looked moodily at Sir Bartlewood's armour, lying on its side on the attic floor, with just the head glinting in the afternoon sunshine trickling in feebly through the skylight. "Well, they won't put me off," he said angrily to himself. "They've no right to come here interfering. This is my argument and I'm going to fight it my way." Once Albert embarked on a scheme he would always see it through, and was not one to be put off easily. Albert had always had a joke in life that if people asked was he talking to himself and did he know it was the first sign of madness, he would tell them he was talking to the little green man sitting on his shoulder. But this time there was no little green man, no fairies at the bottom of the garden…not even anyone wondering why he was talking to himself. He knew the armour was in no position to answer him—after all, he had been its only life force during the last few hundred years. Yet still he spoke to it.

"Well, looks like we've got a gang of flying pickets to deal with. Shall we go and see if they're still around?" He gleeked into the suit of armour and stood up with it, like a second skin, so snugly did it fit him.

On the way to the office to find some paint and several sheets of cardboard, Mr. Cochran had found Gladys, still in a faint. The world record for fainting the highest number of times in a day had not been registered, but Gladys must have been on the brink of achieving it. Mr. Cochran pulled her into a chair, watched by the gang of ghosts, who were gathered together in the corner trying to draw up plans to stop Albert. While the world fainting record had gone largely unnoticed in the greater scheme of things, so it was with the collective noun for a gang of ghosts. While language experts had duly recorded a swarm of bees, a colony of ants, a gaggle of geese and a pair of shoes, they had left off the list a break of winds, a flush of plumbers, an impatience of wives, and a fright of ghosts.

And now this fright of ghosts agreed that intimidation by words was like water off a flock of ducks' backs to Albert, so they needed to find something stronger. "A quick show of muscle might work," said the head. "Obviously we don't want to hurt Albert if we can avoid it, but if he won't see things our way I'm afraid we might have to."

***

Wallace had long held the opinion that there were too many ministries, each with so many staff concentrating on things of no real consequence, that the essential jobs remained neglected. And he felt that one of those essential but neglected jobs was liaison between the ministries. Each one was so cocooned in its own little silo trying to sort out its own issues, that it let the others plod along undisturbed.

"With a little bit of communication through the proper channels this would never have happened," he said. "It could all have been avoided so easily. If the Ministry of Hauntings had been able to secure immediate action from Saint Christopher's Doomsday Ministry, Albert would have been stopped officially."

"As it is, he looks like being harassed and intimidated by a fright of ghosts who shouldn't even be there," snapped Mozelbeek.

"How you turn the tables to suit yourself," said Wallace, searching through his mind for a slice of history he wanted to cut from the cake to illustrate his point. Back through the years he travelled; Albert's life flashing past his eyes with immense clarity. The surge through time stopped as Wallace found a moment from early on in Albert's reign as shop steward.

"Here, take a look at this memory." By the side of the great limpid pool teeming with the waters of life stood a smaller, cloudier pool. Its waters were calm, having remained undisturbed for many a long while. It was a rarely used pool which relived snatches from the past brought into play again by an angel. Wallace plucked the memory from his mind and waved a hand over the cloudy waters. Instantly they cleared, and Albert could be seen in their depths, about to reenact a scene from his appearance in life's theatre, projected from the mists of time through Wallace's mind.

The stage, of course, was Jebsons Glue Factory. The time doesn't matter, other than to say it was during the longest dispute in the company's history. Albert had not long been the shop steward, and was trying to make his mark by refusing to even negotiate with management. He had put his case for more pay and a shorter working week, and was not going to be moved. The management had rejected the claim, so he called the workforce out on strike. His problem was that in those early days only about half the workers were union members. This, of course, led to feelings and tempers running so high that they frayed at the edges. For day after day Albert and his followers stood outside the gates attempting to talk to their fellow workers who went straight past them into the factory every morning.

Tuesday was delivery day, when the mass of animal waste and bones was delivered to the factory ready to be rendered down for the part it played in the manufacture of Jebson's finest traditional glue. Albert could see he would never be able to persuade all his colleagues to join the strike by words alone. The time had come to take firm action. He organised his pickets into a single line with arms linked, barring the entrance.

Eventually the delivery lorry swung off the main road and trundled to a halt inches from the unwavering human chain. The driver thrust his head through the cab window. He had read about the dispute in the *Brindon Herald* and thought Albert was backing a hundred-to-one loser. "Get out of my way," he thundered. "I'm behind schedule as it is, without farting about with you lot. Now move, or I'll drive over you."

"Just a moment, brother…" Albert strode over and clambered up onto the footplate. "This is a strike of the Amalgamated Glue and Adhesive Workers Union over a perfectly reasonable pay and conditions claim. The management refuses point-blank to listen to our case, so as a last resort we've had to withdraw our labour. Can I ask you to support us by not delivering materials for the blacklegging scabs inside to work with, please?"

"You can ask all you like," the driver responded. "But I'm giving you just ten seconds to get them men out of my way, then this lorry goes in." He slammed the cab window shut. Albert used his ten seconds to keep protesting and knocking on the glass. Suddenly the driver crunched the gears in and moved forwards. The pickets scattered like ninepins as the revving monster ploughed its way into the factory. The driver had had enough of Albert clinging for dear life to the footplate and door handle. He swerved, causing Albert to lose his grip and fall heavily on to the concrete yard.

Albert groaned as his colleagues helped him gingerly to his feet. "Did you see that?" he demanded painfully, rubbing a rapidly colouring bruise. "We'll stop him next time. He won't get away with that one again."

Even the local trades council was divided. Some felt glue workers had been exploited for too long and that Albert was doing a fine job, while others felt he should at least negotiate with the management in seeking a solution.

Come Friday, the next delivery day, Albert had two hundred staunch unionists from the trades council behind him. They had foregone a morning's work from their local mines and factories to lend support to the glue strike. But Albert had decided against having them at Jebsons. He felt that as the suppliers had failed to be sympathetic the pickets could do more good by refusing to let any delivery lorries leave their depot.

So all two hundred flying pickets crowded into the narrow gateway of Jebsons' suppliers. It was the same lorry driver as before, making the same threats as before. This time his bosses came out to tell the pickets he had many more deliveries to make as well as the one at Jebsons.

"You should have thought of that," yelled Albert, "before you sent this scabbing blackleg round on Tuesday. Let me tell you, you won't be making any more deliveries on Tuesdays and Fridays until the dispute's settled. We'll be here to make sure of that."

While the driver went off to have a cup of tea the works foreman continued the argument with Albert. "We're not involved in your dispute; that's between you and your company. Why drag us into it? The other companies we've got to deliver to today need their materials quickly. Neither they nor us have harmed you in any way."

Mozelbeek angrily waved a hand above the pool. The waters instantly clouded over, drowning the scene being played out below. He rounded on Wallace: "What do you think you're trying to prove?"

"Just that Albert has been in exactly the same position as the ghosts he's now facing. He has played both roles now and knows what that supply company and their other customers went through at the hands of his flying pickets.

"All I'm saying, Mozelbeek, is that Albert is now angry that someone's doing to him exactly what he's done to others. And if you examine it carefully you can see that the ghosts have more right to pester Albert than he did to picket the supply company, because they're responding to action which is disrupting haunting routines. Albert is far from an innocent party here, yet still he's protesting."

Mozelbeek rose to the defence. "How can any upper-class management be as innocent as you try to make these companies out to be? Okay, they may have been innocent as far as this particular dispute was concerned, but they all had the same unrelenting views as Jebsons about their own workers. Albert was fighting for an overall principle for the downtrodden masses. It's the old, old story of the wealthy upper classes against the poor working class.

"So, while on the face of it it appeared to be just for the glue workers in conflict with Jebsons, Albert was really flying the flag for his whole social class. He wasn't bothered if the whole of the upper class suffered; he felt they'd caused his people to suffer enough and he was just repaying them a little."

"That's nonsense," said Wallace. "And you know it. Look what happened the following week." Again he waved over the waters, and the drama continued in their depths.

The old rag and bone man always came on Mondays and Wednesdays to take away the remnants of the glue-making process. He was onto a good thing. Jebsons paid him to come and collect whatever he could use, and in return he let them have a quantity of bones at cost price whenever he could get them.

His horse and cart was a familiar sight in Brindon, having worked the patch for many years. But his horse's temper never got any better and was the scourge of local schoolchildren. They liked the rag and bone man, Paddy Briers, who told everyone he was eighty-six, but they didn't like Dusty, his horse. And Dusty didn't like them. In fact Dusty didn't like anyone except old Paddy, and even then it was cupboard love because he knew Paddy fed him and probably wouldn't if he didn't pretend to like him.

So when Paddy and Dusty rolled up on Monday it was from a distance that Albert called to him: "Why, hi there, Paddy. How're yer keepin'?"

"Oh, foine, foine, to be sure" came back the drawling Irish brogue. "Oi'm just going in to collect me bits and pieces, don't yer know."

Albert ventured a step or two nearer. "Paddy, you know we're in dispute with the management here. Can I ask you not to do any business with Jebsons until it's all settled?"

Dusty snorted, his fiery breath making a beeline for Albert.

Albert shot back, alarmed. Paddy ruffled the horse's already tatty mane. "Now then, Dusty, take it easy me old feller, he'll not be meanin' it, don't yer know. He knows we rely on Jebsons for a good slice of our livin' and he wouldn't be wantin' us to starve, now would he?"

"But Paddy, if you do anything for them you'll be helping them against us, your old mates."

"Now then, yer may be me mates, and the management ain't me mates, but it's the management that be payin' me. It ain't you who be payin' me. Oi've to keep the old wolf from the door o' me poor old run-down shack, now ain't Oi?" He patted the now docile horse who widened his eyes with a saddened expression.

"It ain't just for my sake, yers be understandin', but for the sake o' me poor old 'orse. Oi couldne be seein' Dusty goin' hungry, now coulda?"

Paddy led Dusty and the cart through the gates, Dusty snorting and chomping as he went, twisting his head from side to side, eager to get at the pickets, who just as eagerly pressed themselves into the wall to get as far away from him as they could.

After three weeks of picketing Jebsons on Mondays, Wednesdays, and Thursdays, and the supply company on Tuesdays and Fridays, Albert began to get suspicious. Jebsons appeared in no way to be running out of material; yet their normal supplies did not usually last even a week.

He woke up in the middle of the night with the answer on his lips. "Paddy Briers," he yelled at his wife, sitting bolt upright in bed. Abigail was getting fed up with it by now, as were the other men's spouses; living up to their collective noun of an impatience of wives. As the housekeeping had long since run out and the bills were mounting, they were putting increasing pressure on their men to go back to work. But the men stood firm.

The next day being Wednesday, Paddy turned up as usual at ten o'clock. The pickets all had sticks this time in case Dusty was hungry and fancied making a meal out of one of them. Albert stood a good five yards away, noting unhappily that Dusty was eyeing him rather balefully.

"Paddy, I'm afraid I must ask you to lift the cover on your cart."

"Oi'll be doin' no such t'ing," retorted Paddy. "Oi've got me work to be doin' and Oi'm goin' to be doin' it." The pickets didn't move as Dusty snorted towards them. They stood firm, sticks held in front of them. With a savage twist of his massive, powerful head and a snap of his teeth, Dusty bit through Albert's stick as if it were straw.

As well as breaking the stick, Dusty had also broken the pickets' nerve and gritty resolution. The grit in it was squashed as if underfoot, and they leaped back as Paddy tunelessly whistled his way past them and disappeared inside.

It had been the works manager's idea and Nethanial Jebson dubbed it "a brilliant wheeze." Paddy brought their materials in on his cart and took out barrels of the finished glue which he promptly delivered to the distributors. The factory was only producing less than a third of its normal amount of glue, but Nethanial Jebson said that was better than giving in to the pickets.

Albert had remarked that Paddy had taken to lashing down the tarpaulin which covered his cart, but until that moment of divine inspiration in his bedroom, he had not suspected what Paddy was doing. Actually, for "divine inspiration" read "a hint implanted by Mozelbeek."

Now Albert changed his plan. On Tuesdays and Fridays they would still picket the supply company, but on Mondays and Wednesdays they would picket Paddy's scrapyard and not let him out. And on Thursdays they would picket Jebsons. Foolproof.

Which meant Albert was all the more infuriated when it didn't work.

The company should be grinding to a halt by now and management wearing out their trouser knees by grovelling to the strikers to go back to work. But instead the factory chimney continued painting the sky with its thick grey smoke as if nothing were wrong.

Okay, so the scabbing blacklegs who carried on working were putting in a hell of a lot of overtime, but it still begged the question, just how were the supplies getting in? Albert couldn't fathom it at all. It suddenly came to him in another Mozelbeek-instilled flash. Had he been a mathematician named Archimedes taking a leisurely bath in around 242 BC he may well have called "Eureka," but as it was, he just called a union meeting.

"Now, brothers," he began. "As you know, thanks to our blackleg friends who persist in carrying on working, the management is having a measure of success in breaking the strike. The only way they can be getting materials into the factory is still through Paddy Briers. It seems picketing his yard has not solved our problems—he must be taking the stuff to them at night."

There was a murmur of agreement.

"Obviously this must stop. We can't keep the strike going for much longer, we're all just about broke. Something's got to be done, and quickly. I don't propose that we extend our picketing to the evenings and weekends, but I do think we should stop Paddy by equally drastic measures.

"What I propose we do it this..." He paused for effect, looking round at the expectant faces. He needn't have worried about effect. His next words had their fair share of that.

"I suggest we steal Paddy's horse until the dispute's settled. Without Paddy's help Jebsons will quickly come to a standstill and the management will have to give in to our claims."

"Steal that little monster? You must be joking." It was a solid and unanimous protest, but Albert was not to be put off.

"I've got it all worked out. If we go in when he's asleep, armed with plenty of carrots, we can wake him up and start feeding him straight away. He won't have time to be angry, and we can lead him away with the carrots, like you do with donkeys. He'll be docile then, and we can get him out with no trouble.

"My back yard's completely walled off. He can stay there until everything's settled. As long as we keep feeding him while we take him there I'm sure it'll be alright. I've seen old Paddy slip him a sugar lump or a carrot when he's been getting a bit frisky, and after that he's as good as gold."

There was a stunned silence while everyone weighed up the pros and cons. No-one relished the idea of stealing Dusty, but neither did they relish the idea of the financially-crippling strike carrying on one moment longer than necessary. They finally agreed that stealing Dusty was the lesser of two very nasty evils.

So the following night found the horse-napping team cutting their way with a hacksaw through the chains on Paddy's gate. They crept into the yard towards Dusty's stable, perfect camouflage provided by cloud cover blacking out the moon. Albert inched the stable door open and slipped inside, carrots at the ready.

But he hadn't bargained on Dusty still being awake. With a characteristic snort and snap, Dusty bolted forwards and gripped Albert's hand firmly between his teeth.

It's a wonder the whole population of Brindon was not awoken by Albert's agonised yell: "Let go, you little bugger."

And it was no use the others desperately telling him to shush—it wasn't their hand being crunched in a vice-like jaw.

Wildly Albert kicked the horse's leg. Dusty opened his mouth in pain and surprise, and Albert was away like the nine-forty train to Kings Cross. He slammed the stable door shut and fled past his astonished colleagues as if his tail were ablaze. Albert spent the rest of the night at Brindon General Hospital waiting his turn to have several stitches put in the wound. By now he had had enough, and decided on the spur of the moment that enough was very definitely enough. It was time to call the strike off.

So next morning, with his arm in a sling, he told the men he was calling it a day.

That afternoon he went in to tell Nethanial Jebson they were returning to work. Mr. Jebson smiled and said that sadly it was too late. They were so far behind with orders that it was impossible to keep the factory going: there was no alternative but to close it down and make everyone redundant.

"The only way we could possibly keep it going," he said gently, "is if everyone does a couple of hours unpaid overtime for a few weeks. That way, we might just scrape through. But everyone must work extra hard to get us back on our feet again."

Wallace and Mozelbeek watched Albert's shoulders slump as he slouched forward. On behalf of the men, he accepted the conditions.

And Mr. Jebson never did tell him that since they had left the factory unguarded on Mondays and Wednesdays by picketing Paddy's yard, he had arranged for the supply company to deliver their normal quota of materials on those two days instead of their regular Tuesdays and Fridays.

The waters clouded over again and Wallace looked up at Mozelbeek. "That's the sort of person you're guardian to," he spat contemptuously. "A man who would deliberately try to deprive another man of his livelihood by stealing an animal from him."

Mozelbeek had forgotten that episode and did not take too kindly to being reminded of it. "Okay, okay," he snapped. "Taken out of context it does look bad, I agree. But that rag and bone man was siding with the capitalist management, so he deserved all that Albert tried to do to him."

An exasperated sigh escaped Wallace's lips. "It illustrates my point perfectly, highlighting what I was saying earlier about loyalties. You can hardly call Paddy Briers an upper-class member of the management. He's barely able to scrape a living together, but Albert was quite prepared to deprive him of the means of making any money at all. And that horse means more to him than anything else in the world. It's the only living thing he cares for, and probably the only living thing that cares for him.

"As well as that, he's got his loyalties right. It was the management who paid him and who deserved his loyalty. I was glad to see he remained loyal to them in the face of intimidation from Albert and his gang."

Mozelbeek did not want to get involved in another argument with Wallace. And if truth be told, neither did Wallace. Neither really knew what he was striving for, nor what the other had in mind, but they felt it important to show strength whenever they could and to score victories in as many clashes as possible. Like lawyers they protected those in their care with an all-embracing arm wrapped passionately around their shoulders, caring little for truth, justice, or the opposition's viewpoint. It was their job to highlight the good points of their humans. And they had to ensure that their charges went through their earthly lives with more than a fifty-fifty chance of avoiding trouble and temptation, to get to heaven. Neither stuck too closely to the morals which tripped easily off their tongues when defending the actions of an earthbound soul in their care.

As guardian angels they were regarded by their superiors as being rogues and renegades. But on the whole they did a good job, recognised as being moody, brilliant mavericks who always strived to be unconventional.

They each had the flair to pull it off, not like many a plodding, nose-to-the-grindstone angel who could not achieve all that Wallace and Mozelbeek had, even if they devoted their entire life after death to it.

During their earthly lives the sparring partners had missed each other by several hundred years, but on becoming guardian angels they quickly realised they were the perfect foil for one another. Their arguments were, on the whole, one-sided using the philosophy of "to each his own." To a bystander it made for a more interesting tussle—the coming together of two powerful minds, each an irresistible force and immovable object at the same time. Each an individual, while at the same time an entire tribe, country, and nation. In every battle they had they made peace with their souls—even guardian angels have souls—by telling themselves they were representing others, and their actions were open to deeper interpretation than a simple battle of wits.

Both Wallace and Mozelbeek had become totally involved in the battle at Marlston Manor. It presented the opportunity of eternity. Not every day did ghosts choose an earthbound site for a conflict between themselves. And when they did, how often could it be said that one of the parties was also in conflict with a mortal? No, indeed, it was too good a game to miss, and the angels were determined to make the most of it until it was time for Fate to blow the final whistle.

But Fate had no intention of ending the game for a while to come. There was still plenty to be played out yet before Fate could say she was satisfied.

***

Mr. Cochran had a habit of letting his tongue protrude slightly from the corner of his mouth while concentrating, and right now the pink tip could clearly be seen. He stepped back from his desk to admire his handiwork—the black-painted lettering shining damply on the cream-coloured cardboard.

"Yes, that's fine," he said to himself.

The door opened and Lord B-P came in, smiling. "Gladys is on yet another brandy in the drawing room," he grinned. Then he turned to more serious matters.

"The paper's going to run a piece tomorrow, so if we can get this notice on the gate as soon as possible we'll have a good breathing space." He looked down at the cardboard. "Yes, that's fine, Cochran. Let it dry, then at the end of the day take it down and lock the gates. Fasten it above the brass Marlston Manor sign, and we're in business. Or should I say temporarily out of business?"

***

Albert had gleeked carefully around the house still inside the armour, looking for his adversaries. He peered down from the picture gallery and saw the fright of ghosts huddled in a corner talking. He was too far away to hear their conversation but guessed they were drawing up new plans to stop him haunting. And with him having only just discovered the powers spirits have he wondered if the fright had any others he did not yet know about.

Suddenly he decided to risk everything and snapped the visor shut with a vengeance.

"Now listen to me," he boomed at the top of his voice. The ghostly gathering stopped their furtive whispering and whirled to face him as he floated downstairs.

"I'm the resident ghost of Marlston Manor," he cried. "Albert Carter is working here with me. We have a mission, and you have no right to interfere with our work."

The fright didn't need any time at all to see through Albert's disguise. They realised straight away who it was.

"Come on," cried the head. "Get him." Albert instantly knew his strategy was undone, and gleeked.

And thus began the most incredible chase through Marlston Manor that its exotic and ancient walls had ever seen. Had any wandering spirit been passing through they could have been forgiven for thinking the world had gone mad. Albert's pursuers had one power unknown to him. For a few seconds after a ghost gleeked, their vibrations remain in the air, and experienced spirits can latch on to them, following them through the mystic veil to their landing place.

On arriving in his attic Albert breathed a sigh of relief, thinking he had escaped. He could hardly believe it when the dismal room was suddenly full of the angry-looking fright.

"Bloody hell," he cried, gleeking again. This time he found himself standing in the B-Ps' private drawing room, but before he had time to look around his pursuers were there too. From room to room he flitted, but a few seconds after arrival they were there too, every time. He tried the summer house, but still they followed. And so back to the mansion itself, into the old part, the original house. Over the years various extensions had been added, but they were all in keeping with the splendid magnificence of Marlston. The styling throughout remained exquisite; the only difference being that none of the additions had the twenty-two-inch-thick walls of the original.

Albert materialised in the old dining room, whose ceiling displayed the massive oak beam running through that entire section of the house. He was standing alongside the dark oak refectory table and ladder-back chairs. Even as he looked across the room, the head and his troops appeared.

On the opposite side of the hall was the smaller of a dozen or so sitting rooms. The feature which caught Albert's eye as soon as he gleeked inside was the natural stone fireplace with a tall hood of beaten brass. And brass hangings adorned the same major oak beam, common to the dining room, running crossways to the rest, and was twice their thickness.

The windows in both the south – and west-facing elevations opened on to breathtaking views of the rolling Marlston countryside, the deep sills demonstrating the unusual thickness of the walls. Once more the room became full of the spectral beings forcing Albert to quickly be on his way again.

This time he arrived back in the hall where a few remaining visitors were wandering through. The suit of armour suddenly appearing in front of them out of thin air had the effect Albert had come to expect. First they stared in complete disbelief which swiftly turned to a more basic primeval fear. As he floated towards them they gasped, then screamed.

Out of the corner of his eye he saw the fright arrive, and in desperation tried something different, gleeking out of the armour and back up to the attic. Without its life-giving force the armour crashed heavily to the floor and lay still. But the tourists were no longer around to see that it was now just a harmless shell; they were fleeing hysterically back to the car park.

While the chase was going on, Bobby and Daphne had gone back to the attic. They had no desire to get involved with a routing of Marlston which seemed to be in full swing.

"For God's sake, help me," pleaded Albert. He knew now

how the fox felt when the hounds were closing for the kill. "Where can I hide?"

Daphne suddenly felt a twinge of pity. The wild hunted look in Albert's eyes twanged at her heart strings like an out-of-tune guitar. And she felt sanity and peace may return to Marlston if they got him out of the way for a while.

It was a strange and wonderful power, only told to souls who had committed suicide on Earth, and Bobby and Daphne had been ordered to use it regularly while serving their sentences as earthbound spirits. Saint Christopher had told them it would give them a chance to think again of the wrongs they had done and help them focus on the error of their actions. But it was a power which would enable Albert to escape, albeit temporarily, from his relentless pursuers, and Daphne had no qualms about betraying the secret.

"Gleek into your own mind, your own brain and thoughts—quickly, before they get here," she cried urgently. "There's no way they can follow you into the very fibre of your own being."

It only took Albert a fraction of a second to understand. He had no idea what would happen, but if Daphne said it would help him escape he needed no further prompting.

As Albert gleeked he got the distinct impression of falling; at first oh, so slowly, more as if he were being lowered from the hook of some giant crane. Then suddenly he was speeding, ever faster, engulfed in thoughts and memories, some recent, some from his deep past. He remembered vividly his mother feeding him for the first time; then he plunged even further back, curled warm and snug in the security of the womb. Instantly the cycle began again, remembering Georgie coming to fetch him when he died. Almost momentarily the thoughts flashed by, intermingling with each other until none was legible in its own right. It seemed to the startled Albert that he was trapped for centuries in the ever-increasing spiral of memory. But it was only a few seconds before reality was restored. That is if there is such a thing as reality in the murky world in which Albert had just arrived. He had no idea how he got there. It was when he had lain immersed in the womb for a fourth time on the cycle of memory that he suddenly cracked.

"My God, stop it," he cried, whirling helplessly through space—through the space of his mind; inner space, another world he knew nothing about, living deep within him.

Bobby and Daphne had been closely briefed as to how to use this extraordinary power and were told how it would benefit them. For hours they sat literally lost in the maze of their own thoughts reliving parts of their lives and realising with mature afterthoughts where their hearts and feelings had misled them. They came to learn more than most about the folly of mankind, quickly realising that given time their true love for each other and Bobby's innocent sincerity would have won Daphne's father over. Eventually he would have given his consent and blessing to their union, but they had acted on a foolish impulse, such as befits the young. They had followed their hearts, not their heads, having seen just one way out—suicide—and were ignorant of the consequences of their action, the consequences they now knew so much about. But for them there was to be a happy ending. Once their sentence was served they would find eternal happiness in heaven; not an ending everyone found.

So often mankind acted without realising the full consequences, without knowing what he was letting himself and his contemporaries in for. Learning of one's mistakes afterwards won't undo the damage already caused, but mankind's greed usually ignored the wishes of others, giving misguided strength to press on regardless.

At that moment Albert was wondering if perhaps he had not committed a rash act by gleeking into the fire over the side of a sizzling frying pan. He was surrounded by nothing but greyness; a thick, festering greyness of fog that swirled and swept and licked at his spirit. Taking a few paces forward he found the fog turning to mist. He was astonished to find his thoughts so cloudy. He had always regarded himself as having crystal-clear thoughts. Instantly the haze evaporated and he saw he was standing by a brook in a wood, the water gurgling happily past him. Was this idyllic scene of the peaceful countryside really deep inside him? And if so, what was it doing there?

At the edge of a clearing stood a tall oak tree, whose roots burst through the banks of the brook to drink of its waters. Suddenly Albert was aware of someone standing behind him. Spinning round to face the newcomer he found himself staring straight into the eyes of…

…himself!

"What the hell…?" he began.

"Greetings, Albert," said his mirror image, who was even wearing the same clothes, and now holding out his hand. "I'm very glad to meet you at last. I've been a part of you from the moment you were born—even before that, in fact. This is quite an honour for me, you know. It isn't very often a spirit bothers to look in on its soul."

"But who are?" Albert managed to ask.

"I'm your soul," said Albert the Second.

"But how…? I thought I was my soul?"

"No, no, no, you're the spirit; I'm the soul."

"We're not one and the same, then?"

"Well, yes and no," conceded the soul. "We're one and the same person, one and the same being; Albert Carter. But we're different parts of him. All through his life—our life—there've been three parts: the body, the spirit, and the soul.

"The body, which is so prone to the earthly impurity of disease, is sadly no longer with us, having fallen victim to one of those impurities, pneumonia. You provided the life force for that body in the same way that I provided it with feelings, ideals, and a conscience. This is where Earth-based teachings fail in their accuracy. They confuse the spirit with the soul. Many strains of religion acknowledge the afterlife and the existence of a soul, but they believe the spirit is the soul, and that's not right. I live within you, just as you lived within the body."

Albert was confused, but fascinated, wanting to know more. "You're the power behind all my thoughts then, and everything I feel?"

"I AM your thoughts, I AM everything you feel," said the soul. "I'm what made Albert Carter who he was in life and what is making you, the spirit, who you are in the Condition Of Transit.

"Our true resting place is the settlement of either heaven or hell, whichever the powers greater than us decide is to be our destiny. If I have done enough during our body's lifetime we shall win a seat in heaven. If I've failed and the evil which lies in both spirit and body has impressed a stronger presence upon Saint Christopher, then we're doomed to hell."

The soul held up his hand as Albert began to protest.

"Please do not take offence," he continued. "You don't understand. The very purpose of the soul's existence in man is to temper the wickedness of the flesh and the raw spirit, such as yourself. If I've worked well, then day by day throughout our entire life a little more of my personality wears off on you, which you, in turn, pass on to the body. Now the body is dead, but we live on, and our true place in heaven or hell is still to be won or lost, dependant on your actions, guided by me."

For the first time Albert began to have doubts about his haunting of Marlston Manor.

"Do you think I'm doing the right thing, then, in frightening people away from Marlston?"

"That's not for me to say. I'm just your conscience and your feelings in this matter. But I will say this; I have always instilled into you a singleness of purpose and you have reacted well. I've passed on to you my feelings that you should fight solidly towards your target and your ideals, and not be put off by any other considerations.

"I believe I'm right in those beliefs because what you've been doing in our earthly life wasn't just for your benefit. You were acting on behalf of many of your colleagues and you were doing your best for them. So often people fight for a single goal just for themselves, without any other consideration. It's that which I believe is wrong, but if you fight for others, then I feel it's right.

"And look at this…" The soul turned to indicate the huge oak tree and brook. "This tree was nothing but an acorn when you—when we—were born. This is Albert Carter's tree of wisdom, and the brook flows with the waters of life. See how the roots quest out from the tree and drink of those waters, and how the waters give life and strength to the tree." He kicked the trunk fiercely. "See how sturdy and firm it is. It thrives on that life which it sucks up. Now my theory is that if those waters, that life, weren't good for the tree, it would turn rotten and shrivel up.

"I see no reason to deviate from the path we're set upon. Go, Albert Carter, back into the Condition Of Transit, fearing no man, no spirit, no soul, in the quest for your heart's fulfilment."

The soul smiled, strangely but knowingly, before being suddenly engulfed in the fog which descended once more to the clearing.

Again Albert was alone, for a moment feeling unusually humble. The soul had said it wasn't often his kind met their spirit, but Albert was thinking about it from the other point of view. How many men could say they've met their soul face-to-face and had a chat with it?

A new feeling surged through him exciting every fibre of the spirit. He felt his soul had given him renewed confidence for his battle at Marlston Manor. And he was no longer unduly worried by the presence of flying pickets. He now knew how to escape from them if necessary. And if they tried to interfere while he was in the middle of scaring people away he could turn that to his advantage, remembering how Bobby and Daphne had unwittingly helped him when they tried it.

He gleeked out of himself straight to beneath the four-poster bed in the King Charles I Room. He felt he would be safe from the fright of ghosts under there.

***

Mozelbeek sighed with relief as Albert reappeared in the depths of the limpid pool. "He's come out of himself. Thank goodness for that. I wonder who, or what, he came up against inside?"

"Perhaps it's a good thing we haven't the power to see within a spirit," said Wallace, turning from his harp, where he had been retuning a middle string. "If we could actually know what a human was thinking and feeling, the temptations would be too much for even the hardiest guardian angel. I'm sure too many of us would use it to stamp our own personalities on our mortals."

"Yes, I think you're right. It's okay us putting in a prodding suggestion now and again, but if we could see into their very minds we could counteract their own thoughts."

Wallace smiled at the implications which would arise from that. "We could make sure everyone got to heaven," he grinned. "Put the devil and his dark abode out of business—to say nothing of Saint Christopher and his Doomsday Ministry." He chuckled. "Perhaps that's why communication with an earthbound soul is still shrouded in mystery, even to us."

A bright, faraway look glimmered in Mozelbeek's eyes as he stared dreamily into the water. He had lost count of the number of times people had denied the existence of a god in the face of great tragedy, asking themselves how a loving god could let such dreadful things happen. Mozelbeek felt he now had the answer to those criticisms. "Just think of the benefits that would bring. We'd all be acting in unison for the benefit and good of the world and mankind." The spark now blazed and became a raging inferno. He leaped to his feet, nearly bumping his head on his halo.

"We could counter every evil thought born in the whole of mankind. Don't you see, Wallace, this is what it's all about? This is the break Destiny has been waiting an eternity for. And I'm the one to find it."

All the stars in all the spangled skies were nothing compared to those blazing in Mozelbeek's eyes at that moment. "No more wars or uncertainty." His voice was almost a hushed and reverent whisper. "It'll be the perfect world. Everyone will always have pure thoughts and clear, untroubled consciences. It'll be the ideal world—it'll be…it'll be…heaven on Earth."

The paradox was too frightening for Wallace to handle. "It'll never work, I'm afraid," he said sadly. "It sounds a nice idea, I admit, but imagine what would happen to the balance of Destiny. Her scales would tip uncontrollably to one side and—"

Mozelbeek cut in quickly. "But that wouldn't matter any more, would it? It would be a whole new concept. No festering maggots of evil anywhere. Just think of it, don't the possibilities excite you?"

"Of course they do, but it's all so impossible."

"Why is it? We don't know until we try. Who knows what could be waiting for us within these unexplored lands?"

"I can think of many pits the explorers of your brave new world could fall into. Pits dug by the natives themselves. For instance, once a soul gets to heaven its guardian angel loses control over it, so the dominant evil and wickedness that will have lain dormant within it while it's been manipulated for goodness on Earth will awaken," said Wallace. "And it'll probably have a lot of pent-up frustration which it hasn't had a chance to get rid of. Such a soul, and certainly those which were originally destined for hell, would never be happy in heaven. During its earthly life it would think it was happy, but in the end would it really be worth the angels cheating just to find short-term happiness for their charge?"

Still Mozelbeek's eyes blazed, even as Wallace continued. "And picture the scene, Mozelbeek, in three, maybe as little as two, generations' time. The evil souls who've found their way into heaven by our kindness will eventually realise there's only one way out for them. They'll get together and take over everything—life, heaven, the universe, even Destiny herself will fall under evil's controlling spell. Everything that God and his chosen guardians have striven so hard for across millennia will be destroyed in the wink of an eye.

"The process will begin with quiet infiltration into key positions. They'll become guardian angels themselves and as they'll be able to see clearly into the thoughts of mortal men they'll know which souls really belong to their clan. Of course they'll guide them with goodness on Earth, but as soon as they arrive in heaven those souls will be reunited, and the mould will spread as swiftly as if its sperms had been cast to the wind.

"Eventually they'll be in total control and then they can turn their attentions to the earth. Instead of countering evil thoughts with good ones, the guardian angels will counter all good ones with evil. Mankind will be ravaged by wickedness and the devil will have won.

"He'll come from his own dark domain to rule the cosmos. The spectrum of life will lie in tatters, eaten away from the inside. And all because of one guardian angel's good intentions.

"You think now that you've found a way forward. A way that can lead to good triumphantly dominating evil. But evil is crafty and will always find a way of surviving. If anyone, even guardian angels, achieves the absolute power that your idea would give them, they'd run the risk of becoming corrupted. But even that risk is overshadowed by wicked souls finding their way to heaven and then realising their true potential.

"No, Mozelbeek, your idea is too dreadful to contemplate further. Evil already has a stranglehold on Earth, and it's only by the careful selection of souls that it hasn't got into heaven. But let anyone into heaven who doesn't deserve it, who hasn't earned that place because of the way their soul behaved on Earth, and the decay will start."

Mozelbeek hadn't stopped to consider it from that viewpoint, but he now realised that Wallace was absolutely right. Evil was an integral part of life that had to be lived with and could never be totally destroyed. The way to combat it was not to try and stamp it out altogether, or it would inevitably rise from the ashes like a shining phoenix, but to wage small-scale individual battles with it.

Wallace continued: "And I'm sure your idea must have been thought about before and rejected. If there were another way of handling life, on whatever plane of existence, it would surely be in use by now. This just has to be the best known way. The only way.

"There must be a reason we can't follow a spirit into its own soul, and why we can't communicate with a soul. And I think that's the reason."

Mozelbeek sighed again. His dream and visions of a perfect utopian world with eternal happiness for everyone, were lying crushed and broken in his vase of Christmas Roses.

Wallace was talking again: "We must remember above all that no-one has the divine right to find a place in heaven, which your idea would give them. It's only as humans strive to achieve their place there that they make the Earth a better world to live in."

He looked up, grinning at the dejected Mozelbeek. "Anyway, there's a much more fundamental reason why your dream will never become reality." He paused as Mozelbeek glanced quizzically in his direction. "And I'll tell you why. Angels just don't have the power to see and talk to a mortal's soul, and no-one is inclined to give us that power. So all the dreaming in eternity will never bring it to fruition."

Mozelbeek smiled. He had been too carried away with his utopian dreams to think of that. Then he grinned. Then he laughed. Laughed until the tears were rolling down his cheeks, threatening to rust his harp. As he wiped his face with the back of his hand he managed to utter a few strangled words between his shrieks of uncontrollable laughter. "Wallace, you old bugger. You really are an old bugger…ha, ha, ha, ha, ha."

CHAPTER 8

In which our hero becomes the first ghost to broadcast live on the radio

ALBERT COULDN'T UNDERSTAND it. Here it was, eleven o'clock on a Saturday morning in the school Easter holidays and not a tourist to be seen. He knew he'd done well yesterday in frightening people away, but he hadn't expected word to travel so fast, warning everyone to steer clear of the evil at Marlston.

In fact he was quite disappointed. He was just getting into the swing of haunting and now there was no-one to haunt. In a scary, squeaky-bum sort of way he had also been looking forward to the challenge of pitting his wits against the picketing ghosts.

He eased himself out from under the bed and peered through the window. The car park was empty and there wasn't a soul to be seen anywhere. Albert was not given over to a quick sense of humour—his little green man joke being the summit of his witticisms—nor was he appreciative of puns, but he had to smile to himself at the thought which passed for a fleeting moment across his mind: Marlston was silent as the grave, almost like a ghost town, which was certainly an apt description seeing it *was* full of ghosts on that sunny April morning.

Keeping a careful watch for his spectral opponents, Albert gleeked into the main tourist spots. The ice cream man was nowhere to be seen and the snack bar was shuttered and locked. Albert got the distinct impression that something was *going on*, and set off to look for Lord B-P. He didn't have to look very far. Gleeking into the drawing room he came across Lord and Lady B-P, Mr. Cochran, and Riley the butler.

Riley had taken an awful lot of convincing that a ghost really was on the loose in the mansion. Lord B-P had been against Riley being in on the discussions, saying he would be neither use nor ornament as a ghost hunter. But Lady B-P and Mr. Cochran persuaded him that if they were having a council of war they must do it properly and involve the head of the estate's domestic staff.

As Albert arrived they were in the middle of deciding how to track him down.

"We've got to engage him in conversation and get him to meet us all," Lord B-P was saying. "And the most important thing now is not to be scared of the blighter. We know why he's here and we've got to be able to talk to him to show him he's wrong, without us being frightened or getting angry."

"I think we've got to appear really interested in him," agreed Mr. Cochran. "Hopefully we can get him talking about himself, who he is and why he's targeting us."

"But how do we find him?" Riley wanted to know. "It isn't as if we're sure to find him just by searching thoroughly. He could be anywhere. He could even be in this room now, listening to us." Riley shivered at the thought.

His Lordship smiled grimly. "Once he gets wind that there aren't any tourists here today, I have a feeling he'll come looking for us."

So, there aren't any visitors today, thought Albert. *I wonder how he's managed that?* Although reluctant to leave the conversation, his curiosity got the better of him, and he gleeked outside. There was nothing at the main entrance or the tourist entrance to show why everyone was keeping away, so he started walking down the long, winding drive. Every so often he strayed from the path, choosing the gladed countryside, eventually coming to the imposing double gates which opened on to the roadway. They were shut and padlocked, and there was a piece of cardboard tied on to the left-hand gate with a length of gardening twine.

Albert gleeked to the other side of the gate. He pursed his lips, then read aloud what was written on the card: "Temporarily closed for renovation work." He smiled to himself.

"So he'd rather close the manor than face up to me and let me have the run of the place while it's teeming with visitors, would he?" Albert registered the victory and rested on his laurels. There wasn't much more he could do without visitors. He felt pleased at having achieved so much in a relatively short space of time. Suddenly a frown twisted across his face. He knew what he'd achieved, and so did Lord Barrington-Pottsherbert. So did the tourists who had visited the mansion yesterday. But to all the would-be visitors of today, tomorrow, and the next day it was a different story. To them the manor was closed for renovations and although they would think it inconvenient that they had had a wasted journey, they would probably come back when the work was complete—in reality, when Albert had gone. To them there was no ghost. They weren't to know Marlston was haunted.

Albert needed more people to know about it than just one day's trippers. Thinking about it he decided there were two courses of action he could embark upon.

One: he could keep in the background and not appear to the B-Ps again until they thought he had gone and they reopened Marlston. But the problem with that was he could be recalled to Saint Christopher at any time and not be able to continue his plan.

Two: he knew the B-Ps wanted to see him, so perhaps he could talk to them and convince them he was leaving immediately. That way they would reopen sooner and he could be more selective in his hauntings; try to wait until there were visitors who might spread the word. Because that was what he wanted: to discredit Marlston in the eyes of as many people as possible.

It didn't really need thinking about further. He gleeked back to the drawing room.

One moment there was no-one standing by the window; but the next, Lord and Lady B-P, Mr. Cochran, and Riley could all see a smoky, shimmering figure which solidified slowly before their eyes.

Riley and Lady B-P froze, their gaze locked on Albert who waved cheerily at them. "Hi," he called nonchalantly. "Have you had a good breakfast?"

Lord B-P repressed both a shudder and his anger, slapping a warning hand on Mr. Cochran's shoulder just in case the estate manager should let his feelings run away with him. He gave a nervous laugh. "Ah…er, y-yes, a very n-nice breakfast, thank you. You know my manager, and myself, of course, we met yesterday. Allow me to introduce my wife, Lady Sylvia Barrington-Pottsherbert, and another member of my staff, Riley, our butler." Then he looked around at his wife and Riley, then back again to Albert. "I'm afraid I didn't catch your name yesterday."

Albert decided to play along with them, and play it straight. He nodded politely. "Albert Carter. Good morning."

Lord B-P gave an embarrassed cough. "Er, I want to apologise for my rather violent behaviour towards you yesterday. I rather flew off the handle, but you must realise I'd never seen a ghost before and I'm afraid you unnerved me a little. I do hope you'll forgive me."

Albert gleeked into the chair next to Lady B-P and said he did forgive His Lordship. Four heads instantly whirled to face the chair, eyes now focusing on it, rather than the spot on which he had stood just a split second ago.

"Oh!" squealed Lady B-P, leaping up. The ghost smiled at her before turning to look at her husband.

"I see you're cheating and lying to the public," he mused, quietly. "Closed for renovations, indeed."

Lord B-P swallowed nervously as he felt himself starting to sweat. He tugged at his collar. "Ah. Yes. You see, you told us yesterday why you were here, and I couldn't afford to let you frighten any more people away. You'll ruin us if you do it anymore. I had to stop people coming in while we talked to you."

Albert was enjoying seeing Lord B-P sweat, and decided to let him carry on. And Lord B-P dutifully obliged. "I'd like to talk to you about this business. Can we come to some agreement?"

"What sort of agreement?" Albert asked. "What can you possibly offer me?"

That one threw His Lordship. "Well, I, er, I thought perhaps if we gave you the suit of armour you were playing with yesterday you might go away and haunt someone else? No…? Oh. Oh dear." His voice trailed off as Albert shook his head, trying desperately not to smile.

"Or you could—you could…" He broke off. What could he offer to a ghost? "Well, what would you like?" he continued in a small voice, rather like that of a timid child.

Then, slightly less subdued: "But please don't scare my visitors any more."

Albert felt he could do no better than to tell the truth. At least part of the truth. "I'm just passing through Marlston on a long journey." *But by no means all of the truth.* "So my time here has been limited and is now at an end. I'm afraid I must move on towards my final destination."

A sigh of relief escaped from each member of Albert's audience, which he pretended not to notice. "My job here is incomplete, but that can't be helped. I must leave here straight away."

Despite his exhilaration at the thought of getting back to normal, Lord B-P felt too many questions were left unanswered to let the ghost go without some explanation. "Before you depart, could you tell us why you came to Marlston? I want to be able to avoid the wrath of any more ghosts who happen to be passing this way in the future. If you tell me what I've done wrong I'll try to put it right."

"There was no particular reason for choosing this place for my campaign, other than it was a spot on my journey where I had to take a rest. All such homes which are open to the public at a price are as bad each other. I now leave you in peace, Lord Barrington-Pottsherbert, to reopen Marlston Manor, if your conscience will allow you to. But take heed of my message— don't exploit the working classes."

Albert instantly shimmered into nothing. He was still there, but had merely become invisible. Resisting the temptation to call a ghostly farewell he contented himself with listening to the deep silence he left behind.

The silence which was only broken by Lady B-P shaking herself vigorously. "What a dreadful creature. Is that the ghost we were up against, then?"

Riley had gone as white as a bride's proverbial dress, and for a second or two appeared to have been struck dumb. "Good God. It really was a ghost after all," he eventually managed to stammer. Looking up at Lord B-P he asked what they should do next.

"I think the problem's ended," said His Lordship happily. "You heard him say he was going. And it seems he's gone. I think we can remove the notice from the gates and open for business as usual."

Albert smiled. It was just the reaction he was hoping for. All he needed now was a constructive form of haunting and Marlston would be finished forever as a tourist destination.

Lord B-P rubbed his hands briskly. "Off you go then, Cochran. Open up and find Gladys. Tell her not to worry about the suit of armour. It'll be back in its regular place shortly, as harmless as it ever was."

Albert gleeked out to the summer house to draw up some double-pronged plans. One prong would be the actual haunting, while the second would keep one step ahead of the fright of ghosts.

As Mr. Cochran climbed into the Land Rover to drive the mile down to the gates he was suddenly engulfed in a wave of grim realisation: the realisation that things were not quite as simple as Lord B-P thought on hearing that Albert was leaving. He drove like a man possessed, hoping against hope he wasn't about to find evidence proving the problems were not over. He would know within two minutes when he reached the mailbox at the gate.

The fright of ghosts were also wondering why Marlston was lacking in visitors, and were taking a stroll by the lake pondering on what could have happened. They were convinced Albert's hauntings could not have become so notorious already that no-one dared come to the mansion.

"There must be a logical explanation," said a ghost with a chain. "Perhaps Lord Barrington-Pottsherbert has closed the manor for some other perfectly good reason."

"Look there," cried another ghost, pointing to the summer house. "There's Albert."

Suddenly they appeared directly in front of Albert, who

looked up, somewhat surprised. *Play it cool,* he told himself. "Good morning. Lovely day, isn't it?"

They made a slightly threatening move towards him. "It's alright," he said, hastily. "You needn't worry. I've stopped haunting."

The fright stopped in their tracks and the head was laid down by his body on the seat next to Albert. "What do you mean, you've stopped haunting?" he demanded.

"Just what I say. I've had a long talk with Lord B-P and he convinced me I'm wrong." Albert explained that Lord B-P had been so afraid of him ruining his tourist business that he'd temporarily closed the mansion. "But no-one has anything to worry about anymore. Lord Barrington-Pottsherbert convinced me he's done nothing wrong in charging people to visit his home, so I'll spend the rest of my time here watching the visitors enjoy themselves until I'm called to my rightful place in heaven or hell. You can all go back to your own hauntings now."

However, the head wasn't so easily convinced. "How do I know you're telling the truth?" he asked suspiciously.

"Just ask Lord Barrington-Pottsherbert why he closed Marlston and why he's now decided to reopen it," answered Albert, keeping his fingers crossed.

The head was as cunning as Albert. "Alright, I believe you, but now we're here we'll take advantage of the peace and quiet and stay for a couple of days for a nice rest."

Albert's heart sank. A couple of days might be too late; he might have been recalled to Saint Christopher by then. But he smiled. There was no alternative, and he might be able to avoid the ghosts if they believed his haunting days were over.

"I'll be pleased to have you around," he lied. "You'll be able to tell me so much of the mysteries of the afterlife. I'm still very new to this game."

The head exchanged swift glances with his cronies. "We'll see you later," he said, as they gleeked, leaving Albert alone with his thoughts in the summer house.

"A penny for them…," said a finger of sunlight, creeping up his leg, having sneaked between the trees and shown its passport to the glass in the window.

Albert shrugged his shoulders. "Oh, it's nothing," he sighed. "I was just thinking about the attitude of those ghosts and of something Bobby and Daphne said to me. Somehow the two things just don't add up. Here we have these ghosts who've come from various haunted houses throughout the country. They're very strong-willed in that they don't want me to show myself as a spirit because they say it's affecting their colleagues. On the other hand, Bobby and Daphne don't like me haunting here because they're afraid of Saint Christopher thinking they've had something to do with it when their day of judgement comes.

"It's a poor state of affairs when the simple action of one person—such as myself—can have such a far-reaching impact on both camps: these other ghosts and Bobby and Daphne.

"Each has their own reasons for being frightened of what my haunting might do, and that's not right; it can't be. Why should my haunting Marlston so radically affect ghosts in places hundreds of miles away? And why should my haunting affect Bobby and Daphne? Something should be done about it."

The finger deposited its radiant wares on Albert's seat. "You can only see things from one side," it said. "Every action has a reaction and they all have a purpose to justify their existence. There's a far greater depth of knowledge than you can understand at the moment. You're not seeing the opposite side to your opponent for the simple reason that it hasn't been unveiled to you yet. But no reasonable entity will argue a point without listening to the opposing viewpoint and understanding why that opposition's there.

"We all appeal to you, Albert Carter, to stop haunting Marlston and give the natural balance of the universe time to put itself right. Who knows, you may be able to persuade Saint Christopher to grant you leave to ask the Ministry of Hauntings for permission to haunt here legitimately. If you can show a good reason why Marlston should be haunted you might be seconded officially for several months, or even years, before you take up your place in the afterlife."

"What a bloody complicated fuss," protested Albert. "Just to be able to do exactly what I'm doing now. What a load of useless red tape—applying to Saint Christopher first, then applying to...what did you say it was, the Ministry of Hauntings?"

"But then you'd be haunting officially," argued the finger, which had now turned into a wider ray of light and warmth as its creator stepped out a little further from behind the trees.

What little patience Albert had suddenly snapped. "Look!" he cried. "There's far too much bureaucracy and little people employed just to delay things from getting done in the living world, without having to put up with it here as well."

He recalled the conversation with his soul. "I'm here at Marlston now, and wherever I am I'm going to carry on doing what I think is right. And that means putting a stop to this wicked exploitation. Let me tell you..." Albert pointed an accusing finger at the expanding light. "I've hardly started my haunting yet. My God, you'll know what haunting really is by the time I've finished here."

"But—" began the sunlight.

"What's going on here?" screamed Mozelbeek, returning earlier than anticipated from making his latest batch of angel cake. "I can't leave you for five minutes without you getting up to something."

Wallace whirled around guiltily from the limpid pool, hurriedly clouding over the waters of life, his long-standing and often-used ventriloquist act with the sun as his dummy coming to an abrupt end. He thought Mozelbeek would have been away longer.

"You've been talking to my client!" thundered Mozelbeek. "You know that's illegal. You've gone too far this time, Wallace. I'll have you for this, see if I don't."

"Now just minute—alright, I admit I've used the sun to talk to Albert." He thought back to when he had hummed "The Red Flag." "In fact I have done on several occasions. But it's in everyone's best interests that I've done so. He's getting too dangerous and must be stopped. You're doing nothing to help sort out this problem, so it's left to me."

"He's my charge; I'll look after him and do what's best." Mozelbeek was still angry, feeling himself justifiably so.

But Wallace felt he had two reasons to stoutly defend his dubious actions. Firstly, he believed Albert really was too dangerous to be let loose at Marlston much longer. And secondly he had been caught doing something highly illegal, so if Mozelbeek could prove it to the authorities he was in deep trouble.

"Sometimes, Mozelbeek, the rules have to be bent a little to stop people being hurt. Rules are made to protect people, so sticking to them is usually in everyone's best interests. But there comes a time every now and again—and this is one of those times—when a new situation arises; a new problem that couldn't possibly have been foreseen raises its head and the solution to it lies outside the boundaries of the accepted laws and regulations. If the laws can't be changed in time to stop any damage the only thing to do is to step outside them. That's all I've done in this case. By breaking the law I was trying to uphold another section of it, the law which says only authorised spirits shall make themselves known to those still living their mortal lives. I was simply trying to prevent untold damage from being done by persuading Albert to end this foolhardy campaign."

Mozelbeek was far from impressed. "A right isn't found by putting together two wrongs. But if you're using that argument so shall I. Albert hasn't been made officially aware of the law prohibiting him from a physical haunting. He was sent to Marlston to fend for himself, and like a baby just becoming aware of the world around him he is learning to walk and talk. He's also battling for what he thinks is right, and if he has to step outside the law to do it, so what?"

And so the angels' battle, which had begun down the ages, continued with each side putting forward moral ideals as to why they were right. One day, of course, the line would be drawn and one side declared the winner. But that day was still long way off.

***

The door burst open as if it had been the victim of some ancient battering ram.

"Good Lord, whatever's the matter?" cried Lord B-P as Mr. Cochran almost fell into the drawing room clutching the early edition of the evening newspaper.

"It's the paper, my lord; they're carrying the story you gave them about Marlston being closed for renovation work."

Lord B-P groaned, dropping his head into his neatly manicured hands. "Oh no, I'd forgotten about that." He took the paper which Mr. Cochran had picked up from the mailbox at the gate. It had been the newspaper story that Mr. Cochran had suddenly remembered while climbing into the Land Rover. The paper was open at page seven and Lord B-P groaned as he read aloud first the headline, "Repairs Shut Marlston," and then the story: "Marlston Manor, the ancient stately home of Lord Maxwell and Lady Sylvia Barrington-Pottsherbert, has been closed indefinitely for essential renovations.

"The popular tourist spot, which attracts thousands of visitors daily in the summer, has been hit by rising damp in many rooms, and much of the outside stonework has started crumbling.

"Lord Barrington-Pottsherbert says the work will take several weeks, but there is no telling how long Marlston will be closed. There is also no indication how much the work will cost. The manor will only be reopened once it's deemed safe for the public to go in."

Lady B-P broke the short silence. "Well, now what do we do?"

"I suppose we'll just have to stay shut for a few days at least," said His Lordship, throwing down the paper. "Damn. During a holiday period as well." An exasperated sigh whistled from his lips. "There's no way we can bluff our way out of this one."

A fuller version of the story appeared in the late final edition, running to twelve paragraphs on the middle pages, giving a brief history of the manor as well as including a photograph taken last year of His Lordship standing by the steps to the main entrance.

Mr. Cochran elected most wisely not to show the full copy to Lord B-P and decided to get home to his wife early for a change. Locking his office door he hurried the three hundred yards to his cottage behind the manor.

Albert picked up the late final which Mr. Cochran had left lying open on his desk. His heart sank. Like His Lordship he felt there was no way of bluffing out of this one. The manor was shut and that was all there was to it. And he didn't feel Bobby and Daphne should be so angry with him.

"You should be ashamed of yourself, bringing poor Lord Barrington-Pottsherbert to this," Bobby told him. "He's a good man who doesn't deserve to be treated like this by the likes of you."

Albert started to interrupt, but Bobby was well into his stride and not to be put off. "And I'll tell you this, while ever you're here, if there's anything Daphne and I can do to help Lord Barrington-Pottsherbert get back his tourists, we'll do it." Bobby's eyes spat fire. "I'm not bothered now about how it'll reflect on us because I'm sure it'll be seen as an act of goodness to help counter the evil you've brought here."

And with that, Bobby and Daphne gleeked, leaving Albert's "now hang on a moment" echoing hollowly around the walls, evading all ears.

It always seemed to Albert that coincidence was too much of a coincidence for it to be coincidence. He felt there was always something much deeper behind it and that someone, somewhere, was engineering things. And this time there could be no doubt about it. It surely couldn't be coincidence that he was in Mr. Cochran's office when the telephone rang the next day, Sunday morning.

He watched intently as Mr. Cochran's face turned a colour that would put any blushing bride to shame. The manager seemed to lose the power of clear coherent speech as he began babbling into the telephone. "No. Only His Lordship can answer questions like that. I'll see if he's available today and ring you back."

He slammed the handset down with such force it was a miracle he did not chip a piece off it, then leaped up, heading for the library. During the last couple of days Lord B-P had become used to sudden and noisy entrances from his staff.

"Yes, what is it this time, Cochran?" he asked wearily as his estate manager burst through the door, one of his large ears twitching as if under the relentless touch of a stray lock of hair which had lost its way on the wrong side of his parting.

"The newspaper's just been on the telephone, sir," he gasped breathlessly.

"What did they want?"

"They say that since they published the story of Marlston closing for renovations, their switchboard has been flooded with calls from people who've visited us in the last three or four days."

Lord B-P groaned. He knew what was coming next, but let Mr. Cochran tell the story without interruption.

"They say those people claim there's an evil ghost here and you're closing Marlston because of that, not because of renovation work."

"I hope you denied it all, Cochran."

"Well, no, sir. I didn't say anything because the reporter told me they're going to run a story tomorrow based on the interviews with the people who've seen the ghost. They want you to comment on it."

"I'd better ring 'em and deny it. I'll tell 'em what I told those people who saw the blighter in his suit of armour, that it's my nephew fooling about."

Mr. Cochran, ever the quick thinker, had a more inventive idea. "But my lord, the evidence against us would seem to be too overwhelming. Why not tell the truth, with a little embellishment?"

Lord B-P could see his cosy little world disintegrating around him and was prepared to clutch at any hope which would give him a chance of emerging unscathed. "What do you have in mind?" he asked, a little uneasily.

"I thought that perhaps you could tell the newspaper that there was a ghost here who had been determined to scare everyone away, and you felt it was your duty to protect your visitors by keeping them away while you tried to get rid of it. I'm sure if you say you didn't want to see them frightened or upset by this horrific apparition and felt you had to tell a white lie about renovation work in their best interests, you'll come through as a hero.

"Just think of it, sir. You'll be the lord who got rid of an evil spirit single-handedly. The tourists'll flock here to see you."

"Yes," mused Lord B-P, rubbing his chin. "I like the sound of that. It might just work. I can tell them I've got rid of the ghost, so there's nothing more to worry about. I do believe we're going to come through this okay, Cochran. Well done. I don't know what I'd do without you."

Mr. Cochran smiled. He felt he was well worthy of the pay raise he intended to ask for when this whole dreadful business was over and life at Marlston settled down to normality once more.

Reaching out for the library telephone, he dialled the newspaper, telling them that Lord Barrington-Pottsherbert would prepare a statement for them.

Mr. Cochran wasn't the only one smiling. Albert was positively grinning from ear to ear as within the hour he heard Lord B-P tell the reporter that the ghost had been forced away from Marlston forever and that it was now safe for the public to return.

"Oh yes," Lord B-P's honeyed tones drooled into the telephone. "I was so concerned about the safety of my visitors with a ghost loose in the house that I thought it best to shut up shop until I found a way to deal with it. But now it's gone and things are back to normal, so we reopen for business as usual first thing tomorrow morning. Now, let me tell you how I got rid of it."

Albert kept clear of the other ghosts for the rest of the day. He saw them from time to time wandering aimlessly about the extensive grounds or through the seemingly endless corridors of the house, and quickly gleeked out of harm's way.

He had never been what one could call a really active person throughout his life as far as physical exertion was concerned. If he could get away with not doing as much work as he should, he would, and his Sundays were spent in a leisurely repose in front of the television. He had never been bored with doing nothing because he was always too busy enjoying not doing anything. But boredom set in now with a startling jolt. At home it had been different. He could relax or go to sleep. But here in the afterlife where sleep was a thing of the past with the spirit never tiring, he was at a total loose end. There was so much about life after death that he wanted to ask the ghosts, but felt the wiser course of action would be to stay away from them for a while longer.

How he managed to pass the time he never knew, but somehow he made it through the night to the following day.

The visitors started to trickle in again as they found the gates open and everything back to normal. Albert could hardly wait for the thousands he was sure would come after reading that Marlston was safe and ghostless once again.

Mr. Cochran could scarcely believe what he saw when he gathered up the midday newspaper from the mail box. Right the way across the tabloid front page was a headline, story, and another picture of Lord B-P standing in front of the manor.

Lord B-P smiled widely when he saw it. "The front page main story," he exclaimed radiantly. "I didn't think we'd manage that." He scanned the words quickly to make sure he had been quoted correctly and that he hadn't said anything that sounded too outrageous. But he felt that even the truth was so incredible he would not have believed it possible a week ago.

The newspaper faithfully reported the absolute nonsense he told them about how he exorcised the ghost with an ancient incantation picked up years ago in Africa.

"This is good stuff," he exuded, then turned, full of smiles, to Mr. Cochran. "D'you know, I reckon this is the best thing to happen to Marlston for years. It's given us wonderful publicity." Rereading the paragraphs quoting the angry visitors describing the ghost, then the bits about how he exorcised it single-handedly, he was happy with his deception, believing it had turned a near disaster into great success.

And Albert read it over this shoulder with equal happiness, pleased with his own little deception. He could already see how this was going to play out. If things went according to plan he need only appear at one more haunting session for his task at Marlston to be complete.

When Marlston was thronged with tourists again he would embark on another spectral episode. Having read about the all-clear, the visitors were bound to let the paper know that the ghost was still there, discrediting Lord B-P and the mansion forever.

Mr. Cochran hardly had time to settle down to his work again when the office telephone rang.

"Hello," crackled the voice at the other end. "This is Mike Phillips of Moorside Radio. I'd like to talk to Lord Barrington-Pottsherbert about getting rid of his ghost. It's quite an interesting story in the paper and I'm sure our listeners would be very keen to hear about it."

Moorside Radio was a successful commercial station with a wide transmission area. *More publicity*, thought Mr. Cochran.

"Just one moment and I'll see if His Lordship's available."

Mr. Phillips explained to Lord B-P that there wasn't time to send a reporter out to Marlston Manor for their lunchtime news programme, but he would just ask a few questions to do a holding piece and then send someone round to do a special live interview into the afternoon music and local current affairs programme.

Albert listened along with the others as the newsreader began the story at one o'clock.

"There are claims today that a local stately home has been plagued by a ghost. But its owner says he's now exorcised it. Lord Maxwell Barrington-Pottsherbert was so worried about the effects the ghost was having on visitors to his beautiful ancestral home, Marlston Manor, that he closed the mansion while he carried out a special African exorcism to get rid of it.

"The ghost has now been banished, and we'll have a live interview with Lord Barrington-Pottsherbert in our mid-afternoon programme, 'More About Moorside,' here on Moorside Radio.

"Now the dispute at Jebsons Glue Factory, and the strike continues despite the death of…"

Lord B-P snapped the radio off with a flourish. "Well, what d'you think of that?" he beamed.

Albert was keen to hear the latest about the strike at Jebsons, but didn't want to turn the radio back on, or Lord B-P would know he was still around. He had no intention of spoiling the wonderful plan lined up for the afternoon.

It was an exciting lunchtime for the B-Ps. They invited Mr. Cochran to eat with them while they practiced what they were going to say on the radio.

"This just could not be better," smiled Lord B-P. "The tourists'll flock here in their thousands after this."

But Albert had other ideas. By the time he finished his day's work he expected that no tourists would ever go to Marlston again.

The Moorside Radio interviewer arrived at about quarter to four. He was a tall, thick-set man in his mid-twenties with blond blow-dried hair curling neatly over his collar. He introduced himself as Paul Evans, and soon relented his half-hearted protest that it was too early in the day to accept Lord B-P's offer of a glass of single malt whisky.

Flopping down heavily in a library chair, he crossed his long jean-clad legs as he took a sip of the fiery amber liquid.

"Right, we'll be on the air at about ten past four. I'll want you to describe when the ghost first appeared and what it did. Then I'll move on to the effects of its visit and how you handled it all. We've got plenty of time for a change, so you can go into as much detail as you like."

They trooped outside and saw a Land Rover at the bottom of the steps, with a mast extending thirty feet from its roof. A man stood by the open tailgate, wearing a pair of headphones and talking into a microphone held in his hand.

"This is my engineer," said Mr. Evans briskly. "What's the signal like?"

"It's perfect, Paul. They're hearing me loud and clear."

A few moments later Mr. Evans handed a pair of headphones to Lord B-P and donned a set himself. He took the microphone from the engineer, who jumped into the back of the vehicle and knelt in front of a control box packed with knobs and gauges.

"Right, stand by to go live on air," said Mr. Evans, briefly clearing his throat.

The engineer turned a black knob, causing the headphones covering Lord B-P's ears to instantly spring into life, thumping the latest hit record deep into his brain. The music began to fade, then the disc jockey was talking.

"And that's gonna be a winner—already riding high at number three, it's my tip for the top. By this time next week it'll be number one; of that, my friends, I'm sure...oh yessiree, 'Mysterious Love' by that up and coming group The Campsite Dreamers is destined for greater dreams than only making it to number three. And it went out today especially for Melanie." The DJ deepened his tones to a hoarse whisper. "The message to you, Melanie, my love, comes from fiancé Bob. Hugs and kisses, says Bob, until he sees you tonight. Oh, Melanie, tonight's the night by the sound of it. Well, I'll leave you to your dreams.

"That song was all about mysterious love, and talking of things mysterious, what about the ghostly goings-on at Moorside's favourite stately home, Marlston Manor? The story goes that for the last few days visitors to the mansion have been spooked out of their minds by an evil spirit. I'll tell you who first introduced me to the spirit world: my father. He gave me a whisky when I was twelve years old. But, of course, that's not evil. Whisky's a good spirit.

"But anyway, back at the ranch—we've sent our reporter Paul Evans along to Marlston to find out just what's going on down there. Hello Paul, have you seen a ghost yet?"

"Good afternoon, Johnny. No, I haven't seen a ghost yet, for the simple reason that there isn't one. Lord Maxwell Barrington-Pottsherbert, who lives here at Marlston, used a special African exorcism to get rid of it. And Lord Barrington-Pottsherbert is with me now. If I could ask you, my lord, to tell me when you were first aware of the presence of the ghost?"

"Well, it was last week…," he began.

Lord B-P embellished the tale a little until he got near to the end when it bore no resemblance to the truth whatsoever.

"Having had experiences of black magic and spooks in Africa, I drew on an old spell I picked up one night. Many years ago on a safari through that darkest of continents one of our guides fell ill. Or so we thought. Suddenly he dropped to the ground and began thrashing about with his arms and legs like a man possessed—which, of course, he was, but we didn't know it at the time.

"So you can imagine my surprise when he began talking in a voice so unlike his own that it was difficult to believe it came from his very own lips. It took five of us to hold him down while our interpreter prepared himself for the ceremony. The exorcism began with the interpreter starting to speak in a slow, crystal clear voice, but the words were in a language none of us had ever heard, and appeared to be meaningless. Gradually the pace of the incantation picked up until it became a garbled jumble. Then, instantly, seemingly in mid-sentence, he stopped, just as if someone somewhere had pulled the plug from his power supply.

"For a second a deathly hush fell upon that jungle clearing. But it was just for a second, no more, before a wind whipped up, lashing the trees into a violent frenzy. A crash of thunder rolled through the heavens as we stood there, petrified, unable to move. The man on the ground moaned uncontrollably, then a thin wispy haze began to force its way out of his mouth. We looked on with horror as it turned to a foul smelling black gunge in the air, taking on a vaguely human shape. There was no face as such, just a dreadful black mass. But near the top were two pinpricks of light which became piercing, blazing eyes.

"A fork of lightning divided the skies, striking deep into the heart of the shimmering black shape, which disappeared in a blinding flash of light and an ear-splitting scream. Whatever that dreadful thing was that came from within our poor unfortunate guide, it had gone forever.

"Well, I was so intrigued by it all that I learned a lot more about spirit exorcism on that trip. So when Marlston became infested by a spirit from beyond the mortal veil, I called upon those powers I'd learned and banished it from this kingdom, back to its own dark abode.

"And really, that's all there is to it."

Albert had been interviewed on Moorside Radio many times as Jebsons' shop steward, but never by Paul Evans, for which he was now eternally grateful. It meant he could carry out his plan without being recognised. But he decided to let Lord B-P milk the cow dry before pulling the hangman's lever on the trapdoor beneath him, which would surely result in the irascible lord being hoist with the length of rope he'd unravelled.

The rope might be unravelled, thought Albert gleefully, *but the plot was so interwoven there would be no chance of His Lordship slipping the knot and escaping.* The battle of Marlston was almost won.

Albert's smile broadened as he heard Paul Evans's next question. "So what did you actually see when you'd completed the exorcism?"

Lord B-P had it all worked out. His lunchtime discussion had not been wasted.

"I'd gone outside the house to perform the ceremony, and saw the spirit suddenly surge through a window, looking as if it were bleeding heavily. Red rivers flowed down its form, dripping into nothing underneath it; the blood, or whatever it was, just disappeared as it fell from the shape.

"And the look of pain and horror on its face—well, that sight will stay with me for as long as I live. Whatever effect my exorcism had on it, was certainly painful for it. The being hovered over the house for a few seconds, though at the time it felt like an age. Its eyes held mine in a wild clinch before it seemed to explode into a thousand wisps of smoke, with a shattering scream. The smoke swirled before me, then merged into a thick black pole which shot upwards and vanished in the clouds.

"At that second a powerful wave of relief broke over me, as I knew I'd rid my home of the evil presence that had haunted it for several days."

Albert had heard enough, and decided it was time to act before the fright of ghosts turned up to ruin his plans. He materialised into a transparent figure alongside His Lordship.

"Now, that's not strictly true," he said into the microphone.

No-one realised it at the time, but at that precise moment history was being made. Although the record books failed to show it, it was the first time a ghost had broadcast directly on the radio. The expression of incredulity on Paul Evans's face was matched only by that of utter defeat and sickness on Lord B-P's. Neither of them appreciated that finer point of history, or that they might be remembered as having their interview interrupted from beyond the grave—they were far too astonished at the sudden sight and sound of what could only be a ghost.

Usually a professional broadcaster like Paul Evans would have been worried by the silence, but at that particular moment he could do nothing other than stare with eyes and mouth agog.

"The spirit haunting Marlston Manor hasn't gone at all. As you can see, I'm still here," said the ghost.

Mr. Evans desperately tried to recover his composure. "I…I'm not sure what's just happened," he finally managed to coax from his throat into the microphone. Frantically his mind scrambled to articulate what he was seeing and hearing. When the words eventually came they were a little haphazard and shaky, but they were certainly among the most stunning and devastating ever broadcast on Moorside Radio.

"I think I'm looking at a ghost, a spirit. And the last few words you heard were spoken by that spirit. Standing not two yards from me is the figure of a man, and yet I can see straight through it, as if it were made of some finely spun lace." Mr. Evans was swiftly taking command of the situation when something suddenly snapped within his aristocratic interviewee.

Lord B-P's chin was quivering and a nervous twitch tugged remorselessly at his left eyelid. "You evil bastard," he cried at Albert, the veneer of His stately Lordshipness now stripped completely away, and totally oblivious to the fact that his words were being carried on high to the eager ears of thousands.

"Why don't you leave me alone? You've done enough damage." Tears of rage and frustration streamed down his straining face as Lady B-P and Mr. Cochran rushed forward to grab him.

Mr. Evans pressed on valiantly: "Lord Barrington-Pottsherbert, is this the ghost you thought you'd exorcised?"

"Yes" came the strangled answer. "The bastard's come back. I'm ruined."

"This really is the most amazing development." Mr. Evans began to realise he may have stumbled on the scoop of the century. "I can hardly believe it, but there really is no doubt that it's true. I'm witnessing it with my very own eyes and ears. There is a ghost here.

"If I can turn to the ghost—what are you doing here, sir?"

Before Albert could answer, Lord B-P was led away into the house by Her Ladyship and Mr. Cochran, quietly sobbing. "It's all over," he sniffed. "Marlston's finished." The rest of his words were carried to the trees by the wind, but no-one cared any more. The radio listeners had heard Paul Evans ask a ghost a question, and they listened intently for the answer.

Throughout the district it seemed that wherever a radio was tuned into Moorside, life had stopped. The factory girls listening to it being piped overhead stopped their machines. Car drivers quickly pulled over and turned up the volume. Housewives laid down their irons and bricklayers laid down their mugs of tea. Thousands upon thousands of people waited breathlessly as the silence spread like a shock wave after someone carelessly tossed a pebble into the mirror-surfaced face of a pond. Then they finally heard the ghost speak.

"Yes, I'm the ghost of Marlston Manor, and it's my job to haunt this place of evil forever, to try to protect it in the face of dreadful adversity. Wicked things have happened here across the years and many more wicked things are yet to happen. It's as well for the public to stay away. It's hardly…" Albert broke off, suddenly finding himself surrounded by a full complement of the fright of ghosts.

"What are you doing?" cried the head, held firmly under his body's right arm.

Paul Evans did not bat an eyelid. It was clear he could neither see nor hear the spectral gathering.

Albert turned again to the microphone. He knew it was no use trying to tell his unseen audience that another dozen or so ghosts had suddenly arrived. And, after all, he had set out to do a job, and felt he must have succeeded. Never again would a tourist come near Marlston Manor, of that he was sure. So he could see little point in staying to hear what the ghosts had to say to him or find out what they intended to do to him. The world now knew Marlston was haunted, so Albert could fade, quite literally, into the background once more.

But just before gleeking into a treetop on the other side of the house where he hoped the fright would never find him, he could not resist a final shot.

"I can't stop at the moment. Even as I speak I feel a new wave of evil surging around Marlston. I have to go back inside and help fight it off. Marlston will soon become a battleground for evil forces. For God's sake, keep away from here."

And then, for all intents and purposes, Paul Evans was alone.

CHAPTER 9

In which we find the ghosts getting militant

ALTHOUGH A FULL two minutes had gone by since the waters clouded over again in the pool, Wallace still stared into the limpid liquid, as if trying to count the elusive ripples which gently rocked their way to the edge.

Mozelbeek drained a goblet of chilled nectar before clanging it down on the table with a flourish. Rather mischievously he had offered a goblet to Wallace, proposing a toast to Albert's glorious success. Wallace's goblet remained untouched where Mozelbeek left it.

"Come on, Wallace, don't be a sore loser. You've got to admit that Albert won by his own initiative. Oh, how refreshing to see someone use initiative nowadays. There's far too much stodgy tradition followed in the world for my liking. I'm proud to say I am Albert Carter's guardian angel."

But Wallace wasn't to be drawn yet. He listened in moody silence as Mozelbeek enthused further.

"You know, I was beginning to have my doubts about whether he'd succeed. It was never in any doubt that he'd win the small skirmish, but I don't know how far ahead he looked. He may well have scared visitors off for a while, but things could have possibly started slotting back into place after Albert has to leave Marlston at the end of the ministry strike. Mankind has such a short memory to go with what little insight he possesses. It wouldn't have taken long to forget the ghost of Marlston Manor, just as both Albert—in his earthly life—and

Nethanial Jebson, kept winning various skirmishes against each other, forgetting the lessons they should have learned. So each skirmish came round again, such as the annual fight over pay where Albert started with an unacceptably high demand, while the company's offer was far too derisory.

"After the usual non-cooperation and strike they met in the middle. Then the ritual was reenacted again the following year. They never learned.

"Well, I was afraid something like that was going to happen here. I thought Albert might only win a short-term victory, but now, thanks to his master stroke of broadcasting, the world thinks there's evil at Marlston.

"I'm convinced now, though, that he's achieved what he set out to do, and demolished the opposition entirely."

Had Lord B-P heard the last part of that one-sided conversation he would have agreed wholeheartedly with Mozelbeek. He considered he had taken some knocks in life, but this was without doubt the most serious. Almost in one fell swoop his livelihood had been snatched from him as efficiently as an owl dives for a mouse.

He spent the next two days in a waking nightmare. It seemed every time he turned on the radio or television the newscaster was talking about the ghost of Marlston Manor, and every time he opened a newspaper he saw a story about his unsuccessful exorcism. For two full days the gates were locked and the telephone handset lay on the table alongside its cradle. Lord B-P became a virtual recluse, only opening his door at six-hour intervals to take in a fresh bottle of single malt he insisted be left there on the maid's tray.

Albert, on the other hand, found enforced idleness did not suit him, and that worried him a little. At work he had always been looking for excuses to slow down his pace, or even to stop altogether if he could. He had not realised it at the time, of course, but the reason he always felt happy taking two hours to do a one-hour job was because he was beating the system.

But now he had nothing to do all day he was getting desperately bored. There was no-one to cheat. Yet still he felt something was not quite right—here he was worrying because he had no work to do. *And that's not like me,* he thought.

His hours were spent wandering the house, moping about on the hills outside or sitting brooding in the summer house. From time to time he would drop in on Lord B-P drowning his sorrows (and almost his sanity) with a tumbler of single malt in his bedroom.

Something began to poke and prod at Albert's conscience as he saw His Lordship's trembling hand link his ashen face to the whisky glass like a mechanical conveyor belt every few seconds.

He hadn't thought a man of such aristocratic steel could have been reduced to a wreck in so short a space of time. Swiftly he gleeked away—he didn't mind where, as long as he was out of the gloom penetrating his soul when he was in Lord B-P's presence. He tried to put the pathetic sight to the back of his mind, but with nothing else to occupy his thoughts it remained as firm as if it were glued to the scenery in front of his eyes.

While the sight remained, the pity didn't. It went as soon as he began to think about the thousands of people Lord B-P had exploited during his reign at Marlston Manor. *Ah, yes,* he thought. That definitely tipped the balance back. Hardness steeped into his eyes and he smiled once more, until he chose to call again into the bedroom a couple of hours later.

Lord B-P was slumped drunkenly across his bed, an empty bottle on its side on the floor. The feelings of doubt crept back. Had he done the right thing in his campaign of terror at the stately home?

Then he remembered all the things his soul had told him about a singleness of purpose, and he instantly dismissed those nagging fears as his confidence returned.

The last few hours had seemed like a pair of scales that could be tipped by the drop of a crumb into either cup. A crumb of doubt, a crumb of confidence; either sent the sands scurrying to a downward drop. Albert felt the confusion and indecision was there because of the dire lack of competition in his mind. There was nothing else jostling for place; everything preying on its emptiness, magnified to many times its real importance. His thoughts wandered to the fright of ghosts. However did they manage to survive the interminably long years of their hauntings, he wondered.

Now he had finished his haunting he had nothing to fear, and decided to find them to try and talk to them. Perhaps they could tell him some of the mysteries of the afterlife which were still cloaked in darkness to him. He found them sitting round a table in one of the public rooms of the West Wing.

"Hi there," he called nonchalantly. "Mind if I join you?"

The head was lying on his right ear on a cushion placed just within reach of his body. He glared up at the newcomer, then snapped, "Don't you think you've done enough damage? I've just come from Lord B-P's bedroom."

Albert's retaliation was swift. "I told you I had a purpose…a mission…here. My actions have been to repay the thousands of people he has walked over, and to safeguard the future for many thousands of others. But I don't have to justify my reasons to you, you who have come from hauntings throughout the country. How many innocent people have you frightened in your time?"

His barbed arrow struck home but did little damage to the head, whose response was swift and straight to the point: "We have official sanction for our hauntings, but you are carrying on illegally."

"A ghost is a ghost, surely," protested Albert. "Why do we have to go through all this and be burdened with officialdom and bureaucracy wherever we go?"

"There are far greater powers at work here than you know of, Albert Carter, and any interference or meddling of any kind can unleash havoc as a backlash. Take the case of our old sea-salt here." The head indicated a figure sitting at the opposite end of the table. A figure Albert hadn't noticed before. Though why he failed to spot him, he couldn't begin to know, because he seemed distinctive enough in his faded sailor's uniform.

"Old Walter, here, was killed in an accident on board his ship, and buried at sea." The sailor nodded mournfully as the head began his tale: "He always had the wanderlust, even in death. He was intrigued by the state in which he found himself and wanted to find out more about the Condition Of Transit. But he quickly reached the head of the queue, coming face to face with Saint Christopher, who told him a place was allocated for him in hell.

"Old Walter was having none of that, and he fled back to Earth. A search party was dispatched, but they couldn't find him. He would haunt ships, houses, castles—anything and anywhere he turned up. His travels took him far and wide, and no sooner had the balance tipped one way than old Walter was off somewhere else. By the time he'd finished, the very essence of life had twisted in on itself by trying to keep things on an even keel. The entire equilibrium became unstable, causing an horrendous crack in the earth's crust. You know the rest, it's history. The island of Krakatoa was blown off the face of the earth. Old Walter and his innocent hauntings were responsible for that."

Albert reeled in the face of what he heard. "But you can't mean that my actions here could have a similar effect?" he stammered.

"But of course. Who knows what might happen? There's a force of life even greater than those we know of. We don't understand why these things happen. The physics behind their cause is far too complicated, but we do know that if anyone messes with those forces an entire area can become terribly unstable with dreadful consequences."

It was all too much for Albert, who began to wonder if they were trying to blind him with science. But before he could raise any questions, the head carried on: "In the afterlife the Ministry of Hauntings sorts out which ghosts can go where. If a spirit has a natural affinity for a place it is undoubtedly sent back there if it wishes to go. For instance, a murder victim might want to go back and haunt the scene of the diabolical crime. Ministry staff will check that the forces of nature can be balanced somewhere else, and then give the go-ahead for the haunting to start.

"Spirits are sometimes banished to Earth for a specific period of time as a punishment, like Marlston's official ghosts, Bobby and Daphne. But they can't just be sent back without the balance being rectified somewhere else. In their case things were easier because they had no desire to show themselves to the living. That's one of the biggest problems, the link between a visible spirit and the mortal world. Every time a ghost is seen by a human eye it takes up a tremendous amount of energy from its surroundings to break the barrier. It might seem easy to the ghost, to appear on the whim of a thought, but it dents the fabric of the airspace it pushes out to become visible. That dent has to be balanced somewhere.

"Are you beginning to see the problems you're causing?"

Throughout his earthly life Albert had caused many problems for many people, sometimes without even knowing it. And that's how it was now in his ghostly life.

"To hell with the consequences," he cried. "How many more times do I have to spell it out? I'm doing this for the benefit of those who can't fight for themselves; for those who've been exploited to keep families like the Barrington-Pottsherberts in luxury. Well, their reign is over. They won't be taking money from the pockets of my people again.

"I've finished my job here, now, so as soon as the dispute at the ministry's over I'll leave here forever and take up my rightful place in the afterlife. And in the meantime I've no need to show myself to the living again. So your worries are over."

"You told us that before…," began one of the other ghosts.

"That was to get you off my back until I'd finished my work. Now everything's completed I don't need to appear again. I'll stay in the background now, I promise you."

A deep silence descended over the meeting. Never before had such a diverse group of spirits sat around a table. Some came from way back in the mists of time while some came from not so long ago. But each was linked to the other by an invisible chain stretching across the ages to draw them together. And that bond between them was that they were all destined to spend eternity haunting the earth.

Some had originally, and rather unwisely, chosen to return to Earth; some sentenced to it for dark and dire crimes during their mortal existence. But a unanimous thought now surged from one to the other: how they all secretly envied Albert. Between them they had notched up thousands of years of hauntings and were as bored by it as Albert had been after just a few short days. For them, though, there was to be no rest in heaven or damnation in hell. They were trapped in a vortex midway between the two, and they hated it. They wouldn't have minded one way or the other, heaven or hell, just so long as they could have had a spiritual home instead of being permanent lodgers on Earth. And here was a spirit soon to take up his home, yet he was able to spurn the rules and get away with it.

No-one wanted to be the first to voice the view that they were fed up with the mind-numbing routine which filled the days of all ghosts, and that they all felt they had been dealt a poor hand. One by one they unfolded their stories to Albert and he noticed that each story held the common theme of dissatisfaction. It was the first time the ghosts had been brought together and as they listened to the private sorrows of their neighbour one thing remained etched clearly in their minds: the underlying theme was the same.

For the first time in as long as any of them could remember they began to realise what a widely spread place the world was, and how each problem could be broken down to the common denominator. The tales of battles over politics, money, and love that flowed from the group all bore that same mark of conflict, many with the individual losing out to the massed ranks.

As their stories unfolded one by one they each discovered they weren't the only one whose brave face hid a grieving heart.

Albert saw the opportunity appear before his eyes, and grabbed it quickly with both hands.

"And you've put up with that for all these hundreds of years," he spat contemptuously. "What are you, ghosts of men, or ghosts of mice?"

Their voices blended into one as they did the unforgivable, answering one question with another. "But what can we do about it?"

The words flowed freely from Albert's lips now. It was the

same formula he used on Earth, just adapted a little to take account of the spiritual position he now found himself in.

"Your combined force will be far greater than any pressure you could bring to bear in smaller groups or as individuals," he recited. "Just remember that, and you're on your way."

Thus began the first lesson in trades unionism the fright had ever had. As Albert unveiled the possibilities they began to acknowledge what they may be able to achieve.

"You say the powers of nature are made unstable if spirits act out of character," said Albert. "But what would happen if you could gather as many of your fellow ghosts together as possible and you all appeared at once in a crowded place, say the House of Commons or a football field in the middle of a match?"

The head took just a few seconds to weigh up the possibilities. "The amount of energy required would be incredible," he mused. "It would probably rip a hole in the fabric of space. At the very least it's likely to cause chaotic storms across the world for about twelve hours."

"There you go, then." A hint of triumph crept into Albert's voice. "Go to Saint Christopher and threaten to do exactly that if your cases aren't reviewed. Tell him you feel you've been punished enough by your banishment to Earth down the centuries and you're ready to take up a place in the afterlife. If the consequences of a mass haunting are as dire as you say, he daren't risk you carrying it out."

"You know, you could be right," said the head, smiling up at Albert. "All these years we've meekly stayed on Earth, putting in a ghostly appearance every now and then, and hating every minute of it, when all along we could have got together and forced changes in our favour."

The headless body leaped up, crashing a fist heavily into the other palm. "Come on," cried his head. "Let's go and find recruits. Albert, we'll see you back here when we've tracked down enough spirits to cause havoc if our demands aren't met. We'll get our rightful places in heaven or hell yet, and it's all down to you. See you soon."

The body snatched up his head and the fright of ghosts melted away before Albert's eyes.

***

"The bloody sheep," wailed Wallace. "Whatever do they think they're doing? They're just following on mindlessly. They can't possibly be irresponsible enough to let the forces loose on the world that a mass haunting would produce. The polar ice caps would start melting, there'd be floods in places, droughts in others, English summers would hardly see the sun—where would it all end?"

"I'm sure it won't come to that," said Mozelbeek. "Whether it's a real threat or a bluff, Saint Christopher will have to give in. He daren't risk anything else. This is a great day for earthbound spirits. The official ministerial domination of them will soon be over.

"I've always thought it unfair that they've never had any collective weight behind them. They've always been the forgotten minority. Everyone else has a strong union body to fall back on, but the earthly spirits have never really had the chance to see that they could have the same. The very nature of their existence—the fact that they're often isolated in groups of only two or three, or just as individuals—has never really let them get together to see how they all felt about the conditions forced on them. This gathering, and the meeting with Albert, has done wonders for them."

But Wallace was thinking of the consequences facing others. He regarded earthly ghosts as being at the bottom of the ladder, both for intelligence and status, and he had grave fears about how they would handle their newfound powers.

"The reason no-one's told them they could become powerful by joining together is because everyone's afraid of what would happen. Ghosts aren't responsible enough to be given that sort of power."

"But you see what that attitude's led to. They're not waiting to be given it, they're taking it for themselves," said Mozelbeek. "And if someone snatches power they're more likely to use it to its full potential than if someone gave it to them. If you try to deny someone their rights they'll seek vengeance when they take those rights. And they have as much right as everyone else to form a united body to further their interests."

"Rights!" sneered Wallace. "There's enough claptrap and hot air spouted on Earth about rights without it filtering through to everyone here as well. If people got on with what they were supposed to do instead of making sure they took advantage of every so-called right they thought they were entitled to, everything would be so much better."

"You've got to agree that the haunting system is a little archaic, though. There's been no change in the law governing it for many hundreds of years. Surely if a ghost spent his time doing what he was sent back to Earth to do, he should be entitled to have his case reviewed to see if he's become a fit and proper soul to take a place in heaven or hell. He shouldn't be expected to spend eternity roaming aimlessly among mortals.

"It doesn't take infinity to be punished for a crime. Take two souls like Bobby and Daphne, for instance, sentenced to a hundred years on Earth. They quickly realised the foolishness of their youth and are fully repentant already. Is it right, now they've paid for their crime, that they're still being punished for it? All these spirits are asking is that they have a second chance; an opportunity to correct the faults of their mortal existence when they get to the afterlife and then move on to a permanent home. What's so terrible about that? Why should they not press for that basic right, the right to prove they've achieved something and haven't wasted their time on Earth, but have actually learned something about life?

"Let the fruits of those enforced labours be harvested and let them taste sweet. They haven't even got that as a right, so let them join forces to seek it."

Wallace remained silent. Civilisations had risen and fallen through similar ideals. Eventually he put his thoughts into words: "But will it end there? Once they see their demands are met, what's to stop them carrying on and asking for more? Collectively they can build tremendous power. They could hold the entire world to ransom with their threats of mass hauntings."

He could have continued, but Mozelbeek motioned for quiet. The waters of life were stirring again in the limpid pool. Something was happening at Marlston.

***

Moments earlier Mr. Cochran had ushered Lord and Lady B-P out into the grounds for a breath of fresh air and he felt it high time the phone went back on the hook. He agreed with his lord and master that Marlston Manor was finished as a tourist attraction, but life had to go on. The mansion was still their home while they were deciding what to do, and a home needed fuelling and its larder restocking.

So while Lord B-P was still in a drunken stupor Mr. Cochran had persuaded Her Ladyship to take him for a walk while he made a few hurried calls to their regular suppliers.

Now, replacing the telephone receiver with a sigh, his thoughts turned back to the ghost. It was the first time anyone had had a chance to actually think about the haunting. As his mind retraced the events of the last few days he realised what a whirlwind trip the ghost had made. It had blown onto the scene, creating almost instant havoc. But what had happened to it now?

He began to think it odd that no-one had heard a whisper or caught a fleeting glimpse of it since it pulled off its coup de grâce with the radio broadcast. *Wasn't a haunting supposed to go on and on, with the ghost only showing itself every now and then?* he thought. A ghost was a slow, sedate character, very mysterious and often sad and pathetic. Certainly not a boisterous, flamboyant spectre that the spirit of Marlston had been.

It was as if Mr. Cochran chose those thoughts extremely carefully, with the phrase "had been" turning itself around and around on the pivot of his brain. He had no idea where the deep feeling could have come from that the ghost really had gone this time. Even if it had crossed his mind that his employer's guardian angel might be up to his old tricks again by firing a thought like a thunderbolt across the skies, he would have dismissed it as being entirely preposterous.

All he knew was that he clearly discerned a voice within him urging that the ghost had gone for good and now was the time to reopen Marlston and try to forget the horrors of recent days.

Then Mr. Cochran spoke aloud. Perhaps he knew the same little green man who had never sat on Albert's shoulder. "Maybe the ghost was telling the truth when he said he was just passing through Marlston. It does seem strange that he hasn't shown himself for a while."

Despite the encouragement of the silent voice inside him, Mr. Cochran slipped into a melancholic slump over the table. Even if the ghost had copied the moving finger and moved on after writing, its words remained behind, and the damage was done. Thousands of people had heard the ghost say on the radio he was haunting Marlston forever, and there was growing evil in the house.

The telephone bell was a welcome interruption to Mr. Cochran's gloomy thoughts.

"Marlston Manor," he said into the instrument, his crisp tones belying his sluggish feelings.

"Well, at last," cried a man at the other end of the line. "Hello, Your Lordship. My name's Maurice H. Liddy. The *H* stands for Henry, but I don't do much talking about that. Your Lordship, I'm telephoning you from that quaint little ol' village of Stratford upon the river Avon—"

"Hey, now wait a minute," Mr. Cochran cut in over the strong American drawl. "I'm not Lord Barrington-Pottsherbert. He's out at the moment. Can I take a message?"

"Well now, you must be His Lordship's butler, then; else why'd you be answering his telephone? Now, Mr. Butler, you listen carefully to what Maurice H. Liddy's got to say to you."

Mr. Cochran shrugged to himself, thinking about interrupting again, but decided just to let Maurice H. Liddy wade ahead.

"Just wait till I tell the folks back home in West Virginia that I've been talking to a real-live lord's butler on the telephone. Why, they'll just turn all green with envy, that they will.

"Now you listen to me good, Mr. Butler, and be sure to tell Lord Barrington-Pottsherbert what I'm saying the second he comes in, right?"

Maurice H Liddy didn't give Mr. Cochran the chance to say whether it was alright or not; he covered the mouthpiece and called to his wife in the bathroom of their hotel in Stratford: "Hey, Barbi-Lou, I'm talking to a real English butler. Make sure you put it down in the diary for the folks back home.

"Well, now then, Mr. Butler, I want to make an appointment

to see Lord Barrington-Pottsherbert as soon as he's free. Me and my wife Barbi-Lou's touring this little island of yours and I've seen on the television as how there's a real live ghost at Marlston Manor.

"Well, siree, my friends'd never forgive me if I went home to West Virginia without popping over to say hi to this ghost of yours. Can you just picture it; me and my wife Barbi-Lou'd be proper celebrities back home if we met your ghost. A real British ghost, wowee—you've got to let us come over. We'd pay His Lordship a handsome fee to see it, you know."

It felt to Mr. Cochran as if centuries passed. It was, in fact, quite a long time. Almost ten seconds. The pause was just long enough for Maurice H. Liddy to think he'd been cut off or that Mr. Cochran had gone away.

"Hello Mr. Butler, are you still there?"

Mr. Cochran swallowed hard, realisation mingling with wonder and excitement, like a spoonful of sugar melting into a cup of scalding tea. Perhaps Marlston was not yet dead as a tourist attraction, after all. Somehow it had escaped everyone's attention that although the visitors had been frightened of the ghost, there must be a vast number of people who would travel a long way to see one. Maurice H. Liddy had just shown that.

"Let me take your number and I'll get His Lordship to ring you back," bleated Mr. Cochran excitedly. Suddenly he saw a brave and bright new future for Marlston, and hoped against hope that Lord B-P would view it in the same light.

He danced around like the proverbial dog with two tails, hardly able to contain himself until Lord and Lady B-P returned from their stroll.

It seemed to the aristocratic pair that their estate manager had turned into a foaming sea as he washed over them the second they walked through the door.

Lady B-P reeled at the verbal onslaught. "Just a moment, Cochran; calm down and start again, a little slower and a little less excitedly this time, if you please."

Mr. Cochran gathered his wits and thoughts, not letting his brain race ahead of his words as it had done before, jumbling everything he wanted to say.

Lord B-P's eyes, dimmed by the single malt, were once more shot with a dash of sparkle as he listened to Mr. Cochran explain Maurice H. Liddy's request. His mind, also still firmly in the grip of the contents of more than a few bottles of that excellent beverage, strived to make practical sense of the idea swelling within his breast. Some might say his breast was a strange place for an idea to swell, but his brain was in no fit state to handle it—a point Lady B-P quickly grasped, almost as swiftly as she grasped her husband's arm to check his violent sway and arrest in mid-flight his crashing date with the floor.

But whether the thought nestled in breast or brain, Lord B-P began to realise that, like the phoenix, Marlston Manor could rise from ashes to glory.

Albert could not understand the feverish activity that suddenly seemed to engulf Marlston Manor. Lord B-P's drunkenness vanished as if it had been put there by a hypnotist who then told him to wake up and remember nothing about it when he snapped his fingers. *Snap!* And Lord B-P was back to normal. Servants ran backwards and forwards, cleaning things, changing the furniture and generally acting like new brooms sweeping everything dazzlingly clean. Albert wandered into the drawing room as His Lordship was ending a telephone conversation with Maurice H. Liddy.

"Yes, Mr. Liddy, I look forward to seeing you at half past ten tomorrow morning. That's just in time for coffee, by the way. I know how much you Americans love your coffee. I do hope the ghost will be around for you to see him."

"So do I," said Maurice H. Liddy. "I don't want me and my wife Barbi-Lou to have a wasted journey."

Albert had spent so much of his time at Marlston making people watch and listen in horror. Now it was his turn to be on the receiving end. Was this man coming to Marlston just to see him?

But the horror soon disappeared. *So that's his little game, is it?* he thought. *He's after promoting me as Marlston's latest tourist attraction, is he? Well, we'll see about that.*

Albert had told the fright of ghosts he had finished his work at Marlston and wouldn't appear to the living again. He smiled. *I can hardly break my word, now can I? The ghost of Marlston Manor has gone for good.*

Lord B-P was certainly a transformed man. There was a new spring in his step, a gleam in his eye, a curl in what little hair he had left, and no glass of single malt in his hand. He was back in command.

"Right, we're reopening straight away," he snapped. "Cochran, change the boards at the entrance hall; we're putting up our prices. From now on we'll charge four pounds for admission. That's still a modest sum for a genuine haunted house.

"While you're doing that, I'll draft out an advert for the paper, and I might even buy a minute's airtime on Moorside Radio. This'll do wonders for us—the money'll soon be rolling in. What blind beetles we were, not to see the potential of this ghost from the outset. Instead of trying to hide it, denying its existence, we should have been promoting it. People will flock from all over the world to see a genuine ghost."

He slapped his forehead. "All that worrying over the last few days for nothing. Oh, if only that ghost knew what he'd done for us. He'll double our income overnight."

Lord B-P had never been one to put all his eggs in one basket, let alone count their offspring before they cracked the shells, but this time he felt there was nothing in his way. The ghost had declared its own existence to the world, and the world had never been anything if not sceptical and cynical. So a deluge of people could be expected at Marlston to see for themselves before they believed.

***

There was a nagging feeling at the back of Mozelbeek's not insubstantial mind that one man's poison might well be the main meat dish for another man. Such was the complexity and diversity of the human brain that what one man worshipped, another feared. For every mortal who had run in terror from the ghost of Marlston Manor, there were ten more who would welcome the chance of meeting it.

But the laws governing the absurd and chance being what they were, there was no way that anyone who had seen the ghost so far had welcomed the opportunity, while many a frustrated ghost hunter would have given both their spirit and soul to witness such a phenomenon.

Wallace had the same feeling, but to him it represented pending victory. The swings and roundabouts had had their ups and downs and turns aplenty, and while the losers had lost, the victors had also won.

It was the obvious which was so often overlooked and forgotten, for the simple reason that it was so simple.

Mankind's cynicism made it impossible to accept at first glance that the obvious answer was the one being sought. Mankind always felt that his own humble brain should not arrive at the correct solution without dismissing a host of possibilities first.

Mozelbeek's feeling indicated another fact of life, which was that no-one could be sure of anything. That's the only thing that anyone could really be sure about. Not so long ago he would have said that Albert had won his fight, but now it looked as if the tables had turned and Albert's own petard was poised ready to hoist him neatly aloft.

***

Albert spent the rest of the day in the grip of almost uncontrollable frustration. There was nothing he could do to prevent the staff getting Marlston Manor ready for its hordes of people, all anxious to spend money to catch a glimpse of its ghost. The only thing keeping him from flipping his lid altogether was the thought that they would all have a wasted journey, because the ghost of Marlston had taken his last bow.

CHAPTER 10

In which we meet the Scribes and Overlords, on an even higher plane

ALBERT EVENTUALLY CAME to accept that his plan had gone a mite haywire. *Okay*, he thought, *so while some people will come for a time just to try to see the ghost, word'll soon get around that they never do see anything. Marlston Manor and Lord Barrington-Pottsherbert will be exposed as phonies. It'll all be seen as a gigantic publicity stunt and they'll lose credibility.*

The dawn's arrival saw Lord B-P up and about, rushing back and forth checking that everything was okay. As he came to the bottom of the stairs he patted the suit of armour, listening intently to its hollow ring.

"Don't let me down, old boy. Make sure the ghost's around when those Americans get here."

Being born sans silver spoon in mouth Mr. Cochran always regarded himself as being a little more on the practical side than Lord B-P, so it came as no surprise to him that it should be he who quickly realised the consequences of the ghost not showing up. He felt it would be no use trying to explain to His Lordship. When such bees were buzzing remorselessly within His Lordship's bonnet, neither gentle persuasion nor brute force could press home an argument. It was Lord B-P's way, or it was the highway.

So Mr. Cochran decided to take matters into his own hands once more. As the Americans were coming to see a ghost, he would make absolutely sure that, one way or another, a ghost they would see. It meant that he, too, was up at dawn, hard at work in his office.

In another part of the house Lord B-P happily munched his way through an early breakfast. He was on top of the world; not only was it dawning a new day, it was also dawning, for Marlston at any rate, a new age—a new era.

At 10:15 a.m. he looked in the mirror, straightened his tie and smoothed down his hair. In a few short moments Marlston Manor's new career as a genuine haunted house would be launched, with the arrival of Maurice H. Liddy. Lord B-P wondered if a bottle of champagne would be appropriate. He could picture himself standing outside, smashing the bottle against the west wing wall, declaring: "I name this haunted house Marlston Manor. Good luck to her and all who haunt in her."

He waited proudly by the front door as Maurice H. Liddy's huge black Cadillac swept up the drive; the American's battleship-grey jacket and bow tie shouting at the flowered shirt and red-green-and-yellow striped trousers to turn down their volume. But even the outrageously loud clothes paled into nothing more than a faint whisper compared to the hale and hearty booming welcome which growled its way from the bran-induced flatulence of the stomach they worked so hard to cover.

For a man of such wide girth Maurice H. Liddy lifted himself from the body-hugging cling of the contoured car seats with amazing alacrity and lumbered forward like a drunken grizzly bear.

Lord B-P viewed the outstretched sweating palm with more than a little distaste, but felt obliged to take it. Bracing himself, he repressed an agonised yell as his fingers were apparently grasped by a bone-crushing boa constrictor.

"Why, hi-yar, Your Lordship. I'm Maurice H. Liddy, and this li'l ol' lady's my good wife, Barbi-Lou."

Albert looked on from across the table as Lord B-P chatted about the ghost over coffee. He felt happier now, reflecting on changing fortunes. His short-lived career as the ghost of Marlston Manor had been satisfactory, and his equally sudden disappearance would have the same effect. His initial ambitions at Marlston were fulfilled, meaning he could turn his attentions now towards getting a better deal for ghosts.

Although Maurice H. Liddy was enjoying his coffee and Lord B-P's enthusiastic chatter about the wonders of Marlston Manor and its resident ghost, he was anxious to see it for himself.

"You must understand," said Lord B-P, "that I can't just take you to a certain room and summon the ghost at my will. He appears when and where he wants to."

Albert smiled. "And he's not going to appear at all," he said to himself. A sudden movement behind him caught his ear and he spun round to see Bobby and Daphne standing by the window, framed in the streaming sunlight.

"Oh, hi," he called. Catching their angry and disappointed looks he tried a different gambit. "It's okay. I've stopped my haunting, just as you asked."

"Don't you think it's too late for that?" fired Bobby across the broadside. "The damage has been done now. It'd be better to continue your haunting. Lord Barrington-Pottsherbert might recover a little from the damage you've already caused."

He and Daphne had been talking about it and arrived at the same conclusion as Albert. It was now the other side of the coin, and unless Albert continued to appear as a ghost, nothing could save Marlston's reputation.

"I couldn't do that," said Albert innocently. "I've given my word to stop. And after all, you told me to stop; the sunlight told me to stop; those other ghosts told me to stop." He grinned mischievously. "You surely can't want me to carry on?"

"Why must you be so awkward?" cried Daphne. "You know what we mean. Your little plan of scaring people away from here has gone wrong. You've actually succeeded in turning Marlston into an international tourist attraction—just the opposite of what you wanted to do." She pulled herself up to her full height. "Why can't you admit defeat gracefully? Throw in the towel and be the ghost the tourists want to see."

Albert felt the time was right to hear the swish of a curtain falling on his charade. "My plan's not gone wrong at all," he gloated. "The tactics of war are to build up your opponent's confidence until they overreach themselves. That's what's happened here. I declared my existence to the world and now the world is anxious to see me. When they never hear from me again they'll believe the whole thing was a hoax—a huge publicity stunt—and the Barrington-Pottsherberts will be totally discredited.

"It's not my fault I've become a tourist attraction. I was just doing my job here, and Lord Barrington-Pottsherbert tried to exploit me. He's trying to use me unfairly to make money, but it won't work. I came here to stamp out such exploitation, and that's exactly what I'm going to do."

There seemed very little for Bobby or Daphne to say to that. They simply couldn't understand Albert's attitude at all. It was as if they were at opposite ends of the pole, as black is to white.

***

Wallace felt more than a little morose as depression, a rather uncommon complaint for the superior race of guardian angels, descended like a dark thunder cloud upon his brooding head.

Which made Mozlebeek's cheerfulness all the more like a bloodied rag to a bull. Mozelbeek sang and whistled while tending his window box. The window itself had long since gone. Indeed, so had the whole building, but the window box remained as a somewhat staggering memento to the ancient days of grab and greed and materialistic possessions. The ancient days, that is, to those in the afterlife. Mere mortals were still plunging headlong on their materialistic course to Armageddon, not caring whom they trampled in the rush. And until they could leave their earthbound existence to those who really were wicked enough to deserve it, they were doomed to suffer the slings, arrows, bee stings, dog bites, and mule kicks of petty materialism.

But those minor irritations were not for the likes of Wallace and Mozelbeek. Death and the life thereafter can, and usually do, radically change the designs of a mortal's mind on crossing from one level of living to another. When mankind first evolved on planet Earth he was a somewhat happy-go-lucky but dim-witted character intent on being the master of all he surveyed. To a certain extent he still is. But down the centuries evolution did make a few changes, especially to man in death, rather than to man in life.

When those early humans found themselves in the Condition Of Transit they couldn't understand where they were or what had happened to them. As the new recruits became more intelligent—in their eyes, anyway—great palaces, indeed whole townships, followed by whole civilisations, sprang up across the infinite reaches of the Condition Of Transit. Mankind made his mark in the afterlife. As neither heaven nor hell had the resources to combat these early bands of renegades who insisted on living outside their boundaries, they were left very much to their own devices.

But then, many centuries ago, the Doomsday Ministry decided that too many souls were slipping through the net, making the bureaucrats look inefficient. Something had to be done.

First of all it had to be done at the point of death on Earth. Instead of just letting a soul and spirit quietly cross the great divide alone, leaving it to fend for itself until an inspector had the time to find it and bring it before Saint Christopher, it was decided to send guides to meet it on Earth and take it instantly to learn of its fate. That way the renegades had no chance of getting to it first. It meant a lot more work for a lot more people. It also meant setting up a whole new workforce: the guides. But everyone felt it would be worthwhile.

Secondly, something had to be done about the renegades themselves. So, like those early missionaries in darkest Africa, a group of inspectors sallied forth into the deep wilderness areas of the Condition Of Transit to find the renegades and convert them to the truth.

Many were found and saw the light. But even to this day it is not known how many escaped the inspectors' clutches to flee even further into the wild, uncharted countryside to set up new civilisations. Some souls in the afterlife speak of those unaccounted-for renegades in the same tone of voice as mortals speak of the Abominable Snowman, the Loch Ness Monster, and Robin Hood. Others just can't think of them as romantic legends, saying they escaped back to Earth to live new lives as politicians and lawyers.

Parts of their civilisations remain, however. All the ministry buildings were once the fine houses or town halls of those ancient people. Some buildings, though, crumbled with age or neglect and the only thing left, from one of them at any rate, was Mozelbeek's window box which he nurtured with tender, loving care.

"Can't you shut up that row?" grumbled Wallace. Mozelbeek responded by pulling up a weed and hurling it at his colleague to the accompaniment of a rather shrilly whistled rendition of "The Sailor's Hornpipe."

Wallace's black mood had been brought on by the work

he was doing, and continued unabated. He was logging Lord B-P's movements over the last few days and charting the amount of astral pull encountered from outside sources. Those sources were almost exclusively Albert and, somewhat surprisingly, Maurice H. Liddy. Albert had been the main reason for His Lordship's recent actions up to yesterday, but the whole complex position had changed when Mr. Cochran took the American's telephone call.

"They do say the forerunner to a fall is pride, and Lord Barrington-Pottsherbert is certainly proud now," remarked Wallace, looking up from the limpid pool where the waters showed the aristocrat beginning a conducted tour of the mansion for Maurice H. Liddy.

"I feel so helpless. Here I am, his guardian angel, and I can't do anything to stop him from making an utter fool of himself."

"Don't blame yourself too much." Wallace would rather do without Mozelbeek's gloating sympathy. "It's just that he's letting circumstances control him, instead of him controlling the circumstances, which is a common folly among mankind. All too often they get caught up in the tidal drift of life around them. Then they feel the power is too great for them to combat, not understanding that if they were to mould their ideals into a working proposition and really think positively, they'd be able to beat circumstances into submission.

"Of course, those positive thoughts must be accompanied by positive action, and the target must always be one that can be reached with a little work. A far-set ambition with the sights too high can be a wonderful driving force for a while. But only for a while, because when it palls, as it surely will, it can be as destructive as negative thinking. If a mortal plods through life with an ultimate aim he must always stop off on lower perches on the way up. So the thing to remember is to set a goal which is within your reach. Then, when you've reached it, savour its sweet success for a while before moving on, while you're preparing to ascend to the next level. That way the journey seems not as long, tiring, or unrewarding as it would be if you were consumed with an all-embracing passion to hit the high spot directly.

"And you don't become twisted, bitter, and frustrated as you see yourself vainly trying to inch forward on an unrelenting treadmill. The path to success is through moderate ambitions which are constantly being reviewed whenever one is achieved."

"Moderation is for fools and monks," hissed Wallace under his breath. "Everything to excess." But in his heart he knew Mozelbeek was right.

In a strange and mysterious place twice as far removed from the limpid pools as the limpid pools were removed from Earth, sat two Elder Scribes. They were watching Wallace and they were watching Mozelbeek. The elder Elder Scribe turned to the younger Elder Scribe.

"Ah, that was always coming with Wallace," he sighed. "He's hardly done a stroke of work in guiding Barrington-Pottsherbert. If he sees a need to work hard he'll knuckle under straightaway and do it. But he's always thought that with Lord Barrington-Pottsherbert being born with the proverbial silver spoon in his teeth, he wasn't in need of such guidance as a more lowly-born mortal would be."

"Yes, I'm afraid you're right," nodded the younger Elder Scribe. "What he doesn't realise is that people with a high birthright have to be strong and firm in their battle to retain it. He's largely let Barrington-Pottsherbert wander through life without a mentor, and he can see now how the mortal's mind has been moulded as a result. Let this be a lesson to all guardian angels—no matter how strong they think those in their care are, let them guard and guide each one with perfection. For each human life is as important as its neighbour's, neither more nor less, regardless of its mental and physical limitations and of its station."

In an even stranger and more mysterious place, four times as distant from the strange and mysterious place which itself was twice as far removed from the limpid pools as the limpid pools were removed from Earth, sat two Overlords. They were watching the elder Elder Scribe and they were watching the younger Elder Scribe.

The elder Overlord turned to the younger Overlord.

"Remind me to press for more of an inkling of common sense to be born into the next generation of mankind. If either of these two clowns Albert Carter and Maxwell Barrington-Pottsherbert are anything to go by I despair for the human race. Their selfish single-mindedness can only lead to doom and destruction.

"Their guardian angels are no better either. I just don't know what Wallace and Mozelbeek are thinking of. Their petty sparring has gone down the ages for far too long, and it's time the Elder Scribes put a stop to it. In my day, a scribe would have been struck from the list if they'd let guardian angels carry on in such an irresponsible fashion."

In a place that was nowhere—it had never been anywhere nor would it ever be anywhere, yet it was sixteen times further away from the stranger and more mysterious place, which itself was four times distant from the strange and mysterious place lying double the distance from the limpid pools as the limpid pools lay from Earth—floated nothing. At least to anyone who happened to be passing it would appear to be nothing. In reality it really was something. It was a pure force of disembodied life and thought. And it was watching the elder Overlord and it was watching the younger Overlord.

Albert and Lord B-P did not know that Wallace and Mozelbeek were watching them.

Wallace and Mozelbeek did not know that the elder and younger Elder Scribes were watching them.

The elder and younger Elder Scribes did not know that the elder and younger Overlords were watching them.

The elder and younger Overlords did not know that the pure force of disembodied life and thought was watching them.

The pure force of disembodied life and thought did not know who or what was watching it, because Destiny kept herself very much in the shadows.

What Albert did know, however, was that Maurice H. Liddy was sensing he was near the end of his tour of the mansion and that Lord B-P was desperately killing time, praying for the ghost to show itself.

The elder Overlord would have been proud. The thought was at last beginning to pour over Lord B-P's silver spoon that he might have been led up the garden path, and it made him sweat. There was no sign of the ghost. He pictured the dreamed-of riches and fame that would surely have come with a genuine publicly-acclaimed haunted house slipping from his grasp.

Dear God, don't let me down now. Please send the ghost, please, he thought intently. Did prayers work when you thought them while walking, instead of saying them while kneeling? he wondered.

Lord B-P caught a movement in the corner of his eye as they stood at the foot of the stairs. He was sure there was something on the gallery, but he wanted to be absolutely certain before raising the American's hopes, to say nothing of his own. He cast a surreptitious glance at Maurice H. Liddy and Barbi-Lou. It was obvious they hadn't noticed anything.

But there was definitely a white, vaguely human form, half concealed by the balustrades. *That's not my ghost*, thought Lord B-P. *But no matter. It's a ghost. It'll do.*

"Look there," he cried excitedly. Two pairs of American eyes followed the line of his outstretched, trembling finger.

Almost in unison with Barbi-Lou's "Good God, you're right," came a brilliant bluey-white flash.

"I got it, I got it, bang in the middle," exalted Maurice H. Liddy, lowering the camera from his eye. "I actually got it."

They stood rooted to the spot, watching the ghost move even further back into the shadows. Its strangely muffled voice boomed a grim warning: "You were told before, Lord Barrington-Pottsherbert, about the dangers of lingering in this house of evil. And yet you stay. Not alone, but with guests. For that, you will pay dearly." The ghost made a brave attempt at copying Albert's wild laughter, but this, too, appeared muffled and distant.

Maurice H. Liddy was the first to break free of the invisible chains binding them to the floor. "Come on, after it!" he cried, hurtling up the stairs, not two, not three, but four at a time.

The ghost did not seem to find that quite as amusing as it had the proceedings of the seconds leading up to it, because the laughter abruptly stopped as the spirit took off down the corridor like a ghost possessed.

Albert felt he should find out who was muscling in on his patch, and gleeked up to the gallery, but he had the same view that met Maurice H. Liddy's eyes as he arrived panting and breathless at the top of the stairs. And that was of the ghost disappearing through the door at the end of the passage, slamming it shut behind it.

Lord B-P was perhaps more puzzled by the ghost's presence than was anyone else, except Albert. He knew the ghost wasn't Albert, but couldn't think who else would be haunting Marlston Manor. And like Albert, he felt he knew the voice but couldn't quite place it. As well as being mysteriously muffled it had the sound of a deliberate attempt to disguise it.

Albert fumed. It seemed the best-laid schemes of mice and men and ghosts could easily be unthreaded. How swiftly one was embraced in the crushing arms of defeat so soon after a gentle caress in the tender, soothing arms of victory.

Although Albert could not know it, the new ghost brought a strange twist to Wallace's prophetic mutterings of not so long ago. Pride was certainly the forerunner to a fall. But it wasn't Lord B-P's fall. It was Albert's arrogant pride in his scheme; now it was Albert's fall.

Lord B-P followed the two Americans upstairs at a far more leisurely stride, his head swimming in a sea of euphoric ecstasy as pound signs rang themselves up in his eyes. *Now they've seen a ghost,* he thought, *Marlston's reputation is saved and the future's assured.*

Maurice H. Liddy's angry rattling at the door through which the ghost fled seemed vague and distant. It was only his raised voice which penetrated the financial calculations, bringing Lord B-P back to Earth like the rain from cloud nine.

"This door's locked," grumbled the American. Turning to Lord B-P he asked suspiciously, "What sort of ghost locks doors?"

"Oh, he does it all the time. It's just an annoying little game of his," came back the casual answer, accompanied by an equally dismissive wave of his hand, while at the same time Lord B-P's second prayer inside two minutes asked that he be believed. And to create an added measure of luck he crossed his fingers.

"Well I don't like it. I wanna see that ghost again. If it was a ghost."

"It certainly looked like a ghost…" began Barbi-Lou, but Lord B-P raised his hand.

"Say no more, my dear. If your husband doesn't believe in my ghost, that's up to him. But I'm having no Doubting Thomases in Marlston Manor. Ghosts are extremely susceptible to the thought vibrations around them. If you had doubts about the ghost's existence it's no wonder he fled from you. In fact it's a wonder you even saw it at all. To see a ghost, you have to believe in them."

But Maurice H. Liddy was not for turning so easily. Recalling the ghost's words sent a shiver down his spine. "The ghost didn't seem to mind what we thought of him, but he was pretty explicit about what he thought of us—or of you, at any rate."

"If you don't believe he's genuine or if you're afraid of him you'd better leave my house. I can handle him; he's harmless, you know. He just likes to try and frighten people with his big talk. But I'm not having your doubting thoughts flying about the place. You'll upset him. Now I really would like you to leave, please." Lord B-P amazed himself. Without having to think about it, the words almost tumbled over themselves in their bid to provide an explanation. He knew there was no way the Americans would want to leave until they got to the bottom of it, and even if the ghost failed to show up again, at least it had appeared once to sow the seeds in their mind.

Barbi-Lou took her husband's arm. "Don't be so cynical, dear. You wanted to see a ghost and now you've seen one. Accept it for what it is and be thankful you've seen it."

"I'd like to get closer to it. All I saw was a white shape that has now locked that door." Then he held his hands up in resignation. "Okay, Your Lordship, I'm sorry. It's just that I didn't expect a ghost to run away after delivering such a grim warning, and I'm really quite excited about it all. It just got to my head for a few seconds. I'd still like to get closer to it and see if it'll talk to me. If that's okay with you, of course?"

Of course it was okay with Lord B-P. He wanted the Americans to leave Marlston Manor absolutely convinced it was haunted and then tell the world.

Locked doors posed no problems for the ethereal Albert. He must have a word with this ghost; tell him he was trespassing. He walked through the door into one of the show bedrooms with its valuable pottery two yards inside the boundary of red plaited rope. The door at the far side was wide open but there was no sign of the ghost. However, wandering through into the next room Albert found the ghost…or at least what was left of it: a crumpled sheet with two eyeholes cut in it, lying on the floor. And lying on the bed, panting, was Mr. Cochran. Albert smiled. So Cochran was the ghost. *Well, well, well.*

Albert weighed up what he should do next. If he unlocked the door and lay the remnants of the ghost at Lord B-P's feet, Maurice H. Liddy would wonder who had unlocked the door and put the sheet there. Suddenly he was seized by what he considered to be an almighty brainwave. *There's no reason why it shouldn't work*, he thought, instantly beginning to put his master plan into action.

Mr. Cochran's eyes were screwed tightly shut and his heavy breaths didn't appear to become any shallower as Albert solidified at the foot of the bed. Slowly Albert reached out to pick up the sheet. He didn't make a sound. He didn't want Mr. Cochran cottoning on to what was happening and trying to stop it. Slowly, slowly, he lifted the sheet off the floor, cursing silently when two folds rubbed against each other. Instantly Mr. Cochran opened his eyes, sitting bolt upright. In a second Albert turned tail and ran through the door with the sheet-come-ghost trailing over his shoulders like a cape.

Unleashing a panic-stricken yell, Mr. Cochran leaped off the bed, setting out in hot pursuit. Just as Albert reached the door to the corridor, Mr. Cochran caught hold of the sheet, pulling it towards him with a determined yell.

As Albert still held it in a firm grip, he was pulled off-balance.

"No you don't," grunted Mr. Cochran as they seesawed back and forth with Albert's outstretched hand falling just tantalisingly short of the key. It seemed to be a deadlock for several seconds, when all of a sudden Albert let go and dived for the door.

"*Aaagh!*" yelled Mr. Cochran, tumbling backwards; the sheet enveloping him in muffled, ghostly folds as he struggled on the floor, his kicking legs acting like poles to the ghost of a tent which set itself up over him.

Here we go, thought Albert as he turned the key before throwing open the door. *I've presented Cochran as the phoney ghost to Maurice H. Liddy. I've still won. He'll go up the wall when he sees that a trick's been played on him.*

In the same second that the door flew open, an agonised plea for help shot a hundred, thousand million miles across the universe from Wallace to his final lifeline. The plea was so strong there was no time to question it. Automatic action was taken instantly.

"Stop!!" thundered a voice behind the bemused Americans. As they whirled to see Bobby, standing transparent behind them, Daphne slammed the door shut and relocked it. Before Albert could move she whipped out the key and gleeked into the passage with it.

Lord B-P, Maurice H. Liddy, and Barbi-Lou heard her sigh with relief, and they turned again to face the door. There she stood; the flimsy form of a beautiful girl, through which the wall and door jamb could be seen quite clearly, just as the other end of the corridor could be seen through Bobby. The mere mortals had caught just the briefest glimpse of the white shape thrashing about in the bedroom with Albert standing just inside the door. But now they had more pressing things to think about.

At first Bobby and Daphne were as stunned as they were. An irresistible urge had overtaken them both in the same second, compelling them to help Lord B-P. Now the die was cast and they were standing as ghosts, the first time they had ever appeared in the mortal world during their invisible time at Marlston.

Lord B-P stared in the same disbelief as the Americans at what was quite clearly a ghost in front of them and a ghost behind them.

Again Bobby spoke. This time in quieter, gentler tones than the thunderous roar he had adopted to prevent them staring too long at the apparently human figure of Albert and the phoney ghost in the bedroom.

"Lord Barrington-Pottsherbert, we come to protect you from the evil actions of Albert Carter. We have lived with you in peace here at Marlston Manor down the years. Now Albert Carter's arrival has forced us to show ourselves to you. His plans were to ruin you. We couldn't allow that, so we have risked the wrath of those in the afterlife by breaking through the veil from the world of the dead to the world of the living.

"Have no fear, Lord Barrington-Pottsherbert; we've seen all that Albert Carter has done to you, and until now have felt powerless to prevent him. The fears for our own future were too great and we were too selfish. While we grieved for you and it was in our hearts to help you, we did nothing.

"Now, suddenly, great courage lies within us. The moment of your greatest danger passed just seconds ago, and without our intervention that moment would have consumed your hopes and aspirations, not even spitting out the bones for you to start draping the flesh around again. It was your time of danger that awakened our true sense of responsibility. Like the opening of a door through which floods brilliant sunshine, we, too, can now see the light that brightens even the darkest room.

"While we were serving a purpose only to ourselves by our time at Marlston, we weren't doing anything for anyone else. This has now given us the chance to help you, and we willingly take that chance."

Bobby turned to Maurice H. Liddy, who, like his wife and Lord B-P, stood spellbound, totally transfixed by his words. Although their eyes were wide and staring, and their jaws gaped, there was no fear; only wonder and amazement at the wispy forms of a handsome young man and beautiful girl standing before them.

"You came to see a haunted house, did you not?" he continued. "Well, you've seen one. Marlston has been truly haunted for the last few weeks by an evil spirit whose aim was to cause trouble. Go into the world and tell its people of all you have seen here today. Tell them Marlston Manor is still haunted—not by an evil spirit, for he has been defeated—but by two friendly souls."

Bobby smiled, before turning again to the aristocrat. "While ever you and your descendants live here at Marlston Manor, and while ever our presence as phantoms is welcomed, we shall be here. We are the new ghosts of Marlston Manor."

Daphne stepped forward, pressing the key into Lord B-P's chilled palm. A thought from deep at the back of his mind had niggled him since he first saw the ghosts; a thought that he recognised them from somewhere way back in the past. Further and further his mind probed. Recognition, when it came, was beautiful.

"Of course," he beamed. "I know who you are. You're my friend

Roland Pride's daughter, Daphne, and our gardener Bobby Lewis. Well, well, well, so you've lived here with me all these years?"

Lord B-P was so pleased he positively danced from one foot to the other, totally unable to keep still. The two ghosts smiled warmly at him, and he smiled back.

Yes, he thought. *We're going to get along just fine, and the public will flock here to see you. This truly is the start of a new way of life at Marlston Manor.*

***

By the side of the great limpid pool teeming with the waters of life, and its smaller neighbour – the cloudier pool showing its glimpses of the past – stood an even smaller and more rarely used pool.

"You can't be serious," hissed Wallace. "We can't do that. The Futures Pool should only be used for predicting how to manage situations which could lead to cosmic emergencies. You know the rules."

"I do know the rules," said Mozelbeek. "But I reckon this whole situation with Albert could be classed as a cosmic emergency, don't you? So I sneaked a look, and..."

"You've already looked?" wailed Wallace.

"Yep, already done it," said Mozelbeek. "And there's one particular strand that I really liked. Touched this old heart of mine, it did. That's why I want you to see it. It'll show you how wrong you are."

"But it's not necessarily definitely going to happen. The pool only gives a glimpse of possible shades of time yet to come. The future can still change from what it shows."

"Oh ye, of little faith. I think the cosmic forces will rally round to ensure this possible shade of future time comes to pass. Come on, take a look. It's just a year into the future. Late

April 1981."

Mozelbeek waved a hand over the waters, and together they bent over the pool as the waters cleared, enabling them to witness a possible branch of time yet to come.

Abigail Carter pushed the pram through the cemetery gate and made her way along the path.

She and Timothy – Tiger Tim, she called him – had only undertaken the journey twice since the little boy came into the world. It was a struggle getting the pram on the bus. But all the conductors on the Cemetery Hill run had known Albert, and were only too happy to help her.

"Today's a special day, Tiger," she said, peering under the hood at the little sleeping face. "Exactly a year since your Dad was taken from us."

Daffodils and tulips gave a colourful border to the gravel path which crunched under the pram's wheels.

"Your Dad's up there in heaven looking down on you, right now. And he's so proud of you…the son he never knew." She bit her bottom lip as she recalled discovering she was pregnant the morning after Albert died. She'd had a feeling about it for a couple of days, but wanted to be sure before telling him. The pregnancy test kit was unopened in her bedside drawer when she found him dead.

She turned off the path and stopped by a black granite headstone which had been paid for by the Brindon Trades Union Council. Her eyes scanned every line before she spoke.

'In loving memory of Albert Einstein Carter
A much loved and much missed husband
to Abigail and dad-to-be
Born July 15, 1950
Died April 28, 1980
You clocked off far too early.'

"Hello Albert," she said. "I've got something new for you today."

She pulled a 7"x5" framed photograph of Tim from her handbag, holding it out to face the headstone. "He's three months old now, growing and changing every day."

She bent to place the photo on the granite plinth at the base of the upright, alongside Albert's framed union card.

"I miss you so much, my angel."

She imagined Albert on high, smiling down on them both. "Chin up, girl," he'd be saying. "I miss you, too. And, hey, what a little buster he is. He's going to be a chip off the old block, alright."

Abigail's heart missed a beat. She'd planned how she was going to tell Albert about the future she intended for their son, but didn't know when the time would be right. It might have been today, it might have been in a month, or even on a visit towards the end of the year. As it turned out, it was almost as if Destiny were smiling, or a prod from a guardian angel in some distant mystical place, that led to Albert's words forming in her ear.

Instinctively she knew the time was right. It was now.

"You know you're my hero, Albert," she began, just a touch hesitantly. "And you've been a hero for so many workers throughout your short life.

"In years to come, Tiger Tim will look back on all you've done for the working man, and you'll be his hero, too.

"But I promise you this, Albert...Tim is going to have a job where he doesn't need to struggle for a decent living wage or good working conditions. I'm going to do whatever it takes, whatever is necessary, to give him the best start in life, and get him to university.

"Just think of it...he'll be the first one in both our families to go to university.

"He'll have the world at his feet. And if he chooses a profession he won't need to be part of a union."

She paused, half expecting the grave to split asunder and Albert to rise in a thunderous fury.

Somewhere overhead a bird tweeted to its mate. But that was all, apart from the noise of the traffic on Cemetery Hill, of course.

She ploughed on. "He can be anything he wants; a lawyer or a teacher or a scientist. Or even a junior doctor in an NHS hospital. Definitely no need for unions there."

A slight stirring from the pram told her Tim was awake, bringing her attention back from that utopian future of her dreams, to the present.

She bent again, adjusting the angle of the photograph. Then she stood.

"There. Well. I've told you how things are going to be, Albert. He'll be a real credit to you."

It would be a short visit today. But productive. She'd made sure that Albert knew his son had a dazzling future.

Time to go home.

And as Abigail turned away from the grave, her vision blurred.

She blamed the shaft of sunlight slanting through the branches of the ancient Yew tree. But in reality it was the tear which paused in her eye before trickling its way slowly down her cheek.

She looked back over her shoulder, one last glance at the grave.

"Goodbye my love. God bless."

CHAPTER 11

In which we finally discover what the fuck is really going on

ALBERT STOOD IN the passage at Marlston listening to Bobby swearing allegiance to Lord B-P. He was unsure whether Bobby and Daphne had seen him because they made no signs acknowledging his presence. Perhaps they knew, like Albert knew, that they had won in a blaze of glory.

A wave of power and the desire for revenge had surged through him momentarily, as a fierce battle raged deep within him. His soul was wrestling with a manifestation that had emerged from Albert's waters of life right by his tree of knowledge. In the depths of those waters lay Albert's subconscious and it was from there that the evil being had come.

It was crazed with the thought that Albert had lost and was now bent on a trail of destruction at the mansion. Pure spiteful revenge was the only thing on its mind—revenge that, despite everything, would still leave a bitter taste in its mouth at the end of it all.

The soul was not unduly worried by its presence. He knew he was stronger than the evil emanating from it and he had no fears of losing to it. But first he tried reasoning with it.

"Look, there's no point in doing anything else at Marlston. We put up a good fight but we lost fair and square. We won't be stopping there much longer anyway, so let's just fade away into the background and leave it all to Bobby and Daphne to do as they see fit."

The manifestation turned a fiery, baleful glare to the soul.

"It's weakness like that that's led to mankind being the pathetic creature he is," it hissed. "Just because we've lost one battle doesn't mean we've lost the war. While we're still able to fight, let's carry on. Albert Carter can become a poltergeist. Think of the havoc he'll be able to unleash on the mansion in a short space of time. He can destroy everything of value in the place, everything the tourists go to see. There'll only be the ghosts left. Don't you think that would be poetic justice in the end?"

Still the soul's quiet, gentle manner remained at the forefront while it struggled to quell a rising fury. "But that would be sheer destruction which wouldn't benefit anyone. That's not the way to win battles. Albert won't benefit by it now, because the whole world will soon know without doubt that Marlston is the home of ghosts. He set out to frighten people away, but he's ended up attracting people there instead. There's nothing more you can do."

As he spoke, the soul began to realise that the time was right to reveal the secret he had been forced to keep over the years; that everything had been leading up to this moment, as if guided by some unseen hand. Perhaps the hand of Destiny herself.

"The myth and legend of spirits will be blown wide open. No longer will mankind sit and ponder on the existence of phantoms, ghosts, and spectres. He will know categorically that they do exist. Mankind's spiritual enlightenment will be upon him. The greatest unknown of the ages will become known to those who seek to find it. Many will be sceptical, still refusing to believe. But perhaps that is a good thing, I don't know. Only time will tell.

"So there's nothing more to be gained by Albert seeking revenge. The job Destiny herself gave him—to reveal to the world one way or another—that there is such a thing as the afterlife, has been accomplished. Revenge is meaningless.

Albert hasn't lost. He's won."

The being from Albert's subconscious reeled as it drank in the power and importance of the soul's words.

"All through Albert's lifetime," continued the soul, "I have been moulding his ideas ready for the great moment when the job had to be done. Destiny planned it all. Albert's spirit will never know the immense role he has played in Destiny's game, but that's Destiny's way; that's how she operates. She moves in a mysterious way. Her only servants are the souls of mankind, who, when the spirit takes its rightful place in the afterlife, either heaven or hell, are snatched back by Destiny to be reborn again in another spirit, and another human enters the mortal world."

Albert's soul relaxed a little. It was his first mistake, and the subconscious being pounced immediately, firing a thunderbolt of thoughts about revenge. At that moment Albert felt the momentary surge of power, but the soul neutralised it almost immediately and retook command.

The soul felt he should continue the story. He had always been opposed to keeping Albert's spirit in the dark about his true role, and now seized on the opportunity of giving it a chance to find out.

Soon he, the soul, would depart from the spirit, but the being would go back into Albert's subconscious, and the soul was determined it would take with it the knowledge of its true purpose. *Who knows?* he thought. *Perhaps one day the spirit may dig deep into his subconscious and find the thought waiting there. What a great day that would be.*

He continued his narrative. "Destiny has long since planned for the day when mankind was to be given the opportunity of proving once and for all that there is an afterlife. That knowledge of spiritual enlightenment is essential for mankind to evolve further. When the time was ready Destiny picked the soul to do the job—me. I was trained thoroughly for the task which then lay ahead of me, and I was born into the spirit and body of Albert Carter. It took all of Albert's relatively short lifetime and his somewhat meteoric rise through the local trades union movement to shape his character into the one I wanted, when I could be absolutely sure what his actions would be. Then, when everything was ready, Destiny got a guardian angel to kill him off. The wheels were slowly beginning to turn. Inch by inch they moved round, and everything slotted perfectly into place. The job was done and the trap was sprung.

"Mankind has never before had such an opportunity to prove conclusively on a major basis that ghosts exist and that there is an afterlife. Without the definite knowledge of an afterlife, mankind's evolutionary cycle has halted, and has been halted now for many generations.

"Now mankind has the chance to take the key which unlocks the doorway to the next step in his evolution, and all the wonders which taking that step will bring. Knowledge of the afterlife is that key. Whether he's ready to grasp the opportunity is up to him. Destiny thinks he is, but Destiny's been wrong before.

"Anyway, we've led the horse to water but we can't make it drink. Of course, lesser entities than Destiny herself are unaware of what's happened. Saint Christopher, for example, may well see Albert's actions at Marlston as being against the best interests of the afterlife and decide to punish him. It'll be a tragedy if that happens, but that's his prerogative. He's as much in the dark as to the real reason behind Albert's hauntings as is the rest of the world. Albert could become yet another unsung hero.

"In spite of this great victory, though, his mission is not

yet complete. There is still one more task to be done before Destiny can end the Doomsday Ministry strike allowing Albert to take up his allotted place in heaven or hell."

The being from the waters snarled and turned back towards the banks. But the soul was not to be denied revealing the final part of his plan. He was determined that the full purpose of Albert's life was going to be recorded in his subconscious.

"Knowledge of the afterlife and the many planes of existence within it is like a fan. To most mortals that fan is almost, if not entirely, closed. All they see is the top piece. The rest of the picture lies concealed in many pieces, like a jigsaw, beneath the surface, but it's there all the same. Some mortals have opened the fan a little to glimpse a snatch of what lies within.

"Mankind now has the chance to open that fan to the full and witness the stunning beauty of its innermost layers, which have remained hidden deeply beneath a dull, tarnished exterior for many millennia.

"But just as mortal life becomes thus liberated and takes a step forward in evolution, then so must the lowest plane of the afterlife, holding the spirits which wander the earth. They must become more organised to meet the onslaught which will surely come in the light of mankind's newly acquired knowledge. Ghosts are scattered far and wide about the earthly realm. What they need is a unifying body, if you'll forgive the pun, to give them the strength and resources to cope. Albert is the one to help give them that strength and power. He's already set the machinery in motion; he must now see it through. Only then can he go to his rest while I fly home to Destiny."

The being had halted by the water's edge to hear the conclusion of the soul's tale. For the first time in its murky existence it did not see the evil side of a situation, but only because there was no evil side there for it to see. No matter; it at least had the wisdom not to press a point it knew was useless.

It turned, with a smile, to the soul. "I thank you," it hissed. "In the words of the time-worn cliché you've helped me see the light. I return now to the deepest waters of the subconscious where the knowledge you have given me will lie dormant until it is called upon. Farewell."

With a wave of its hair-covered arm it lumbered out into the deceptively deep waters, ducked under, and disappeared. After just a few moments there were not even any air bubbles to show it had ever been there.

Silence and tranquillity descended once more to the woodland glade, just before they descended on Albert standing in the passageway watching Lord B-P walk away with Maurice H. Liddy, Barbi-Lou, Bobby, and Daphne.

It was a strange feeling to him, one he hadn't come across before. The sensation of utter calm within him was alien. He wasn't to link it with the manifestation of temptation as it sank back into the depths of his subconscious, having realised that purity of intention, even if it's the soul and not the spirit that intends it, can far outweigh any plausible argument put forward by evil.

He was saved from having to ponder his own personal paradox any further, when the bedraggled ghost with its head tucked firmly beneath its arm, was suddenly standing alongside him in the corridor.

"Greetings Albert Carter, we have returned with reinforcements and are ready to challenge Saint Christopher's authority. We've searched the length and breadth of England for disillusioned spirits. It wasn't difficult. Disillusionment comes easily and quickly, even to those who chose to rebel against going to heaven or hell, and not just to those whom the Ministry have sentenced to walk the earth. But now, thanks to you, we'll receive justice at last. We look to you to lead us in our campaign."

***

Like Saint Christopher, like Albert, like everyone, Mozelbeek was unaware that Albert's soul had served its purpose and had indeed won, not lost. He viewed with dismay the meeting between Lord B-P and Bobby and Daphne, and found it difficult to admit defeat to an exuberant Wallace.

He heard the head say they wanted Albert to lead them, which was something he could find solace in, at least. "He may have failed in what he set out to do at Marlston Manor, but he still has the chance to do some good for all the dissenting ghosts," he murmured philosophically. "Perhaps he'll still be able to achieve something."

Mozelbeek and Wallace watched Albert; the elder and younger Elder Scribes watched Mozelbeek and Wallace; the elder and younger Overlords watched the elder and younger Elder Scribes; a pure force of disembodied life and thought watched the elder and younger Overlords; Destiny watched the pure force of disembodied life and thought. Destiny thought she was supreme. Albert's soul served Destiny. Albert watched over Destiny—over his own destiny, anyway. Albert thought he was supreme.

Destiny spoke to Albert's soul in an unknown tongue, but he had no trouble understanding. "You criticise me for not letting Albert Carter know he has been successful in the task I set him…for not even letting him know he was on that mission." She smiled. "But when you look at the achievement of mankind down the ages is it not true of every major step forward he has taken? Has it not been the unknowing, the mystery, which has spurred him on?"

"But at least man has been rewarded for his discoveries down the aeons," countered the soul. "History has recorded, somewhat cloudily, I'll admit, but has still recorded, all his achievements. In this case the achievements will go unrecorded."

Destiny was not to be robbed of something she felt was rightly hers. "But here I am really the achiever. It was I who manipulated Albert Carter; he was merely the puppet and I the puppet-master with the strings. Is it right, therefore, that he should be recognised for something he doesn't even know he's done?"

"But the knowledge that he's done it would be a reward in itself," protested the soul. "And that's all I'm asking for him."

If Destiny had possessed a head she would have shaken it. "No, I'm afraid it's impossible. For evolution to continue unhampered, the afterlife must think their closely-guarded secret became known by coincidence manipulating the wheels and cogs. Once it were to become known that there is divine intervention in the cosmos from me, the need for life to be lived would disappear. Everyone would expect me to do it all for them, and no-one would do anything any more. I'd lose the tools I've been using since the creation to make life happen—life itself.

"Albert Carter will know in time, as will the rest of the afterlife, that it was his actions which led to the discovery. But not for millennia yet. No, let everyone think those actions were stumbled upon and are the coincidence I've contrived them to be.

"You surely see my point that neither he nor anyone else must know he has been an agent of Destiny. It is better this way, my friend—indeed, it is the only way. There are some things that for the good of mankind it is better for them not to know. This is one of them."

And Destiny's ace as far as Albert as an individual was concerned was yet to be played. Here it came: "You know how you've had to mould his character before he was ready for his job as shop steward? It's that character that makes him the leader he is. Think how he would react if he were to discover he's been used all this time…manipulated, exploited… whichever word you want to use."

The ace was played, taking the trick, and with it the game.

***

Even the spacious summer house couldn't hold all the head's reinforcements, so the ghosts gathered outside on the croquet lawn and the next stage of the plan came into being.

"First of all," began the head, "we must have a proper organisation. Is that not right, Albert?"

"Absolutely. A union to represent you all."

"The Union of Ghosts," called a ghostly figure from the back.

"No," called a ghoulish figure from the front. "The Union of Ghouls."

Albert looked at the ghoulish figure who was caked in what appeared to be dried blood. Shuddering, he wondered which chamber of horrors or dark dungeon this character stalked.

Instantly a squabble sprang up. About half those present looked like good, clean-haunting ghosts who opted for the Union of Ghosts. The others, more frightening spectres to behold, demanded to be represented by a Union of Ghouls.

Albert had an idea, but had to keep it strictly within union rules. He held up his hands to silence the shouting and muttering. "Right—those who want to form a Union of Ghosts, move to the right and elect yourselves a leader. Those who want to be in a Union of Ghouls move to the left and also elect a leader."

After five minutes of shuffling into two groups and huddled discussions, the body with head in hand stepped forward from the group of ghosts, while the ghoulish figure with the dried blood stepped from the ghouls. "I am the leader of the ghouls," said the latter.

"And I the leader of the ghosts," proclaimed the former.

"Good. We now have a Union of Ghosts and a Union of Ghouls," declared Albert. "Do you agree that your aims are the same, to press for better conditions for you all, both for ghosts and for ghouls?"

The head said he agreed, and his group of ghosts behind him all nodded in approval. Albert turned to the ghoul. "Of course we agree, Albert, that's what we're all here for."

"Then we mustn't fall out amongst ourselves. I shall arbitrate and reach a decision which I hope will be acceptable to both groups. You are each individual unions and yet you want one and the same thing.

"Therefore, you will join forces and will have joint leaders— you, the head, and you, the ghoul. You will call yourselves the Amalgamated Union of Ghosts and Ghouls."

Albert spread his hands before him as both groups broke into rapturous applause. He looked towards the head and the ghoul who were having another huddled discussion. Then they turned expectantly to him. Cupping his hand, the ghoul shouted above the din of the continuing applause. "You have done so much to help us, Albert, we'd like you to be our overall leader."

Albert smiled, genuinely flattered, but shook his head. He waited until the clapping ceased. "I'm very honoured to be asked to be your leader, but I'm afraid I can't accept your invitation. As soon as the Doomsday Ministry strike is over I shall be taking up my place in heaven or hell. Also, I believe you both deserve the job more than I do. You know a lot more about the afterlife than I do. You've been here many years; I'm just a novice, lacking in experience of ghostly and ghoulish ways.

"I can help you better by being your adviser on how to handle your negotiations with Saint Christopher and on general union practices. I shall be most honoured to accept that post until I'm recalled to hear the judgement passed upon me."

And so it was that Albert became adviser to the Amalgamated Union of Ghosts and Ghouls, and Destiny smiled again.

They had to wait until Saturday before they could pull their coup de grace. Saturday—football day. Albert dispatched the head to find Saint Christopher, and then discovered he had no idea how to gleek to the football ground. The ghoul held out a blood-caked hand. "Here, take my hand and close your eyes. I'll guide you to the ground."

Gingerly Albert did as he was told, and the ghoul looked to see that everyone was ready. "Right!" he cried. "After three. One, two, three."

The ghosts and ghouls had gathered once more on the croquet lawn. One second they were standing there, but after the ghoul's cry of three, only a slight breeze rustled the occasional leaf on the otherwise empty lawn.

Albert experienced the same momentary impression of hurtling through space that he had felt during his original journey to Marlston. Again he felt terra firma beneath his feet, and at the same second his ears were filled with the roar of the crowd. Opening his eyes he saw that he and the rest of the newly formed union were in the middle of the pitch.

The roar of the crowd was like sweet, albeit deafening music to Albert's ears. He was at his favourite football match, the local derby with the highest gate of the day: 57,000.

The game was ten minutes old with no score. But something was happening on the pitch that would soon cause the crowd to become hysterical, and it wasn't a goal.

Albert and the fright of ghosts, accompanied by about

one hundred other spirits who for one reason or another had not taken up their places in the afterlife, remaining in the Condition Of Transit, stood on the field just a thought away from the first mass haunting in the history of creation. The footballers continued their game unaware that anything was amiss, running straight through the unseen spirits without noticing even so much as a chill in the air. There was nothing to show those of the mortal world that all hell—or what perhaps should have been in hell—was about to break loose on them.

Albert had no idea how he got to the football stadium. Although he had mastered the art of gleeking short distances he had to admit it was pretty easy because he just thought exactly where he wanted to go. Which made him wonder what power lay dormant within him, that had he accumulated the same length of ghostly service as his colleagues, he could have executed with the same degree of skill as they had done.

***

The waters of life seethed, frothed, and bubbled as Wallace turned from them to stare grimly at Mozelbeek. Mozelbeek smiled, but it hid a nagging worry that if Saint Christopher failed to meet their demands they might just carry out their threat, appearing to all at the soccer ground.

"See what he's done now," spat Wallace. "This could be the beginning of the end for mankind—and you know it."

"Not at all," grinned Mozelbeek, desperately wishing he could believe his own words. "Saint Christopher's beaten. He'll have to agree to review their cases. He daren't risk the consequences of not doing so."

"He's not the sort of saint to give in to blackmail—and that's exactly what this is: blackmail."

"But again, isn't that the way of the world? On Earth

mankind uses all sorts of blackmail and threats to get his way. It's just the way of life nowadays. You've got to move with the tide, Wallace, or it swamps you, and you drown."

The waters of life splashed over the banks of the no-longer-limpid pool. The reason for their frenzied activity was the imbalance generated by the huge gathering of ghosts and ghouls at the football ground. The image lying within was ruffled and unclear as the waters boiled and thrashed, but the angels could see well enough what was unfolding. The consequences facing the earth if the ghosts and ghouls did all appear at the ground were too horrific for them to contemplate. The energy used to rend asunder the barrier they would have to cross, and the reaction it would spark off around the world, would devastate thousands of square miles with typhoons, floods, volcanoes, and earthquakes. The delicate, sensitive fabric that kept the full fury of pent-up nature at bay would tear like softened butter giving way to a knife.

Unaware of the looming catastrophe, Saint Christopher had been feeling pretty pleased with himself. His negotiations with the inspectors were almost at an end and he felt a settlement was imminent.

He had not been completely successful. He had been trying to persuade the inspectors to accept another ten to their ranks while the inspectors had been pressing for twenty new recruits. They, too, were feeling rather smug, also believing a settlement was imminent, and they were in a better position to judge because it was their decision whether or not to accept what he told their representative was his final offer. That final offer had been fifteen, which secretly delighted the inspectors. Before the talks began they had agreed with each other not to accept less than ten, but Saint Christopher had opened the debate by offering that very number, which they could not accept for two reasons. One, they would lose face by appearing to give in too easily; and two, if that were his starting figure they were almost certain to persuade him to go higher. The inspectors' two representatives glanced sideways at each other.

They would never have made boy scouts, being totally unprepared for this eventuality. Suddenly one of them found himself blurting out: "Ten! Don't be insulting. We'll only settle for twenty, and even then we'll still be undermanned."

Before the talks began Saint Christopher had confided in his close associates that he would be prepared to recruit twenty more inspectors, but as he was prepared to haggle it was a matter of principle for him to halve it. When he realised that was the figure the inspectors had in mind, too, he felt he was almost certain to persuade them to go lower.

And so the ritual began. It seemed the farce had penetrated the boundaries of the earth into the afterlife—the farce which saw two sides dancing around ridiculous starting points before finally meeting in the middle. The happy medium could never be reached without that merry little charade. Neither party could be seen to lose face—to them it mattered not how the game was played.

But when Saint Christopher was confronted with the head's demands on behalf of the Amalgamated Union of Ghosts and Ghouls, it became more than just a game. It was the thing Saint Christopher had been dreading almost as long as he could remember. The ghosts were revolting. Although Saint Christopher felt the Ministry of Hauntings should solve the problem, rather than his Doomsday Ministry, the red tape would become so long, so tangled, and so convoluted that he decided to take action to cut through it before it wound itself firmly around everyone's necks.

"You'd better wheel this headless creature in, then," he said resignedly to his attendant, who had passed on the demands.

As the headless body was ushered through the door and sat down, placing his actual head on the table directly opposite Saint Christopher, Saint Christopher sighed to himself. *No rest for the wicked,* he thought.

"Now look," he began. "You really want the Ministry of Hauntings. They sort out if a ghost can haunt a certain place."

But the head was not put off so easily. "No, not at all. It's definitely the Doomsday Ministry I want. The Ministry of Hauntings only looks after ghosts who want to stay on the earth, and those who've been sentenced to a spell there for their sins. We're asking that our sentences are reviewed earlier. In many cases ghosts pay the full price of their sins long before their haunting is up. It seems such a waste for them to stay there when could be doing something far more useful and their places could be taken by someone who wants to stay on Earth."

"Well, I don't know," said Saint Christopher. "After all, it is the law."

"The law's outdated though. That's why we're pressing for changes. Other laws have changed down the ages, so why not this one?"

Saint Christopher believed a show of ignorance may be the best policy. "Things don't get changed just for the sake of change itself, even if they are outdated. There've been no complaints about this before, so there's never been any need to change it. It hasn't even been a silent majority—it's been a unanimous silence. If you've been unhappy why haven't you come to me before? I'd have considered your points long ago if I'd realised anything was wrong."

The head was stunned. He wouldn't have made a boy scout either. He'd been prepared for a battle with an unrelenting Saint Christopher and had been ready to take him to the football ground to show him what they would do if he failed to meet their perfectly reasonable demands. But now there seemed very little point in mentioning it.

The head felt he had learned something deep and important. In fact, many answers seemed to flash by him as he looked across at Saint Christopher's innocent, smiling face. He now knew that a show of force and blackmail were not always necessary to achieve your aims: if your demands—*Perhaps that's too strong a word*, he thought, *let's call them "requests"*—if your requests were reasonable, a reasonable person on the other side of the fence may well listen to them. Words speak louder than actions. But most importantly, Saint Christopher said he didn't know anything about their grievances and hadn't realised anything was wrong. Yes, the head must tell his union members something about that when he returned.

"You'll review our cases, then?" he asked in a surprised, rather quiet voice.

"Well, of course, the details will have to be worked out. It'll be a long and complicated process to change a law like this, but, yes, I'm prepared to accept your request in principle."

There! That word "request," not "demand," thought the head. But he could still scarcely believe he was hearing right. His body leaped up, reaching for Saint Christopher's hand. "Thank you, sir, thank you very much indeed. I'll pass the good news on to my colleagues straightaway. I'm sure they'll be very happy to hear it."

After the head left, Saint Christopher sent for his attendant. "I've agreed to their requests," he said directly. "You know I've been saying for a long time that a spirit shouldn't be forced to stay on Earth for as long as the initial sentence decrees. But it's important that the spirit learns for itself and thinks for itself. That's why I haven't sought to have the law changed before.

The spirits had to find discontentment themselves and ask for the change. Handing benefits to them on a silver platter wouldn't be good for them. They must work for them and earn them. It seems they're doing that now, and they'll emerge as better, stronger characters, able to stand up for themselves."

And that was not the only philosophy behind Saint Christopher's thinking. "The other point, of course, is the inspectors. After they've agreed to accept fifteen recruits I'll tell them their work programme will have to be changed to accommodate their new colleagues, and as part of their duties they'll have to review every ghost's case to see if they've served long enough on Earth. That way, changing the law won't put too much of a burden on the Ministry. It couldn't have come at a better time, could it?"

Looking across at his attendant, a triumphant smile firmly lodged itself in place. "Taking on the new inspectors to do the extra work will kill two birds with one stone. If we disguise it well enough, by changing the shift patterns, no-one will notice and everyone will be happy."

***

The roar of the football crowd paled into insignificance as the ghosts roared and cheered at the news brought back by the head, who motioned for quiet. "Friends and colleagues," he called. "There is one great lesson to be learned from all this, and it's Albert Carter who's shown us the way. Saint Christopher said he'd have listened to us before if he'd known we were unhappy. How many of us haven't been happy for a long time?"

Not one ghost or ghoul kept its hand down.

"And how many of us confided in someone else that we weren't happy?"

Not one ghost or ghoul put its hand up.

"There lies the answer to our problem, and to a great many other problems. But it wasn't until Albert Carter came to show us the way that we realised what was wrong. We kept our feelings bottled up inside, instead of voicing what we really felt.

"We'll know better than to do that again," he cried. "We know now that it's our heritage to make things work for us as we want them to—or at least to try. It's no use sitting round doing nothing, hoping things will change. We must make things change for the better, we must stand up for what we believe in and make our voices heard."

"I know what I believe in," shouted a ghost from among the crowd. "I believe in Albert Carter. For he's a jolly good fellow…"

The din became overpowering as the ghosts and ghouls sang Albert's praises. Albert tried to make his way to the front to give the speech he usually made on such occasions, when the Amalgamated Union of Glue and Adhesive Workers had won a famous victory. But this time he did not have the chance, finding himself pulled off his feet and hoisted aloft.

"Good old Albert," cried the ghosts and ghouls. "For he's a jolly good fellow, for he's a jolly good fellow, for he's a jolly good fellow, and so say all of us."

"Three cheers for Albert," yelled the head ecstatically. "Hip, hip, hooray!" And Albert was flung high in the air, to be caught safely a second or two later as he fell back into their waiting arms.

"Hip, hip, hooray." Again he was flung heavenward. For a second time he fell safely into their outstretched arms. Albert was their hero.

"Hip, hip, hooray." For a third time they cast him into the air. And then there was nothing. No puff of smoke, no flash of lightning. Nothing. One moment Albert had been in mid-air, all eyes on him, then the next he had completely disappeared.

Each ghost and ghoul turned to its neighbour with a puzzled look. "Where's he gone?" they asked each other. And the answer from each one was the same. Just a blank look and shrug of the shoulders.

CHAPTER 12

In which our hero faces his judgement day

ALBERT WAS HURTLING through space, bright lights flashing around him as he sped on his way. He had no idea what was happening to him. All he knew was that he had been thrown in the air three times and had only come down twice. *So much for the theory about things going up having to come down,* he thought.

Space dissolved before his eyes, turning into a misty hillside, on which stood hundreds of people. In the distance he could see the two-storey whitewashed building where Saint Christopher had sat when Albert first arrived in the afterlife with Georgie. The people stretched in a queue from where he stood down to the building.

Hardly before he had time to realise where he was he heard a rustle behind him, and whirling round, he saw another figure materialise there. A few seconds later there was another. Then another and another and another, all looking equally puzzled. The queue was getting longer. Instinctively Albert knew that the time had arrived. His day of judgement was upon him. *The dispute between the ministry and the inspectors must be over,* he thought.

Indeed it was. The inspectors had brought word to Saint Christopher that they agreed to accept his offer of fifteen more to their ranks and were prepared to return to work straight away. Saint Christopher explained that in future there would be many more cases to review, but as there were going to be more inspectors to do the work, their shift patterns could be changed in such a way that they should all find themselves with much more free time. He had worked out that even with the extra work, fifteen more people helping out could easily cover it.

He shook hands with the inspectors' representatives, and the crippling strike was over.

Instantly Saint Christopher ordered the spirits sent back to Earth to be recalled, and the inspectors fetched their personal reports about the lives of each one. The ministry was back in business.

The call from the Condition Of Transit was as dark and mysterious as space itself. The spirits it was heralding were scattered far and wide about the earth. None could feel the powerful magnetism pulling them; all they knew was that at one moment they were in their haunts, and the next they were speeding across the cosmos to a distant meeting with their fate.

When Albert's call came it was in the split second that he was in mid-air from his third throw, and he departed from the celebrations in the wink of an eye.

Now he found himself in a slow queue waiting to discover if his life had lived up to the expectations of those with the power. The queue snaked its way down to the building where Saint Christopher sat at the top of the steps. As Albert got nearer he could see people stepping from the table to their guides. Some were ecstatically happy, on their way to heaven. Others stepped down with slumped shoulders, utter disappointment and horror etched deeply into their expressions.

A whirlwind of thought blowing both expectation and doubt galloped across Albert's horizon. He felt deadly sick as his stomach tried to escape through his legs.

He recalled his soul's words to him—that his actions on Earth were for the benefit of others. *Surely that's booked me a place in heaven,* he thought. *But then again…*

He snapped out of his dreaming. That alternative just did not bear thinking about.

How long he stood in the queue he didn't know. He took a pace forward every few moments as another spirit learned its fate, and went off to take up its allotted place. Inch by inch Albert got nearer. And then he was there, standing at the head of the queue. His mouth was dry, and if he had a mortal heart pumping mortal blood around a mortal body, it would have been pounding.

"Name?" demanded an attendant.

Albert swallowed. "Albert Carter, sir," he said, thickly, desperately trying to keep his voice on an even keel.

Saint Christopher looked up sharply. "So you're Albert Carter, are you? The ghost of Marlston Manor. Let me tell you, my lad, you've upset the delicate balance of the universe by your antics at Marlston, and the equations of life have had to be altered to keep things straight."

Albert found himself trembling uncontrollably. Saint Christopher's tones were hardly the friendly ones he'd adopted to the soul who'd been in front of him in the queue when he sent him on his way to heaven. But then again, they hadn't been the slow reverent ones he'd used to tell the man two in front of Albert that his was a downwards journey.

Like a drowning man, his life shot past his eyes, burning itself out in the depths of his brain. In a quarter of a second he relived a multitude of victories and defeats; good deeds and bad deeds. And was that a gentle smile on Saint Christopher's face…or a powerful leer?

Wallace and Mozelbeek looked down from the mists of their perch in the perimeter of heaven, and laid bets. Mozelbeek thought Albert had done just enough for his fellow mortals on Earth to warrant a meeting with Saint Peter at the Pearly Gates. Wallace viewed it from a different perspective. While Albert had been doing good for a small minority he had also been upsetting bigger fish in a bigger pond. And, of course he might have blotted his copy book by unlawfully haunting the mansion. Wallace felt the dice were loaded the other way from Mozelbeek's thoughts.

Saint Christopher was talking again: "Well, Albert Carter, we have reached a conclusion. And let me tell you here and now, that for the first time in our long history we have rescinded a soul's right of appeal. My decision is final, you have no comeback at all."

The world exploded in Albert's ears. No right of appeal— that could only mean one thing. He'd lost. He was doomed to eternal damnation, hellfire, and brimstone. Rocking backwards and forwards he scrambled frantically for Saint Christopher's desktop to stop himself falling.

Wallace turned triumphantly to Mozelbeek, just as Saint Christopher resumed. Mozelbeek smiled, laying a gentle hand on Wallace's shoulder. "Wait a moment, my friend, it's not over yet."

"Yours is an unusual case," continued the patron saint of all travellers. "We get many souls here who've held similar posts to yours on Earth, and most have been out-and-out troublemakers. All they've wanted is political and industrial power. They've not cared for the well-being of the people who've looked to them as leaders; the people who've relied on them.

"Too often, far too often, their destructive course has led to war. War between individuals, between groups, between countries. When the talking of the leaders fails, it's left to the masses to take over in the only way they know how.

"There are no victors when it reaches that stage…only losers.

And those losers always feel that the other fellow is better off than they are, so bitterness creeps in and the war continues. Perhaps it's only in the minds of those who've fought, but the spark is there, nevertheless, ready to be kindled again into another flame of aggression at the earliest wayward breeze.

"Look, for example, at the First World War, and how the promised land fit for heroes never came, and how neither side could settle until the talking failed again and the guns had their day, blazing to their full ignominy once more.

"But that's the way of the world, Albert Carter, and neither you nor I will change it, no matter how hard we try, no matter how pure our intentions.

"One man alone can never bring peace. Just as it takes two to make a quarrel and a war, it takes two to make peace. I say this guardedly, and I hope you're taking a firm note of it to see you through the times ahead. You see, Albert Carter, wherever a mortal is, wherever a soul is, it needs another to give comfort. Someone to be at peace with. Because even a man alone is not at peace. The way man is built means he can never be at peace with himself as an individual.

"It is true that your time on Earth was spent mostly at war. You led your followers against what you genuinely believed was the oppression dished out by the ruling classes. But the rulers, too, felt they were doing their best. Not just for themselves, but for the likes of you, who relied on them to keep their factories going to provide you with a living.

"Without them you'd never have survived. Without you they'd never have survived. The race of mankind is like a jigsaw puzzle with many interlocking pieces, all necessary to complete the picture. And that picture can be of anything you want it to be, provided you work for it. But you must always remember that there can only ever be one overall picture. So the picture you want must fit in with the other pieces in the puzzle. It's no use you pulling one way and your neighbour pulling another, or the picture will come apart and be ruined.

"It boils down to a simple maxim that mankind would do well to remember, but one I'm afraid he often forgets. As each individual piece of that jigsaw has to live interlocked with its neighbours, it's better to be at peace and on good terms always, for the benefit of everyone. Or put more simply, work together for the common good."

Saint Christopher paused, probing deeply into Albert's eyes. "You've never been regarded as a troublemaker just for the sake of making trouble. We believe your actions have always had the good of your followers at heart, and you have won better conditions for them.

"So for you, Albert Carter, there is a place in heaven."

Again Albert's world exploded. But this time it was in a celebration of fireworks. For a few seconds the bangers and sparklers danced their booming and glittering paths around his head while Saint Christopher's words struggled to break down the barriers surrounding his mind. He felt numb as the words finally sank in. Unable to contain himself any longer, he began hopping insanely from one foot to the other. The waiting was over, he told himself. He'd done it. He'd got to heaven.

He knew his short earthly life had been devoted to fighting for his downtrodden fellows, but he had wondered at the back of his mind if Saint Christopher would see it that way. But obviously he had.

"I've done it, Abigail," he cried. In his mind's eye he saw her wide smile that showed the slightly crooked tooth that he always said added to her charm.

However, Saint Christopher held up his hand. "Albert Carter, control yourself. I haven't finished."

And Albert's world stood still. What more could there possibly be?

Mozelbeek looked at Wallace, his jubilation also turning sour. Wallace smiled as Saint Christopher continued: "But your recent behaviour at Marlston Manor is inexcusable. Your conduct there was detrimental to both Lord Barrington-Pottsherbert's interests and to the interests of the people who visited Marlston paying their money of their own free will.

"Lord Barrington-Pottsherbert was throwing open to the public the priceless treasures of his ancestral home which would otherwise have been locked away and lost to the public gaze. The visitors were under no duress, no pressure, to go there. They went because they wanted to, and for no other reason. You had no right to scare them away.

"Also, your actions could have had dreadful repercussions on the rest of the world, and indeed, would have done, had the balance not been corrected by other people over and above the call of their normal duties. For all this, you must be punished.

"Listen carefully, Albert Carter, for this is your day of judgement, and you shall now hear how we have judged you.

"For your life on Earth you have been awarded a place in heaven. But you will not take up that allotted place for one year. You will spend the next twelve months in hell, as a guest of my colleague Prince Lucifer, otherwise known as Beelzebub, Satan, or the devil, as punishment for your unlawful haunting of Marlston Manor.

"Once the year is over, your guide will come to meet you in hell and take you to your rightful place in heaven, where you will find eternal peace and happiness. Farewell, Albert Carter. Spend an industrious year in hell musing over your past mistakes, remembering that there are souls who will be spending all eternity there musing over theirs. You are one of the lucky ones."

Saint Christopher nodded to someone standing to Albert's left, someone Albert hadn't noticed before. Albert turned, and there, smiling at him, was Georgie.

"Albert, you old bugger. You've made it then."

Wordlessly Albert took Georgie's outstretched hand, to be led away from the table to a quiet corner on the edge of the mist.

The triumphant smile returned to Mozelbeek's face. He hooked down his halo, breathed on it, polished it on his wing and put it back. With a superior nod to the dejected Wallace he peered down into the limpid pool. Albert was now out of his care. But in a hospital somewhere in the heart of Sussex a baby was born—Mozelbeek's latest charge. Turning his back on Wallace he settled down to concentrate on the new matter in hand.

Albert found himself in total darkness for a few seconds, then he was rushing through space with Georgie, en route to hell.

"What's it like in hell?" he asked, just a touch uncertainly.

"Hell is what you make it," replied Georgie, mysteriously. "You'll see what I mean when you get there. But I can tell you now, there's a string of men who get out of their Rolls-Royces in hell every morning to spend eight hours trying to push an angry, spitting camel through a needle's eye.

"Hell is what each soul thinks it is. The devil just acts as the catalyst, bringing it all together as a working proposition.

"For instance, vandals and hooligans spend much of their time playing Scrabble or watching cricket. A trades unionist like yourself might have to spend three hours a day in the golf club bar sipping pink gins with bankers and utility company chief executives. Those same executives might have to spend another three hours a day in the working men's clubs drinking pints of brown and mild with you.

"Hell can be tolerable, but only just, and you've got to work hard at it. You won't enjoy your time there, but, of course, you're not supposed to. What it all comes down to in the end is that you're forced to do everything you hate…everything that's abhorrent to you."

"But is there really all that fire and brimstone?" asked Albert, beginning to get worried.

"Around the boundary, yes. And it's very much hotter than heaven all the way through. I suppose you could say it's uncomfortably hot.

"Although, the only time I've actually been inside was for a Christmas party, and to be honest, I can't remember much about it."

A party, thought Albert, bucking up a little. Perhaps it wasn't going to be too bad, after all.

They suddenly found themselves on solid ground again, and there, at the edge of a clearing in the mist, was a dark cave. A figure stood just outside, shining a torch.

"This is hell," whispered Georgie. "But it's usually as bright as day in that cave, with flames licking everywhere." Now, though, there wasn't a flame to be seen, and a chill in the air bit deep into their core.

As they strode towards the figure, he turned the torch full into their faces. "Who's there?" he called.

Georgie shielded his eyes. "It's me, Georgie. And for God's sake turn that blasted light off."

"Let's leave my relatives out of this, shall we," grinned the figure, snapping off his powerful beam of light.

Gradually Albert's eyes became accustomed to the dimness and he began to make out the extraordinarily handsome face, the cloven hooves, the tail, and the horns. He was looking at the Prince of Darkness—the devil himself.

The devil turned to Albert. "This must be the notorious Albert Carter, who's been giving everyone such a merry runaround. I've been expecting you. Nice to have you aboard, my lad, even if it is only for a year."

Georgie shivered. "What's going on?" he asked, his teeth chattering as he wrapped his arms around himself. "It's freezing down here. It's usually so hot."

"Yes, I know," said the devil. "It's my boilermen. They've fucking well gone on strike."

The End

Excerpt from To Rise Again

H E GESTURED FOR me to go in. Peering past him, I could see a long mahogany table in the centre of the room. It was much longer than it was wide. Eight dark-wood seats ran down each side of the table, with a carver at both heads. The two mullioned windows at the foot of the room were identical to the ones in the drawing room, and a small shelf ran all the way round, a couple of feet from the ceiling. The shelf was empty now, but I could easily imagine it once displaying a mass of china plates.

As I passed properly through the door a sense of fear instantly hit me. One moment the room was empty. The next it was full of shouting; that deep guttural sound almost unique to the German language. I heard those beautiful dark chairs scraping across the bare wooden floor. My eyes opened wide in a mix of amazement and horror as the room suddenly filled with men. With soldiers. All wearing the sinister uniform of the Nazi.

Each chair was instantly occupied. And after the soldier sitting in the carver in front of the window seemed to spot us, pointing to the door with a yell, all seventeen other faces turned towards us. And with one movement they pushed back the chairs, rising together in a mechanical sweep, rather like a clockwork toy.

The two nearest Germans scrambled forward, reaching for their guns. Time seemed to stand still. An eternity passed and I could sense rather than smell the appetising aroma which sprang from the table. The aroma of a roasted joint.

I visibly leaped as a hand gripped my shoulder. I stared around at the empty chairs and soundless room. Richard released my shoulder as I relaxed. His voice broke the quiet stillness. "Have you seen something else?"

It was no use me asking if he had seen anything. I knew he hadn't. Whatever it was, only I had seen it. I was sure of that.

ABOUT THE AUTHOR

STEWART BINT IS a novelist, magazine columnist and PR writer. He lives with his wife, Sue, in Leicestershire in the UK, and has two grown-up children, Christopher and Charlotte.

While writing, his office companion is his charismatic budgie, Alfie, or his neighbour's cat. But not at the same time.

When not writing, he can often be found hiking barefoot on woodland trails.

CONNECT WITH STEWART BINT ONLINE:

Website:
www.stewartbintauthor.weebly.com

Blog:
www.stewartbintauthor.weebly.com/stewart-bints-blog

Twitter:
Twitter.com/@AuthorSJB

Facebook:
https://www.facebook.com/StewartBintAuthor

90595454R00145

Made in the USA
Columbia, SC
07 March 2018